Fenian Blood

Fenian Blood

by Stevie McEwan

© Stephen McEwan 2020 All rights reserved

ISBN: 9798579116420

He was doing it.

They were *all* doing it.

The Bouncy.

Thousands and thousands of them were off their seats, twirling their scarves and jumping up and down. And they were going BOUNCY! BOUNCY! BOUNCY! BOUNCY! *This* was what it was about. Jackie's Protestant heart was bursting. His loyalist soul was soaring. And the servant to Her Majesty that was his throat? Wounded in action! *What* an afternoon. In the past five minutes alone the Queen had been Saved, the Waves had been Ruled and they'd been up to their Knees in Fenian Blood.

Jackie grinned.

He *really* grinned.

Because he loved this club. *(I do! Come on, youse heard me sing! Almost every word I sang!)* It was a love equalled in fact only by his hatred for *them*. If it wasn't bad enough that the unwashed mob in the green and the grey shared their city, they were *here* in their home.

Aye! Youse saw me celebrate! Youse saw me off my seat!

A verse of The Sash.

A Simply the Best.

A Super Rangers.

Finally, a rest.

The exhausted, contorted muscles in the face of Jackie Aiden Patrick O'Leary sighed with relief.

He blinked up at the scoreboard.

Eighty-seven minutes.

He was nearly there.

He could do this.

He'd get out this place alive.

1

'Still no sign of him.' Brendan dropped the mobile and collapsed onto the stale, crumpled bedsheets. 'That's all she said.'

'Not a peep?' Jackie pulled himself up from the burst couch, nodded at the hole where his head had been. 'Might be down there,' he said, peering inside. He cupped his hands. 'Shaun!...Shaun! I hear some...wait...Nah.' He sat down again, chuckled.

Jackie actually wondered if he was still wasted. No, compared to his wee brother last night he'd barely even drunk, it had just been really easy to laugh these past two weeks. Alright, the rain had poured for most of it *and* he'd missed Nick Cave, but it had been a different world entirely to his last trip back home. The funeral. How awful that had been. Surely no more for a long, long time. By Jackie's feet lay Brendan's flatmate, too scoobed a few hours before to navigate the way back to his room. Around them both was the evidence of the flatmate's three a.m. business proposal, the kebab bits chucked and spat as he'd jabbered on about the exporting of Scottish produce to Egypt. *Irn Bru! In Cairo! It's a winner! Canni fail!* There was a half-smile on him as well, Jackie noticed. The guy's dream still alive.

Meat. Feet. Farts.

He got up and opened a window.

A postcard of a Celtic football player dropped from the sill, Jackie catching it before it fell for the West-End street a floor below. There were tons of football stuff in this flat, and was practically all Brendan and his mates talked about. Had any of them even once had a woman here? Jackie wondered. Or a guy if that was their thing? He fixed the postcard back on the sill. By the time *he* was twenty-four, he'd left all that way behind.

Yawning and stretching across his bed, a crucifix dangling from his wide, milky frame, Brendan slapped on a white and gold baseball cap. 'Amy's starting to brick it. Wants us over, Jackie.'

Jackie gulped at the air. 'Not me, I've said my goodbyes, gonni take a last kick about the town before I hit the airport. Reem wants me to bring back a calendar of Glasgow. Can ye believe that? In April? How am I gonni-'

'-Mr Taylor?' Brendan threw up a hand to shut his brother up. 'Aye...no. No...canni make it. See, I've been up all night with...' At his boss's interruption he rolled his eyes, chucked in a couple of *I know*-s and *sorry*-s. Then, a minute later with a wink, he dropped the phone and fell back onto his bed. Jackie headed for a shower.

Brendan's still bleary blue eyes were gazing at the ceiling when his brother returned. Rubbing at his receding hair, Jackie rummaged around his rucksack, flashed a jubilant smile when he pulled out a fresh black t-shirt. 'A day off then?' he asked, throwing it on.

'Back tomorrow.'

'...But...' Jackie picked up an apple, wiped it on his chest. '...ye willni get paid then, right?'

His brother shrugged, stabbed at his phone again and out blasted an Irish rebel song. It did the trick, with a sigh Jackie shut up and and bit into the apple. Whatever. If his brother was happy to flog crap on some zero hours contract, why should he waste his breath saying otherwise.

8

Brendan trudged to the bathroom then and Jackie returned to the window. Amy freaking out? It was daft. She was the one who should try not turning up for a family lunch, the one who should go and do something mad for once. Their other brother, Shaun, going missing the night before last? Big deal. It had been a holiday weekend, and disappearing in Glasgow wasn't exactly disappearing in Cairo. Torture? Rape? Beatings? Ye go missing in Cairo, everyone *knows* where you are.

'We'll get some grub on the way,' Brendan muttered, having showered and dressed in five minutes. He turned off the music. 'Let's boost.'

Jackie gazed at his brother stepping into the hall. He still looked half-asleep, and his favourite trackie maybe wasn't quite as white as he thought. Jackie followed, then shuffled about the paint-splattered mirror for a proper view of himself. Twisting his black studded earring, he swiped at his black jeans.

Brendan grabbed his keys. 'By the way, Shaun's no turned up for work either.'

'Some time he's having then,' Jackie laughed, grabbing his worn leather jacket and an old paperback. 'Disni know when to stop.' He pointed back at Brendan's bedroom. 'What about your mate? Should we give him a kick?'

'Leave him,' Brendan muttered, opening the flat door. 'He gets up when he wants.'

'The life of an entrepreneur, eh? Not bad.'

The door rattled shut behind them as they headed out to see their sister.

To talk about their brother.

2

From the bay window of her third-floor flat, Amy gazed down at her two brothers leaving the avenue and crossing the street. She'd been there since half-five, throwing down coffee, straining at the radio, grabbing and swiping and stabbing her phone. Jackie let out a laugh loud enough for her to hear and she felt a glimmer of hope. But who was she kidding, she realised, he probably wasn't even talking about Shaun. It was so easy for Jackie and always had been. Thailand first. After that, Malaysia. Then Poland and for years now, Egypt. Unreal, Amy thought, the shades of crap she'd lived through while he'd sun-bathed, smoked and snorkelled. Their dad. Their mum. And *Shaun*, of course. Jackie loved Shaun, she knew that. But he didn't know him like she did.

A gloomy lift of the eyebrows brought Amy's brothers into the flat, and they followed her to the living room. Brendan planked a bottle of Lucozade on the oak coffee table and himself on the couch. Jackie made for an armchair but instead stayed on his feet, he could do with another spy at Amy's crammed bookcase. As Amy drifted off to the window then retreated to the middle of the room, Jackie shrugged. 'Still zilch?'

Snapping her auburn hair into a ponytail, she slumped down next to Brendan, the rise of her denim skirt revealing a freckled ankle and a tattoo. The Chinese word for *understand*, Jackie remembered. Amy shook her head.

'Mobile still off? Bit weird that, I suppose.'

Brendan dropped his cap onto his chest and yawned like he'd just got up. 'Battery.'

'Probably. And I widni worry about him being late for work,' Jackie went on. 'Ye know on Thursday he walked out with a frozen chicken down his boxers?' He laughed. 'It's the way he is. Never going to be trying for Employee of the Month.'

'Saving for his house deposit.' Amy sighed, drawing her hands down her face. 'Every penny counted, he said, that's why he started in that pub as well. And now this.'

'We don't know *this* is anything.'

'But he's done it before.'

'Disappeared?'

'Aye.'

'To London, you're talking about.'

She nodded.

'But he was an addict then, Amy.'

'He still is, Jackie.'

Jackie glanced at Brendan for support but found him only gazing at his phone. 'Alright,' he said, sitting with a sigh. 'But that was *before*. He's going to meetings now, for what, a couple of months? He's transformed, Amy, and that's a word *you* used, remember. Come on, ye spent half of yesterday phoning round hospitals and found nothing to worry about. So…I don't know, how about after his shift ended he headed into town, Easter Sunday remember, the place would have been jumping. He got drunk or say popped a pill and met a woman. And even though he'd much rather sit scanning tins of beans to torn-faced Glaswegians all day, he's no managed to peel himself away from her. Oh aye, and he feels really bad but with his phone on the blink, there's not a lot he can do. How about that?'

'I shouldn't have called him at his work,' Amy said, her green eyes flitting around the room. 'I'd just been waiting so long to hear him say he'd come for lunch. He's so self-conscious about his dyslexia, a bloody smiley would have done. Snapped my head off.'

'But he calmed down, ye said. Everything was cool.'

'But what was I thinking? Having a go at him for not texting? Could I have triggered something?' She sat forward, looked about to get up. 'I need to find him.'

Jackie slapped a knee. 'Okay. So we start with his pals. Brendan?'

Shaun's twin shook himself from his bleary daze and picked the phone up again from his chest. 'I'll check on a couple.' Amy and Jackie watched as he swiped, pressed and listened. One friend then another. After the third he put down the phone. 'All working, I suppose.'

Amy stood. 'So…'

'You're not talking about going to the police,' Jackie asked.

She shook her head. 'Retrace his steps. The pub. Start there.'

He threw Brendan a confused look. 'But ye called it last night.'

Amy picked up a red hoodie, pulled it on. 'He said it was the Black Swan on Paisley Road West. But we checked and there's no such place, even though he gave Brendan the same name. That's bloody weird in itself.'

'Hang on. It wasn't the Black Swan…it was…'Jackie snapped his fingers. '…The Black Dog.'

Brendan grabbed at his half-full Lucozade, it opened with a fizz. 'Black Swan.'

'Black *Dog*.'

'No, man. He told me when he started a few weeks ago.'

'Oh the Black Swan, the Black Dog,' Any snapped. 'Feels like the Black frigging Hole because there's nothing like that on Paisley Road West. I've checked.'

'It's miles long,' Jackie said.

'*Believe* me. It's not an old name either, there's nothing like it past or present.' She fished her ponytail from the back of her top. 'So I'm doing this.'

'You're...?'

'Most places will open soon enough. Look,' she continued, with a look of near apology to her older brother. 'I know this isni how ye planned your last day, Jackie, but I'm going to start at the top of that road and keep going until I find where he worked.' She patted at her jeans, shoved a purse into a pocket. 'Will ye join me?'

'...Well...'

She gave something close to a smile. 'I'd appreciate it.'

He shrugged and stood up. 'Brendan?'

His brother was staring at his phone, open-mouthed.

'Most places are near the start,' Amy said, checking her own mobile. If we have to go further I'll pay for a taxi.'

'No, man...' Brendan started, still staring. '...It's...'

'Full of dives. Aye. We're not staying for drinks.'

'...No...'

'What *is* it?'

He looked up. '...They're Rangers pubs.'

Jackie beamed, threw his head back. 'Right enough, Shaun working down there? He's probably in a sauna scrubbing himself clean. Hey, looking awful white, Brendan. Need a wee lie down?'

'I'm awright...I...'

He drew his eyes up and down his brother. 'Neutral colours, same as myself. Come on, ye'll survive. And it'll be nice to make some new pals.'

'I'm going,' Amy shouted from the hall.

'Wait, Amy. Should we bring some garlic? Just in case? Or a crucifix? What do ye think? Amy? Hang on.'

*

Monday, 18th February

Don't know what to say, really...
My name's Shaun.
I'm...
I'm a compulsive gambler.

I'm alright, I should say that as well, I'm alright cos more than anything I've got a family. I've got a sister and a twin brother and another brother in Egypt, he'll be back for a holiday in a couple of months actually and we're all.. shite, I'm rambling already...What I want...what I want to say is that I'm glad to be here. What I want to say as well is that I've been here before, in this room I mean, a couple of years ago. Aye, I was early I remember, and a guy came in and sat down next to me. Didni matter man that the room was empty and I hadni even looked at him, he just parked himself down and started talking. First thing he said man was we don't come here to please other people, it's got to be about pleasing ourselves. My heart skipped when I heard that. I was like- yes, he knows I'm no into this! He's gonni show me the door! Cos pleasing other people? That was exactly why I was here.

See, I had to get my sister off my case, that was the first thing. She'd been snooping about on Facebook, checking my web history and that, trying to set me straight and doing my head in all round. My older brother man, he was pissing me off as well, sending snidy emails all the way from Cairo. The main reason I came here but was my ma. She was wisni like, a digital stalker, only thing she ever read was my face. Aye, every day she'd pour over it, peering past my lies to get to the truth. She'd never find any but she widni lose her nut or anything, just give me a sad smile and shut her eyes. My ma understood what I was up to. She knew the whole story and forgave me every time.

She was dying, right? She had been for a while and the whistle was about to blow. So I had to do the right thing, or what people would think was the right thing anyway. Amy, that's my sister, she cornered me one night for another chat about this place and I was like- ye know what? I'm gonni go, I'm gonni go cos it'll shut her up at least. Then I'll take home a leaflet, give it to my ma, and she might think I'm no a pointless waster and she could even die in peace.

Anyway, that first meeting, the guy just jabbered on and...I don't think he's...no, he's not here tonight. Anyway, I still hardly looked at him, right? The last thing I wanted was to fall under a spell, I just stared at my baldy napper in that reflection over there. I suppose inside me but there's always been this like, pilot light refusing to go out, and as he talked man now and again it glowed. Was the stuff he said, course it was, but it was other things as well. It was as if he knew what I was scared of, like he'd once been just like me. He'd even leave wee pauses like windows. All I had to do was jump in.

Then the meeting started and I sort of forgot about him, just really sat here no giving a monkey's. But after a bit your man started talking again, and that wee light in me lit up my whole body. It was like I was hearing myself, some successful version of me in the future maybe, a version of me I hadni even dared think aboot. I'm telling youse, just knowing that I could be like that guy, knowing that I could be... it felt mighty. Well, I was like- I need to talk to him, need to get him in a corner, ask how he got so far and if he could help us out. I even switched my phone off. I mean I was serious.

See when my ma died? Everybody was there, there to say goodbye... Almost everybody, anyway. One of us couldni make it. Guess who? My sister, she thought I was away losing somebody else's money and my brothers thought the same. It didn't bother me what they felt, though, we'd have decades to set things straight. But with my ma I didni. Maybe that even killed her, thinking I was away screwing things up as usual. I wisni, that was the last thing I was doing. For the first time in my life man I was trying. I was winning as well. I was in this room, taking it all in, my phone switched off so nobody could distract me.

I was gonni change.

I was.

After that...

Well, ye could say things went downhill.

3

The long road wasn't alone in stretching out before Jackie, half the day did. With the traffic rumbling over the bridge behind them, he peered towards the top and noticed no pubs at all. Fair enough it was early days, but he could already see his afternoon getting eaten up in front of him. On one side of the road stood a massive sandstone restaurant and row upon row of corrugated warehouses, on the other sat a dishevelled café then a turning to a multiplex cinema. Amy gazed in silence as well, and Jackie thought she might just change her mind about doing this on foot. But seconds later still without a word, she started to move, and what else could he do but follow. A moment after that, letting out a groan, Brendan started behind them.

After a couple of minutes however the sun made an appearance, and only Jackie seemed to notice. He gazed up at the shining sky and smiled. This he decided, was actually a perfect way to end the holiday. Alright, it wasn't for the right reason and not exactly in the best of vibes, but a long walk around the south of the city was something he'd never done. It was amazing, Jackie thought as he skipped onto a kerb, how the air was so fresh and the roads were so safe, and the pavements even free of potholes. He wanted to tell Amy and Brendan how lucky they'd been, how lucky *they* still were to live here. But he couldn't of course, *he* was the one who'd done one years ago. He kept his mouth shut and kept up with his sister.

The first pub was a typical old man's joint on a tenement corner, and when Amy spied it she snapped her fingers and quickened up her step.

While Brendan put on the brakes Jackie followed, and Amy clattered the near-closed shutter and stood back, arms-folded. With a screech the shutter was lifted by a grubby-looking fat guy with browning teeth. Amy launched into an explanation and the guy just glared, eyeing up Amy then Jackie, lip curling into a snarl. He didn't seem to be listening or at least hearing the right words, it was like they'd admitted to burning down his pub and were asking for their lighter back. Amy finished and still the guy glared, then began to tremble as well. Jackie sniggered and the guy heard *that*. The two backed away.

'Alright,' Amy snapped after Jackie had pointed out the Union Jack above. '*Shaun O'Leary.* I get it.'

'But ye know what they say,' Jackie said with a wink. 'First they came for the Catholics, then the hippies and old Goths like myself. Brendan's right. Daft trying those pubs.'

'Thank you!' Brendan shouted at the sky.

They carried on. The next place had a cheap nightclubby feel, and all three walked in without breaking stride. Amy, phone ready this time, gave a quick explanation to the young barman and showed him Shaun's photo. The guy smiled and tried to be helpful, he asked questions and stared hard at the picture. But he also slid the phone back and shrugged, he was sorry but he'd never seen Shaun before. Still, outside Amy smiled like this was progress.

For the rest of the block and across the busy road, it was takeaways and bookies and lots of people. The next pub was on the opposite corner and Jackie ran in by himself, then in seconds he was out again nodding at two places in front. Amy entered the first of those and came out shaking her head, and Jackie exited the second doing the same thing. After he'd waited outside each time, Brendan declared he'd had enough, said that to even think Shaun would work round here was to have lost the plot completely. Amy marched straight past him but Jackie knew he had a point, plus no one had been a prick like that first guy but all of these pubs were grim. Throwing an arm around his brother's shoulder, Jackie thought about the coffee house under his flat back home. It was sunlit, gentle and alive. And tomorrow he'd be there.

The pace of the sister and brothers soon slowed, the pubs and shops having more or less stopped and been replaced by warehouses and flats. Ten minutes passed before they reached another bar, a solitary crumbling dive on a piece of wasteground. Sensing possible trouble, for the first time Amy hesitated, she opened the door with the sleeve of her jacket and stepped in like she was entering a crime scene. Behind the squat bar and under a string of Union Jacks, a brillcreamed barman and a tattooed barmaid peered at Shaun's picture. After a moment the woman took the phone and stepped out of Amy and Jackie's earshot, then the two muttered and jabbed like Shaun could be some IRA bomber. Amy found herself hoping that they knew nothing about her brother, the news that Shaun worked in here couldn't be remotely good. The woman returned, and with an unsympathetic shake of the head slapped down the phone.

Moving fuFaFrther south the landscape started to change. More Asian faces. More fruit and vegetable shops. More pubs. The first three of these brought the same results as before, with Brendan now paying more attention to his phone than his surroundings. But when from the other side of the road he saw Amy approach the next, he stopped on the pavement

20

and stood there gibbering. To Jackie, it was like his brother had seen zombies slamming on the windows.

'Gonni get a grip?'

'Fuck's sake, Jackie!' Brendan blurted. 'Do ye no see what's going on in these places?'

Jackie sighed. 'Aye. They have pictures of the Queen and King Billy.'

'You're saying that like it's normal.'

'It is here, Brendan.'

'It's no to me or Shaun.'

Jackie was about to level with his brother, say he might well be right but there'd be no point arguing with their sister, she'd need to reach that conclusion herself. But Amy stormed out then to where they waited and marched straight past to a newsagents. She slid down its wall, her head dropping into her hands. 'Oh, what are we doing?'

Jackie crouched next to her. 'Hey, he might be back home by now.'

'He's not.'

'Ye don't-'

She held up her phone. '-He's not.'

Brendan sat on the other side, and as a tear rolled he placed a hand on her shoulder.

'Brendan?' she asked, gazing at the cracked pavement. 'All the pictures of the Queen, is everywhere like that round here?'

He shrugged. 'The stadium's just up there so I think so.'

She pushed through a smile and looked at each of them. Then she stood, wiped the dust from her jeans. 'We're wasting our time here. Let's move.'

Amy insisted that for the next mile or so they get a bus, and once on one she checked her phone for the next pub that might look someway neutral. Although Brendan was supposed to be doing the same, he was distracted by more bars that they passed, staring open-mouthed at one or two like they were on some haunted history tour. Jackie tapped his shoulder. 'Brendan?' he asked. 'No offence. Have ye *ever* been out the West End?'

Brendan grinned. 'Taking the piss, man?' He counted on his fingers. 'Inverness. Kilmarnock. Stranraer…'

'Right…'

'Ross County. Been there? Magic day out. Bus leaves at seven if it's on the telly.'

He continued counting the football grounds he'd visited, for his own sake now more than Jackie's, only stopping to look at what his brother was now gazing at as the bus pulled into a stop. On the large, standalone rectangular building, *CRAWFORD'S* was splashed in thick white letters, the front and sides awash in blue and red stripes. Below the roof five flags hung on poles. Two Union Jacks, a Saltire, Northern Ireland and Rangers. Brendan yelped like the tour bus had pulled up at the house in the Exorcist. 'Crawford's,' he muttered.

'Looks awright,' Jackie said. 'Fancy nipping in for lunch?'

Amy gave her phone another swipe. 'This isn't right.'

'What?'

'I thought there'd be loads of pubs further on.'

'There isni?'

'Three. Another couple on side-streets.'

Trudging through the traffic for the next fifteen minutes they continued to gaze out and around. Jackie had still half-expected to spot at least one unmapped bar, and was up for jumping off at any he could see. But there were none. There were tenements and open spaces and Bellahouston Park, then more tenements, schools and shops. But there were no pubs. The bus turned into the final stretch and they finally got off. Inside the first place the barman put on his glasses, then stared at the photo but apologised. They took another bus to the next pub, and got such a quick knockback from the woman there that they ended up on the same bus. The last bar was half a mile away and Jackie was in no hurry to arrive, in fact he was starting to dread it. The moment he'd heard the name he'd known it was a non-starter, a well-known southside madhouse that Shaun would at least have joked about. More than that, it hadn't changed its name in decades.

He knew Amy had guessed the same. It was why, after they'd jumped off at the greying two-storied dump, for the first time she stopped rather than went in. Taking a tissue she dabbed at her eyes, gave her brothers an embarrassed smile. 'I'll go,' Brendan said. 'Youse wait here.' He bounded inside and upstairs, and Jackie put his arm around his sister. He wanted to say it'd be cool, that Shaun would turn up soon, that he was young and a bit mad *and* there'd been a holiday weekend. But for the first time Jackie had his doubts, so he said nothing. Then Brendan came out shaking his head.

*

Monday, 18ʰ February (cont'd)

My da, he's dead as well.

That happened before my ma.

Ten years ago.

I was fourteen.

No fishing for sympathy here, no making excuses. I went to London after my ma died and what I got up to was my fault alone. I just need to get my head right, need to unravel all this stuff, cos only when it all makes sense will I be able to move forward.

Before I talk about London, I need to get this out.

He was a gambler as well, my da. A different kind to me and, I don't want to assume anything, but probably all of youse as well. Wisni in it for the money, he never placed a bet in his life in fact, cash didni interest him, he was on a completely different plain. I know what you're all thinking, if he didni lose cash then he wisni a gambler. But he was addicted, addicted to a system that he was trying to build. For the football. And see when something's taken over your life and ye forget what's important? Seriously, what does money matter?

He'd stay up through the night trying to work it out, this system.

One morning he drove to work, fell asleep on the duel carriageway.

Bang.

That was it.

But it was how he got there, how he arrived at that point.

That's what's important.

See, my da had been damaged. His own da had been a real psycho, a violent bevvyier and mad for the horses. For years my da had actually been against gambling, when we were kids he'd warn us all about that and the drink. He wisni even that keen on football, had one love and that was maths. Honest man, we'd all sit watching the telly and he'd be there but ignoring it, instead into his wee book of equations. He'd had ambitions of being a professor I think but like I say he wisni right, he ended up a welder on building sites. He hated it. Maybe no the work, but I know even at fifty-three he couldn't handle it, the smirks and comments at the non-drinking, non-gambling maths geek. Did his nut right in. Then when I was twelve he got a new job.

His workmates there asked him to take part in their Fantasy Football league and of course he knocked them back. But they kept at him, just widni leave it and finally he agreed, paid the minimum stake. Then at some point it clicked that he could use his maths to enjoy it, finally man he could put his skills to the test. He got right into it, my da, within weeks there'd be spreadsheets and post-it notes sprawled around the spare room, and he'd be somewhere underneath, muttering and writing stuff. Algorithmic probabilities is what it's called, creating a formula built on things like teams and players. He was good at it. No, he was brilliant. Before long he was out of sight from his workmates and he was only getting started. Pretty quick he needed a bigger challenge.

So the next season he took part in the same competition, only this time in a newspaper against thousands of other folk. It was up a few levels and that meant more research, so we'd barely even see him, he'd be shut in the room. Soon he had the beating of most of those players as well, out of like ten thousand he was in the top fifty. I'm no kidding, one day a fridge arrived at the door and he'd no idea he'd won it, it might sound funny but none of us were laughing. The quiet-spoken da who'd dance with my ma in the kitchen had gone, replaced by this frazzled, red-eyed weirdo drowning in pointless numbers. It was no fun for him either. He'd sometimes stare at that table man in total despair, not able to get how he wisni top five or ten. Of course he knew what he'd turned into and he'd be all apologies. After he saw out the season, he'd get back to normal.

But, well...

He didni.

At first, as far as I was concerned those gamblers had put my da in his grave, the guys on that site who'd chipped away at him man until he'd eventually cracked. But then I came round, realised he'd had a choice, it was his rabbit hole and no one else's that he'd decided to jump down. But this didni make me feel better, in fact I only felt worse, knowing he'd got so close to success but left the world with nothing. Then a year or so went by and I thought, hey, I can keep it going, I can dig out what's he'd left and understand it and build. A project it'll be, like a massive family mission, something to make sure my da's work widni be in vain. I was just a wean really, no much of a clue. But I suppose that was me on the road to ruin.

Anyway, I'll continue next time if that's alright...

I'm just... that's me for now.

Thanks for, ye know, listening.

4

At least Brendan had got through to Shaun's pals, but each time he could only put his phone down and shrug at his sister. Neither Kev or Alan had heard from Shaun in a week, and the couple of others he'd managed to talk to were insulted to even be asked. Amy pushed away her half-empty soup bowl and drained her tea, then with a faint smile slapped her hands on the table. 'So, a taxi for me and Jackie back to where we stopped. We split up, hit the pubs we ignored first time as well as the side-streets, there's not much online but you never know.' As if expecting to hear a protest, she handed Brendan her keys. 'Check out the flat, ask next door if there's any news. If there's none…' She stopped. '…get back to us. Work your way down the road.' At the chance of disappearing, Brendan gave a thankful nod and was gone.

In the taxi, Jackie felt relieved that Brendan wasn't there anymore to brick it whenever a Rangers pub loomed into view, and as he gazed out one side for any they might have missed, Amy checked the other. Opposite a side entrance to the park she clocked a wine bar, and before the taxi had stopped Jackie was out then starting towards it. But he was inside again in seconds and once more they drove off, and both finally got out again near the stadium. They hugged then, Rangers pubs or not they just do it, and took a side of the road each and began to walk. In a few minutes Jackie realised the online info was right. Beyond his side the streets got so quiet there was no point in straying any further, and he found himself back near where Amy had broken down in tears. He strolled to the first pub and opened the door, and although in a few seconds he was out again, this time he was smiling. The fear he felt earlier had suddenly disappeared. Looking for Shaun in Rangers pubs was actually pretty funny.

Seeing Amy he darted through the traffic, to put an end to all this worrying he'd need something solid. So Shaun had lied, right? That seemed clear enough. But why? Hey, did he work in a gay bar? He'd never had a serious girlfriend so was *that* it? As Amy opened the door to Crawford's he nipped in behind. The pub stretched back deep in royal blue and red, and the walls and the ceiling were crammed with tops, flags and scarves. Above the entire length of the horseshoe-shaped bar hung Union Jack-bunting, and above the mirrored-bar wall hung a collection of assorted-sized photos. But it was the windowless wall at the back of the room that caught Jackie's eye. Far more lively than the scattering of brooding customers, was the giant mural of jubilant fans.

Jackie joined at Amy at the bar and nodded. On his knees filling a fridge, the thirty-something barman in the denim shirt gave a cheery smile and jumped to his feet. Of all the bar staff Jackie had seen, this guy was the only one to seem out of place. Tall and blue-eyed with a mass of blonde curls, he looked handsome enough to bluff his way into Hollywood.

'We're looking for our brother,' Amy sighed, slumped like a far too-regular customer. She pushed over the phone. 'Trying everywhere.'

Rubbing at his stubble, the barman stared. He looked at Amy then stared again, then glanced at Jackie before the photo another time. For a brief, ridiculous moment Jackie thought a break could be coming, that Shaun could be employed *here* of all places. But no. Sure enough, as a barfly

28

shuffled towards them and stole himself an eyeful, the guy pushed back the phone. 'Doesn't work here, no.'

'Thanks,' Amy said, pulling herself up.

'I mean,' he said. 'Not anymore.'

*

Thursday, 21st February

Hi, everybody.

My name's Shaun and I'm a compulsive gambler.

The other night I talked about my da dying when I was fourteen. I'm still trying to come to terms with that, and what happened after it especially. How I was determined to do something worthwhile I suppose, make his death not totally pointless. But how I ended up going to London and that and...I'm actually worried about telling youse what I got up to there. I know this isni a place for judging, but when youse find out what I did I'm not sure youse will let me back in...

I'll worry about that later, I suppose.

So...

After my da died man, things went a bit mad with me and Brendan. He'd been the quiet one, would never give anybody any bother, and I'd always be dogging school, mouthing off to the polis... But Brendan hit the bevvy, would end up steaming in classrooms and that, and I went in the other direction, the right one I suppose. I think I just channelled my anger, I stopped going out and instead got my head down. I took a look at maths first, needed to know if I was up to it, if I could get into my da's work and finish what he'd started. Well in the space of a couple of months man my marks went through the roof, and I wisni just good either, I got some buzz from solving equations. I got into other subjects as well, not quite as on it cos of my dyslexia but I still made major strides. A couple of years later I was on my way to to uni.

My ma, she was dead proud. Amy as well, and even prouder that I was studying something they could barely pronounce. Quantitative analysis. It's what gets ye jobs in finance and that but it's a key to creating sporting odds as well, at its core man is the calculating of likelihoods so for gambling it was perfect. I was buzzing about where it would lead me but it was something I kept it to myself, Fantasy Football could make an interesting study but it's not much of a career move. Thing is, I was zooming past that sort of thing anyway. See, beating the average football fan was fine for my da in his league, and I'd got a lot out of reading his old notes and spreadsheets. But I'd set my sights higher and I needed the ultimate test. To know how robust my system was, I'd have to take on the bookies.

Basically man I'd calculate the likelihood of a result or whatever, then find a bookies with higher odds and make a bet. I widni win every time, that's no how it worked, the secret was just to make sure that I won more than I lost. It was virtual as well, all scribbled down in a jotter, the big total at the back showing the profitability of my system. And it was pretty profitable, with what I learned from my first year I was up a few hundred quid. It didni matter that I was knackered either, the winning was dead rewarding, and I didni care the money wisni real, like I was say it was about something bigger. But then one afternoon I passed the bookies near my house and I stopped and went in. I was after a wee victory dance, there in the land of the enemy and that. But the tension and quiet, I suppose it sort of grabbed me. I placed a bet and I won. But the next time, well, I didni. That was the start.

By this point the uni wisni happy. I was missing classes and deadlines because the data was such a pain, but I didni care, I thought I knew it all. Problem was I didni know it all, I barely even knew my own system. See, the profits were consistent but they were pretty wee as well, it was a matter of sticking to the script and keeping myself disciplined. But I couldni, I'd get impatient, I'd bet more often and I'd bet bigger. Then I'd lose so I'd bet more and...well, we know the script. Second year at uni man and the discipline's out the window, I'm throwing fifty quid on daft games like in the second division in Peru. I've got a job in a pub and it's keeping me afloat, but I end up chucking it to spend more time on my data. I'd lock myself away now, shouting and greeting, then desperate and skint I'd steal from my family and pals. Even now it's hard to think back. There was Amy who'd have given me her last two-bob, Brendan who didni have two bob and my ma who'd just take my hand and ask me what was wrong. 'Nothing', I'd say. Or 'you', once, I'm sure. I hated myself. I'd hit the bottom. Then my ma got sick.

That final year I was consumed man, not just by betting but the process I'd go through. Calculating the odds was like a refuge, then I'd need to step out and see my real world. Failure. Self-hatred. Nae mates. Cancer. Thing is, my ma was dying but she was still living and she wanted to look after us. So there'd be Sunday dinners and trips to Loch Lomond, movie nights and card games, all that. Amy would do most of the organising and my ma would do most of the laughing, and Brendan would do most of the quietly freaking out at how tragic it all was. Me, I'd be doing the turning

32

up late and leaving early, and thinking about my next bet or the cash from when my ma would die. Amy, ever since she caught me rifling her pockets, Amy would try and talk me into thinking about coming here. I thought she'd given up, then the night before my ma died she mentioned it dead casual. 'What's the worst that could happen?' she said.

Well, I told youse about that.

I'm a bit nervous now…about saying what I got up to in London.

I'm not ready yet.

Next time.

Aye, next time.

5

Amy threw her brother a glance, then back to the barman. 'I'm sorry? He worked here?'

Jackie tapped the phone. 'Look again, mate. Seriously.'

'It's him.'

'Alright...so...' Amy's mouth froze.

The barman grinned again. 'Must be a terrible shock.'

'No, it's...When did...?'

'Till Sunday night. Believe me, this place can be wild enough without a Timpostor in pouring the pints. Let's say it was for the best.'

'Timpostor..?'

He waved at some of the memorabilia behind them. 'A Celtic fan claiming to be one of us. *Tim*,' he said again, mouthing clearly. '*Impostor*. Who they kidding? It's like...' He nodded at a scrawny, no-necked customer and lowered his voice. '...like Skin there claiming he's a sadhu monk. Hey, sit down before youse keel over. What you having?'

Amy took a stool, managed a nervy smile. 'No, thanks.'

Jackie stayed on his feet. 'How long did he work here for?'

With another rub at his chin, the barman leant on the bar. 'Three weeks? Yeah, six shifts all in. It was only a temporary thing, next weekend was supposed to be his last. Some of the regulars wanted to chip in for a wee present, couldn't decide on his head on a stake or in a wheelie bin.'

Amy yelped.

'A joke! Hey, look, by Sunday things had got a bit tasty but he walked out of here in one piece. We're not monsters, we wouldn't have it any other way. Ah, no offence, John had bottle but he was missing something. I let him go for his-'

'-John?' Amy asked.

He spun a glass in the air, held it to the light. 'That's right.'

'No, it's…Shaun. His name's Shaun.'

The barman turned to Amy with a half-smile. Jackie expected him to explode with laughter then, but instead he put the glass down and nodded. 'Shaun? Then obviously not as daft as we thought.'

'You're the landlord?'

The barman held out his hand. 'The owner. Daryl.'

'I'm Jackie. This is my sister, Amy.'

'Pleased to meet ye, Amy.' He lifted a tray of glasses and stepped down the bar.

'So ye sacked him? After the shift?'

He smiled back. 'Too busy to let him go during it. Just a case of monitoring things. *Shaun* was gonni survive.'

'How…' Amy had to speak up over a solitary shriek of laughter. '…How did he take it?'

'Don't know.' Daryl shrugged as he stepped back up. 'I gave that job to my head barman. He's not here. Back tomorrow.'

'So…' Amy started. 'Was Shaun pals with anybody? Is there someone…?'

'Pals?' Daryl chuckled. 'He had a bit of patter, that always goes down well with the troops. But I'm telling you, a few punters clocked him the second he walked in. After that, John, Shaun, whatever…he could only be toast.' He slapped a towel on the bar. 'What the hell was he playing at anyway?'

'…I…' Amy's eyes hit the floor. '…don't know.' Jackie gazed around like he might find a clue on the walls, saw that he and Amy had kicked to life the handful of scattered customers. A few were staring over. A couple were swapping scowls. A fat guy sneered as he talked into his phone.

'Did you advertise the job?'

'Nah. Not really how it works, Amy. Fans travel the world to come here. The slogan on the front? *The World's Number 1 Rangers Pub?* That's not arrogance. This isn't just a pub, it's a pilgrim site. Wayne, he deals with recruitment, just a case of saying the word and watching for the stampede. Not that everybody turns out to be suitable of course, and that's without including Celtic fans with a death wish.'

'Do ye have Wayne's number?'

'Sure.' He took his phone from his pocket. 'But he's a stubborn boy, Wayne, don't expect much back. And he might just have had surgery and be answering to the name of Wendy.' He winked. 'Yeah, he's in for a serious pounding after his mistake.' Daryl read out Wayne's number and Amy stabbed at her keys. 'But whether he's still in touch with your brother? Or how he even knew him?' He shrugged. 'No idea.'

'Not our brother,' Jackie said, quickly understanding that he *might* have to come back here. 'Amy's boyfriend.'

A smile and a raise of the eyebrows. Daryl either fancied his chances with Amy or could easily smell the bullshit. He slid over a pen and some paper. 'Give me your number, just in case.'

Nearing Crawford's and biting into a pie, Brendan would *not* be passing ten feet of that midden. Nae danger. Not. A chance. About to bodyswerve to the roadside, his brother and sister stepped out of the door, and at the sight of them he jumped back. '…Are youse…?' Mince fell onto Brendan's trackie. '…Come on, man…!'

An excuse from Jackie and a lecture from Amy, that was what he expected. But they stood in silence. 'Traumatised, aye?' Brendan said with a satisfied glare. 'Youse are lucky, could have been turned into their soup of the day.' He stuffed the rest of the pie into his gub and wiped his hands. 'Nothing doing up the flat. What now?'

Amy's whisper was too quiet to hear.

'What?'

'In there.' She swallowed. 'Where he worked.'

'Ha Ha. Your arse…'

Jackie shook his head. 'Afraid not, brother. His last shift was on Sunday.'

'Your…'

'It was,' Amy said. 'Honest.'

Pie fell from Brendan's mouth.

Slapped onto the pavement.

6

Jackie wondered if Brendan had maybe misheard and thought that Shaun was dead. Just the way he stood there, his eyes welling and gibbering that he'd seen his twin last week and had seemed fine. Then he started to jabber about their shared bedroom and teenage fights before Amy screamed 'Shut it!' and stormed back up the pavement. Jackie took him by the wrists.

'Wakey-wakey, Brendan. See that place? It's a pub, no a gas chamber.'

'But it's just...he was...That's...'

'Sort it out.' He put on a march and caught up with Amy, but didn't quite know what to say. What he really needed was for time to stop, to get a few minutes to process this shambles. And it was a shambles. In spite of the advice he'd just given his brother, Jackie was getting every bit as anxious. He'd been banking on Shaun turning up or at least Amy chilling out, it was half-past two and he was due at the airport by eight. Fat chance now. In fact, getting himself onto that plane seemed to depend on a total stranger who might just explode when he heard *John's* real name.

At a kerb by an overflowing bin Amy took out her phone. She called the number but got no answer. 'I'll try again in a minute.'

'Amy...' started Jackie.

'What?'

'This makes no sense. This Wayne guy...And that place...'

'We speak to him. *Then* decide if it makes sense.'

Trudging towards his sister and brother while he slapped his cap back on, Brendan gave an exhausted shake of the head, he looked like he'd had his car nicked and had just given up the chase. 'The worst thing, man?' he groaned, stopping with a shrug. 'I don't know what I'm gonni find out next. He's got a season ticket for that mob? A King Billy tattoo? His own Hun family living in Kinning Park?' I know we've drifted apart but what the fuck?'

'Brendan,' Amy said calmly. 'We need to go to the police.'

Jackie had already strode ahead. 'Aye,' he shouted. 'So let's do it.'

In the short walk to the station, Jackie didn't ask aloud why Shaun had chosen to be around bams who'd queue up to lamp him if they knew the truth. But it was all he could think of. Could it have been for cash? Some stupid dare? Had someone even *forced* him to work a few shifts? He drew a blank, then he wondered what might have happened afterwards. A kicking that had gone too far, maybe. Shit, Shaun could be breathing his last in a ditch someplace. *No*, he told himself. *Leave the freaking out for now*. He did just that, and when the police station came into view he even managed a joke about Brendan. But then he got closer and couldn't help but feel queasy.

With barely a glance at Amy, the female desk sergeant asked how long Shaun had been missing. Amy filled a form and gave it back with a photo, and the sergeant asked more questions and jabbed at some keys. Amy then pointed out Shaun's gambling and family history, and it was only when she mentioned that he'd disappeared before did the sergeant look up. Amy explained this was different, the way he'd gone missing and his state of mind, and although she understood how this might look, Shaun wouldn't just vanish like this. The policewoman explained there'd be a visit to Crawford's and they'd be in touch afterwards. But, she said with a sympathetic but official smile, their brother was twenty-four. He could do what he liked.

Outside Jackie heard Wayne's number ring out again, and Shaun's another time. They grabbed a taxi back to the West End where Amy hurried across to her close. In her flat she marched into Shaun's bedroom, and with her brothers behind her, emptied Shaun's cabinet and drawers onto the floor. She stared at the contents: t-shirts and boxers, a passport and a football magazine, a pin badge, a train ticket, pens. Then she marched out again and collapsed on the living room chair. Brendan followed her, flopping onto the couch as Jackie stepped to the window. After a moment he snapped his fingers. 'Hey, this Wayne. Could be another ex-gambler.'

Amy drew her hands down her face. 'Yeah.' She nodded. 'Possible.'

'One helping the other sort his life out. A sponsor, that's what they're called. Much bigger than Celtic and Rangers, that kind of thing. All Shaun has to do in there is keep his mouth shut.'

'They met at a meeting? Okay, but why take the risk? There's dozens of pubs Shaun could work in without worrying about getting attacked or ...*worse*.'

Jackie sat down. 'Okay, so what else do we know?'

She stared at the ceiling. 'London.'

London. Jackie waited for more but Amy remained silent. He knew of course that after their mum had died, it was to where Shaun had made his escape, where wracked with guilt and blazing with anger, he'd be able to keep gambling in peace. That system, they'd all guessed, he was going to perfect it, he was going to get it right and prove everyone wrong. He was secretive too, Jackie remembered, sent hardly any emails and definitely gave no invites. Then last autumn Brendan had gone down to convince his twin to come home, and that's exactly what Shaun did. Jackie had been amazed how this had worked out and had expected an explanation, especially when Amy had remarked how shaken up Shaun had seemed. But no explanation ever came, Amy only ever spoke of her relief that the gambling was over, and Shaun, he barely spoke at all. Eventually Jackie assumed there'd been no massive story, with Brendan's help Shaun had just got a grip. But maybe he was wrong.

'The way he just turned up,' Amy sighed, a half-guilty shrug at her older brother. 'Admitted we'd been right.'

'So he was in trouble? Escaping something?' Jackie turned to Brendan, face now buried under his cap.

'Or some*body*,' Amy said. 'I suspected maybe illegal gamblers, just because he was so jumpy for days. I didn't push him, I gave him time to open up.'

'That system,' Jackie asked. 'Did he ever…achieve anything?'

Amy shrugged. 'Who knows. His gambling was out of control, that was the only thing that mattered.'

'Aye.'

'Anyway, he almost did. Open up, I mean.'

'What did he say?'

'He'd been back a few weeks, came in one night from a pub. Was in a state, very emotional, admitted he'd done something terrible. He wouldn't tell me any more, went to his bed. I didn't fill you in because I was relieved to let it go.'

Jackie bit at a nail. 'Blew a ton of cash, maybe.'

'From mum? More than that, I thought.'

'Then something to keep in mind. But it still disni explain him working in Crawford's. Unless him and this Wayne, like I say, they're pals.'

'Pals.' Brendan mouthed the word like it was week-old milk.

'Come on, Brendan. Is it that hard to believe?'

He pulled away the cap and sat up. 'Aye, it is.'

'Ye know, maybe Shaun kept it to himself because he knows what half this city is like.'

Brendan scoffed. 'Sure, man. Ye saying you'd work there?'

Jackie made to answer but he really had to think. 'No,' he said at last. 'But I'm not an addict.'

With a roll of his eyes Brendan muttered something and sat back, chucked his cap back onto his face.

As Amy went to the kitchen, Jackie checked the time on her phone. Three hours until check-in. For God's sake, it'd be nice if one of them even mentioned the flight. Maybe if he...' The phone rang in his hand.

Jackie stared at the screen. 'That's him...'

'*Shaun?*'

He shook his head. 'Wayne.'

Amy rushed back.

Jackie answered, hit speakerphone. 'Hello?'

'Who's this?' It was a growl that sounded like a threat.

'My name's Jackie. Is this...is this Wayne, aye? Listen, I got your number from Daryl, I'm calling about a family friend, John, his name is. Done a few shifts in Crawford's the past few weeks...'

...

'…The thing is,' Jackie continued over the silence. 'He's gone missing. Nobody's seen him since Sunday and we know he worked in Crawford's that night….I'm wondering if you've got any idea cos-'

'-Missing?'

'Two days now. Not like him.'

'No idea,' the voice said. 'How should I have?'

'Because ye gave him the boot, that's one reason. I'm asking cos my sister, John's partner, she's no slept. And he's a good guy, John, I'm kind of getting that way myself.'

…

'Canni help.'

'Ye took him on in Crawford's, aye?' Jackie asked. 'So ye knew him? You're his mate?'

'No a word I'd use.'

Jackie sighed. 'Look, pal. I'm thinking something went down on Sunday night that ye can tell us about…Hello?...Hello?'

…

The voice again. 'What did ye say yir name was?'

'Jackie.'

'We can meet the morra.'

'We can meet now.'

'The morra. Crawford's.'

'Well…'

'Lunchtime.'

'Alright. Just…'

He hung up.

Jackie dropped the phone onto the couch, shrugged at his brother and sister. 'He's got something for us.'

Amy's eyes widened. She took a relieved breath. 'Well, this is good, right?' Her hand was over her mouth. 'This is good.'

Jackie shrugged. 'Seems it.'

'So, are you coming?' Amy smiled an apology then. 'Tomorrow? You coming with us, Jackie because…'

He nodded. 'I'll be there.'

Amy stepped towards her older brother, gave him a tight hug. 'Thanks, Jackie. I couldn't do this without you.'

'It's cool. I just need to tell Reem. Let me use your phone.'

7

Brendan left Jackie at Amy's and walked towards his flat in a trance, wondering if there'd been any signs in his twin that he'd somehow missed. A memory came back to him and he almost collided with a passing car. The t-shirt Shaun had worn months back. It was unmistakable, that stripe of royal blue. Of course Brendan had been too shocked to say a word but his face had given him away, which was when Shaun had tried to assure him that it wasn't royal blue but *navy*. What sort of tube did he think Brendan was? There was a clear rule about colour, it wisni hard, and if ye chose to ignore it it was the slippery slope. Aye, Brendan decided with a grimace. One minute you're giving it *...it's just wan stripe!...*, the next you're camped out for a Royal Wedding. Or hang on. He stopped in the middle of the pavement. Was this a bit much? Maybe. He needed a drink.

He reached a quiet pub and planked himself in a corner. Maybe he shouldn't judge Shaun. No yet. There were other possibilities. Like blackmail. Aye! Some bluenose had found out a secret and was *forcing* him to work there! But he decided against that in seconds. Like Amy had said before he'd left, Shaun had seemed too content these days to be under any pressure. So what else? Brendan thought, scowling and scratching into his cap. Had he gone undercover? In the ultimate extreme sport known as...Hun Dodging? Ha! He rose a cheeky toast to himself and sat back. But then, as if the other customers had heard and taken offence, he groaned aloud. For the first time Brendan faced the truth. If by lunchtime tomorrow Shaun still hadn't trapped, he'd be forced to go to Crawford's himself. To *be* there. To *exist*. Hun Dodging? Brendan wouldn't last the first round. He felt his pint make a U-turn for his throat and rushed to the toilet.

When Amy woke at eight, she'd had three hours sleep. Three more than the night before at least, and she knew she was alive enough to put up a fight. Although Jackie had asked for a nudge, she'd decided to let him sleep on, he should be at home right now with his wife so it was the least she could do. After she called the uni to explain she'd be taking the week off, she switched on the radio and got herself a coffee. Then her mind got lost in a daze of grim maybes. Shaun as the victim of an attacker who'd nicked his mobile couldn't be ruled out. Or he did another runner to London because the new confident Shaun had been a front. *Or* whatever trouble he'd escaped from had just finally caught up with him. *London*, how he'd left there and had never opened up, it started to bother her. She felt a sickening wave as she checked her phone. Four hours to go.

Jackie's eyes sprung open. On another morning the Primal Scream tune on the radio could have catapulted him out of bed, but now its euphoria seemed to be laughing in his face. He collected his thoughts. Amy and Shaun's age gap? It might be too much for the Crawford's crowd to believe they were a couple but if it stuck, he and Brendan could survive by pretending to be Rangers fans. But would Brendan even be up for going? Fair enough bolting last night, but he'd hit the road so fast it was obvious that he needed time alone. Even though they'd not been close for years, Jackie knew this would get tough for Brendan, and probably tougher than he'd ever admit. His job could cause problems as well if he didn't turn up, could even sack him over the phone. Jackie decided that if Brendan wanted to give Crawford's a miss, he wouldn't make things hard.

But just as he was finishing breakfast Brendan appeared, in the same cap but in another trackie, gleaming white with black stripes. Jackie looked him up and down with an appreciative nod. 'Ye sleep alright?'

Brendan chuckled. 'Few pints sorted me out.'

'Good stuff. This mission widni be the same without ye, be like that guy left orbiting the moon when...' Only then did he notice Amy by the window holding up her phone. 'What? Ye called Shaun?'

She nodded.

'It rang?'

'More than that. Somebody answered.'

'Who...?'

'Then hung up.'

'Me as well, man,' Brendan said, getting out his own mobile. 'Last night.'

'Really?'

'I was in the pub, it was loud, couldni hear anything. I thought it had just gone dead like before. But I checked later and look.' He held up the screen.

10.48pm

Call made: 00 minutes 02 seconds.

'I got background noise.' Amy said, still holding hers. 'What's going on? Dead for two days and now this? She jabbed at a key and waited. 'No answer this time.'

47

Jackie rubbed at his chin. 'Whatever this is, I'd say the chances of him lying at the bottom of a ditch are now a lot less.' He headed to the kitchen. 'Who's for tea?'

Brendan stared munching and slurping into his phone, and Amy kept at her post by the window. Jackie turned the pages on a hardbacked book on Palaeontology, Amy's subject at uni, and to make the day appear remotely normal he chucked her a few random questions. But as she gazed out that window, radio blaring next to her, he could barely hear her answers or even know if she was responding. Brendan's mug clunked onto the table. 'Can we get oot of here?'

Jackie shut the book. 'We're not meeting him for another two hours.'

'Pubs are open. Just...disni have to be a pub. Seriously man, I'm cracking up.'

Amy turned and zipped up her top. 'Let's go.'

Jackie asked the taxi driver to head to Ibrox, then he directed him to the pub he'd come close to missing the day before. A dimly-lit wine-bar, he and Amy got a table as Brendan approached the bar. Then, once he'd joined them, Jackie sat back and raised his Irn Bru. Whatever this Wayne had to say for himself, he declared, at least they'd be a step closer to the truth. With a worried smile Amy lifted her water and Brendan nodded, swallowing his pint. Nachos were half-eaten as they sat and waited and wondered. Soon Amy had given up on Shaun's phone, and she and Jackie were just watching Brendan drink. It was time for Crawford's.

8

The wind around the southside chucked an assortment of smells down the main road. Kebab meat and petrol fumes, chip fat and spices. Around the back of the van, the gusts were strong enough for the beer-bellied delivery guy to pause before letting the barrel trundle onto the pavement. He looked up, and at the sight of the swaying flags his chest filled. 'For God and Ulster', he muttered to himself, nodding. He jumped onto the pavement, stepped towards his bemused workmate and jabbed a stubby finger. 'That's what matters. Fucking *that*.' The Polish man followed him down to the cellar, shaking his head.

Getting close to Crawford's and noticing those flags, Jackie groaned. It wasn't just the flags, it was the clown gazing up there like Jimi Hendrix was playing on the roof. This feeling of dread was weirdly familiar, like he'd been dragged back to his teenage years as he'd slept. He just wasn't into this, he needed to be home, and he reminded himself that soon he would be. He decided then that there'd be no sly line about the delivery guy and no digs inside either, he had to stay focused, had to keep the head. He had to lead by example as well. Brendan had seemed alright before, but he was now edging towards the pub like he was freaking out on a mile-high bridge. Jackie almost gave him his hand.

At the door the three shared their last nods, and at Amy's unexpected smile Jackie felt a bit of a rush. They stepped in. It was busier than yesterday and, maybe because there was a lassie by a window and another laughing with the barmaid, less threatening as well. The handful of screens blinked silent horse racing as marching music played, and Brendan let out a whimper and Jackie gazed around. Half a dozen possible Wayne's were staring back, although by the time they reached the bar the only ones still looking were a jug-eared teenager and the glaikit shell the owner had called Skin. A fortyish barmaid with dyed-black hair and a gaunt, yellowing face looked across and scowled. Before Jackie could open his mouth she nodded towards the back. In the darkness a hand raised.

Down but up again, and was that a snap of the fingers? Amy and Jackie strode ahead as Brendan stood back frozen. With the only lighting coming from the spotlights above the mural, Jackie just saw that the guy on the couch was big. Once at the table, a hand was waved to the stools in front, and Jackie and Amy sat down.

A big guy right enough, and with a pock-marked face, a slap of gelled hair and a fringe that could have been done with a ruler. Wayne also wore two hooped earrings, and below each sleeve of a *Help for Heroes* t-shirt was a British and a Northern Irish tattoo. Through slit brown eyes he scowled and wrapped chunky, sovereign-ringed fingers round his pint. This guy, thought Jackie. He saw him ranting on a radio phone-in, screaming at a teenage defender and fuming at the sight of a priest. Wayne put down his drink, and like it contained the faintest whiff of piss, scowled again. He touched his chest like he was going to burp, but instead said, 'So?'

Jackie gave his hand across the table and was relieved to get it shaken in return. 'I'm Jackie. This is Amy.' Wayne then turned to Brendan, appearing in silence at Jackie's back. 'This is ehm…This…This is Billy.'

Jackie watched Wayne search Brendan's startled face for several seconds then, appearing satisfied, sit back. 'Youse no getting a drink?' he asked.

50

That growl, Jackie thought, he wasn't putting it on. Wayne took their order and shouted to the barmaid.

'We need to know about John,' Amy said with a nervy smile. 'What can ye tell us?'

Wayne shrugged. 'Nothing, turns oot.'

'Nothing?' said Jackie. 'Ye must have an idea. Ye…'

'I put the word oot to the troops there. My duty. But I've got this for youse.' He picked up a grey hoodie and handed it to Amy. 'Daryl found it.'

Amy nodded. 'It's his.'

Wayne's eyes narrowed, the beginnings of a smirk appeared. 'Don't know this place, dae youse?'

'No,' Amy said.

He clasped his hands over his belly and nodded. 'See over there?'

The three peered across the bar to the far corner. 'What about it?' Amy asked.

'A couple of years ago a boy got stabbed there,' Wayne said. 'Know how?' No one replied and he nodded. 'Cos he didni like the new away top. And just under that far away window?' Again the family followed his gaze. 'A guy ended up with plates in his jaw cos he left a game ten minutes early. Aye, we've smartened up our act here,' he went on. 'That shite's rare now, but we need to keep on top of hings, know what I mean?' He flicked a nod at Amy. 'So that stunt your boyfriend pulled? A lot of people trusted him, felt whatdoyecallit, violated. Was up to me to find oot if wan or two of us were carrying a wee secret.' He shrugged. 'Or a big wan.'

'And?'

'Dignity,' he spat, glaring at all three of them. 'We bleed that in here. Even after massive Timmy intimidation nobody touched your boyfriend. Something to be proud of, that.' He took his pint and gulped.

'You hired him,' Jackie said.

'I did.' He wiped his mouth.

'Ye knew him.'

'No. He came in a few weeks ago. Had a pint and we chatted about the Gers. Had some no bad patter, John…Should I call him John? Or do I get his real name?'

Amy gave close to an apologetic smile. 'Shaun.'

'Shaun…? He shrugged for a surname.

'Does it matter? Just…'

Wayne downed the last of his pint, then grabbed his wallet and phone. 'Listen, the years I've been daeing this ye get a feeling, especially when you're spun a line about what sounds like a legit Bears t-shirt business. More fool me, eh?' He leaned over for a walking stick and pulled himself up. 'There's nothing for youse here.'

Amy slammed down her coffee, it spilled onto the table. 'Ye expect me to believe that?'

'Eh?'

'That my…my boyfriend, a Celtic supporter, would choose to work here? Of all *fucking* places?'

Wayne looked to her brothers in the hope they'd reign her in. 'Inside the mind of a Tim isni where I go on my holidays, dear.'

Jackie laid a hand on Amy's shoulder, and gestured to Wayne with the other. 'Mate, come on. We're lost. Fill in some bears about Sunday.'

'Bears?' Wayne shot stares between Jackie and Brendan, before it was an examination but now they were under the knife. Wayne had doubts, Jackie saw, but an even bigger one in saying them aloud. Accusing another bluenose of being a Tim would be like accusing your own mum of being a sex offender.

'Just cos we don't drink here, don't think we're secret mutants,' Jackie went on, feigning as much annoyance as he could. 'Get a grip, I've not been to a match in six years but only because I live in the Middle-East. Billy? A crying shame. He'd love to get to the fitba but he's been priced out the game. Int ye, Billy?'

No, Brendan hadn't imagined it. He threw his startled gaze onto the wall, onto the mural of a crowd who only appeared to be screaming for his death. To save his life he tried to work his mouth. '...Agh...aghg...*aye.*'

'Southside?' Wayne asked, sitting again.

'West End,' Jackie said.

'Some decent Bear shops in Partick.'

'We're not quite...Look, mate...'

The barman rolled his eyes. 'Ach, some of the boys clocked him from the off, awright? But they've got a habit of chucking accusations aboot, half of them would spot a Fenian in their own pint if they looked long enough. A rerun of the Hibs game and a few punters said your man cheered when they scored. I pulled him into the back and had it out with him. He denied it, and since I didni have eyes in the back of my fucking heid on that particular shift, I let it pass. But more and more people complained that he was a smartarse, and aye, one of *them*. I hadni really worked with the guy so I had to ask aboot.' He nodded at the barmaid. 'Maureen there, she didni think he was shady and I trust her. But then Sunday came.'

'What happened?' Jackie asked.

He pointed to the near side of the bar. 'What do ye see over there?'

'A calendar?'

'No. A gaping fucking hole.'

'Right...'

He grabbed a fistful of his t-shirt. 'Where *this* used to be.'

Jackie didn't get it, Amy took a few seconds. 'Help for Heroes? A...?'

'Collection tin. Two hunner quid. Ye trust your own family, right? Aw the way. Unless they're no family. There isni a Bear in the world who'd steal that.'

Jackie was about to agree until he saw Wayne shrink a touch, like he didn't quite believe it himself.

'So it was Shaun.' Amy snapped.

'It was a first, let's say that. By Sunday night the whole pub knew and it was threatening to kick aff, know what I mean? Daryl told me to get shot of him. I didni ask about the cash, I just wanted him gone. Noo,' he grabbed the stick again. 'My shift's starting.'

'One more question,' Jackie said.

'What?'

'Any spare tickets for Saturday?'

With a snigger Wayne hobbled away from the couch, and Jackie couldn't tell if it was because the tickets were like gold or Wayne was no fool. Amy got up to leave and Brendan let out a long, trembling fart, he followed it with a who-can-blame-me sort of shrug. Jackie placed a hand on Amy's arm. 'Wait. Can all that be backed-up? He nodded to the other eight or nine customers, none of them any longer with their eyes on them.

Brendan got off his seat, face twisted by every crack and note of the music. 'Come on! What are we...?'

Jackie threw a thumb behind himself. 'Who of that mob can fill us in?'

Doubting he'd make it out at alone, Brendan fell back on his stool, and Amy and Jackie turned to check out the regulars. The nearest customer, at a table by a window, was a woman. Blonde and friendly-looking and near Amy's age, she'd stuck out to Jackie before, and now even more because she was reading a book. Behind her sat a massive guy in a red stripy t-shirt muttering into his phone, he seemed to be glaring in their direction before turning with a sneer away. At the other side, two middle-aged couples chatted their way through a pub lunch, and an old guy in taped-up glasses sat hunched and alone. On barstools, a second old guy swayed in a dream to the music, and the jug-eared ned was shrieking in the face of the barmaid. Next to him was the only customer paying them any attention. A shrivelled waif of a man with a moustache as thick as the turn-ups in his jeans, Skin raised his pint and grinned. Deciding the guy knew nothing, Jackie only nodded back. If anyone could help it'd be the woman. He got up.

Brendan made for the door.

Got halfway.

'Tim Bastard!'

He froze to the spot but then bolted again. Then as he reached the exit, the ned shouted once more. Afraid that he'd dive from his stool, Amy blocked the guy's way, and as he remained there grinning she followed her brother outside. Jackie continued to the woman. Then he heard a clatter and a yelp.

He too ran outside.

On his back and groaning, Brendan had one hand on his knee and the other at his ear. He sat up and winced. Metres away, a guy was dusting himself down then stumbling off.

'Brendan, ye alright?' Jackie and Amy helped him to his feet. He shook his head out of a blur. '…That…guy…'

Blonde and in a red bomber jacket, he was disappearing up the road. 'Ye know him?'

'He winced. '…No, I don't…'

'He said sorry,' Amy said, examining Brendan's knee under his bloodied trackie-leg. 'Was it an accident?'

Checking his ear, he grimaced. 'We just crashed into each other…'

Jackie handed him back his cap. 'Right. But you're okay?'

'…I'll be fine, man.'

'Good.' Do youse mind?' Jackie said. 'Give me a minute?'

He jogged back inside. The woman wasn't there. No, she was heading to the toilets. Okay, he'd wait. He headed outside again to tell his sister and brother, but they're already moved on. Brendan was holding his head and Amy had an arm round him. 'Wait a minute!'

But with her free hand Amy threw up an apology.

It was time to go.

Brendan had had enough.

9

Brendan sat slumped on the subway as his sister inspected the bloody knee of his trackie. She patted his other knee and smiled. 'White vinegar will sort it.' At this Brendan winced and she laughed. 'For the stain, not your knee. I've got some at mine. We'll head there.'

'There's a bottle in my flat, I think.'

'Are you sure?'

He nodded. 'I need to get out this gear, man.'

Five stations later the three of them exited and travelled up the rumbling escalator. As Amy reminded her brother to meet by gates of the nearby park, Brendan limped alone across the busy road. Amy and Jackie watched him continue over a bridge, pass a newsagent's and turn up a street, then they headed back past the subway and down iron steps. They continued along a cobbled path.

Amy frowned. 'I need that boy to act his age a bit more.'

'He's freaked out like we all are,' Jackie said, arm around her shoulder. 'But we'll find Shaun. And they'll be alright.'

'Ye think that guy's telling the truth?'

He shrugged. 'Don't think he's totally at it. Not wanting violence in his beloved pub? Makes sense.'

Waiting at a roadside for a bus to trundle past, Amy grimaced at the wind, zipped her top up to her chin. 'But Shaun strolling in there when he could work in a thousand other pubs? I find that hard to buy, Jackie.'

'Aye.' Jackie sighed. 'Me as well.'

They entered the opened gates and stepped up a gravel track to a bench, Amy lifting a crushed can of coke and dropping it in a nearby bin. 'Police are obviously in no hurry,' she said, sitting down with her phone. 'I'll remind them.' But with a groan she dropped it onto her lap, hung her head back and gazed at the sky. 'Oh, I don't know.'

'Call them. No harm.'

'I mean Brendan.'

'He's *alright*.'

'No...look, Jackie. Something's been spinning round my head all morning. And it's starting to make me sick.'

Jackie sat up, put a hand on his sister's shoulder. 'What?'

'How do you think he and Shaun have got on these past two weeks?'

He pondered this. 'Not seen them together much. But...I'd say pretty well.'

'How many times *have* you seen them? Considering how excited we all were about you coming back?'

'Together?'

'Together.'

He bit at his lip. 'Your flat, the night I got here, and a week ago today. Aye, Shaun's been working the weekends so I widni expect any more. They were on good form, the both of them. How? What did I miss?'

'They were close growing up, we know that, right? Then dad died and the two of them, well they drifted apart. But even then, and I'm not sure if ye know this, Jackie, they still looked out for each other. That time Brendan had to be carried out drunk from the back of a classroom? Shaun got into shit as well, a boy had laughed at Brendan and Shaun battered him. Then when Shaun became obsessed with that bloody system, ye know he'd sometimes hide in Brendan's room? Brendan was the only one who wouldn't give him a lecture. They suffered alone most of the time but not always.'

'So…'

'So ye'd assume that now they're here, now they're older and sorting their lives out, they'd be getting close again, right?'

'Aye.'

'No.'

'No? Ye sure? Last Tuesday…'

'What? A few laughs?'

'More than a few.'

'Was beer involved? Football?' Amy didn't wait for an answer. 'There's no communication between them, Jackie. They're practically strangers.'

'Okay, but growing apart, it happens. What ye saying, Amy? Brendan knows something about Shaun? And he's no telling us?'

Amy dropped her head into her hands, her fingers dragging down her face. 'Okay. So I sent Brendan to London last October, I told him to tell Shaun we missed him and needed him back. He was so sweet, Brendan, he knew Shaun was forever letting me down with his broken promises about visiting, or else bullshitting about his life and that bloody *system*. He was so worried about failing, about disappointing me.'

'But he didni. Two days later Shaun was back.'

'He was back, alright. Brendan was as well but they didn't come up together, did you know that? The thing is, I don't even think Brendan had anything to do with Shaun coming home.' She shrugged. 'By his reaction when I called to thank him, I don't think he *knew*.'

'No idea at all?'

'Well, the night before Shaun took the train up, I called Brendan. The only news he had for me was that Shaun was staying in London and he was a *fucking loser*. Those words. Laughing as well, he was. He was steaming but still, Brendan was never a vindictive drunk.'

'They had a falling out. He was upset. Natural.'

'Then they were home within hours of each other, but if I still ask either of them why, they run a mile. I just wonder if something happened down there, something that's driven a wedge between them that they won't speak about.'

'I don't really think there's an awful lot there, Amy. I-'

'-Yeah, you know what?' Amy jumped up. 'It's fine, I shouldn't have expected ye to understand, I've obviously just turned into a sad neurotic over the years. Maybe Shaun will turn up any minute and say he lost track of the time, eh? Because it's just me, isn't it? Obviously.'

'No, look…'

She turned around. 'I'm going home.'

'What about Brendan?'

'He's big enough.'

Jackie followed, and on the walk back to Amy's he kept his mouth shut. His sister needed time with her thoughts, he knew, for God's sake they all needed time, *he* should disappear somewhere for a couple of hours. In her flat, Amy muttered to herself about the police as she drifted into the kitchen, and from the living room Jackie heard her plead on the phone then hang up. She made another call then, one where she was near to shouting, followed by a third where she sounded calm but insistent. Finally she marched into the living room, eyes glaring and fists clenched.

'Just spoken to that guy Daryl.'

'About Wayne?'

'About Wayne. And guess what?'

'Tell me.'

'He's a gambler. And more than that? Daryl mentioned the guy might have a problem. Aye, the lying toad goes to meetings.'

10

'It's tonight we need to keep the nut screwed for, no Sunday. That'll be a cake-walk.' The barfly took a slurp, his neck disappearing into his once-white shirt collar, and he resurfaced seconds later with a moustache like a lightly-dipped paintbrush. Holding his grin at the barman's back, he hoped for him to turn around, but then he sighed, lowered his gaze. After eyeing up the carpet like it was an old adversary who might just rip him off, Skin stepped down and shuffled to the toilet.

Wayne stood back from the fridge and grabbed the remote, turned and zapped on a screen. A list of match odds was revealed and he stared at them, licking his lips. Then the door clattered open and a customer marched in. Hitting the *off* button, he nodded at the young guy in the blue-overalls bouncing onto a stool. The guy sneered at the pub's deadness, and Wayne muttered that Skin was in the toilets if he fancied a game of Twister. The guy laughed but Wayne didn't. He didn't have to either. Being known as a miserable bastard had its advantages.

Wayne would have at least maybe felt like laughing if he hadn't got the scoop hours before, that the girlfriend wasn't done, earlier she'd been screaming down Maureen's ear for Daryl's number. More questions for Daryl this would mean, more questions about him, questions that he'd like to remain unanswered, thanks very fucking much. He placed the pint on the bar, spilled some, refilled. How long before the three turned up again with more of their nosey pish? In normal circumstances getting shot of them would be a doddle, his *arse* those guys were Bears. But there was nothing normal about any of this, and telling the punters just wasn't an option. With a ...*fuck*... he slammed the till. Deal with it when he had to.

The customer raised his pint. 'Title's ours, Big Yin.'

Wayne slapped down a towel and scratched his chin. 'No,' he sighed, gazing at the door. 'Bit to go, yet.'

Jackie gave Brendan the scoop around six. Those two would head to Crawford's at eight, and Amy would stay home and wait for any news. His brother sat half-sunk into the couch, gazing at an ancient string of chewing gum embedded in the bald, greying carpet. Jackie regretted not telling him earlier, he could have sent a text or left a message. Then again, if Brendan had had time to absorb this he might have got off his mark. When he spoke up, Jackie could barely hear him.

'Back there.'

'Aye.'

'In...*there.*'

'Brendan? The guy's spinning us a line. We need the truth.'

'The truth, sure.'

'We'll get it.'

He snorted. 'If you say so.'

'Ye should have come to Amy's, by the way. I get ye need time of your own but we're all going through this crap. Talking can help.'

'Didni feel like talking, Jackie. Canni think why. Maybe it's cos my brother's done one or my leg's burst to fuck, or just cos my life's that bit shiter than it was three days ago. Take your pick.'

'Come on,' Jackie sat on the couch next to him, the only one to smile when he almost fell into the hole. 'The first problem will soon be over, I'm sure of it, and your second I can't do much about. But your last? Hey, give yourself a break, come to Cairo when all this is done. On me. There's the Sinai. The Red Sea. Get away fae those-'

'-Look.' Brendan swiped up a hand. 'Enough of that pish. I don't care about a holiday, I hate the sun. Just…Ye want me in there? Fine. Just don't expect me to open my gub.'

Jackie sat back and nodded. 'Deal.'

Brendan stood up, grabbed his wallet from his lopsided bedside cabinet. 'Their game's on the telly so it'll be mobbed. Don't know about you but I'm getting tanked up.'

In minutes Brendan was back, bursting open one can and shoving another in Jackie's chest. Jackie took it without a word, who knew how this would go and a beer or two could kill the edge. But when Brendan moved onto his second before Jackie had even started, he realised his brother would have to be watched. Talking to him about dangers, that would just be pointless. Better to grab some food and make sure it got inside him.

He left for the chippy downstairs, and when he got back Irish music was pumping and Brendan was pacing around like a pre-fight boxer. His flatmate, Gary the Irn Bru fan, had arrived and was on the couch, smiling curious at the midweek state of his pal. As Brendan jumped about, Gary raised a can and laughed. 'Must be some doo youse have got lined up. Where youse heading, Jackie, Playboy Mansions?'

Jackie swung a fish supper under Brendan's nose. 'No. Where we're going, there's gonni be sex *and* intelligence. Right, Brendan?'

'Seriously…?' Gary was almost on his feet. 'Am I getting filled in or…?'

The tune headed to a crescendo, and in the coming pocket of silence Brendan raised a finger. He took a breath, and as the song climaxed the finger came down. Stamping his feet now and clapping his hands, Brendan chanted in Jackie's face, to rouse or offend him Jackie had no clue. There was a whoop and the flatmate was up, pouring vodka Jackie hadn't seen and offering up glasses. Jackie knocked it back but Brendan took his, and once it was downed the pals stood screaming at each other. Jackie just sat and watched, it was like some demented Glasgow opera that might well last for hours. But it was actually done in a minute, and with a pair of victorious roars Gary flopped down and Brendan swiped up his dinner. Gary spoke up again for at least *some* sort of clue. Killing the volume, Jackie said it was a family thing.

Brendan didn't seem bothered about the cutting of the sounds, instead he got into his supper, and for the next few minutes the only noise was him munching through it. Gary got up and muttered a disappointed goodbye, then Brendan tossed away the wrapper and wiped his mouth.

'Aye. The sooner we chin this guy…' Jackie said.

Brendan stood and opened his wardrobe. From the bottom he dragged out a bashed-up shoe box. Full, it looked, and he opened and rummaged around. Jackie noticed football programmes and match tickets, coins and one or two CDs. Probably all were of some value to his brother, but worthless compared to what else Jackie saw: a handful of photos. Flashes of their dad, moustached and smiling; their mum, head back and laughing; all the family in the sunshine camping. Everything that meant something to Brendan was in that shoebox.

With a relieved whistle, Brendan pulled it out.

'Come on. You're winding me up.'

'Nope.' Brendan fastened it round his neck. 'No leaving without this beauty.'

'A crucifix?'

'I'll cover it.'

'With what? A Celtic scarf?'

From the wardrobe he grabbed a black crew-neck and threw it on.

Jackie rolled his eyes. 'Whatever. Let's just do it.'

Brendan took the crucifix from inside his clothes, gave it a polish and a kiss. Then he tucked it back in. 'Right. Let's see what that fat prick's hiding.' He bent down and lifted two more cans. 'Wan for the road?'

11

'*Billy*. That's your one job in there. Ye answer to the name of Billy.' Into the half-light, Brendan bounced up the underground steps like he was heading to a cup final. 'Just get that into your head and we'll be …Ye listening?'

Starting to strut, Brendan threw up an arm at his brother behind him. 'No speako the Huno!'

'Billy!'

Jackie swore under his breath. Brendan, he'd spent one half of the journey muttering Celtic tunes like they were precious incantations, the other doubled-up and groaning like he'd just been poisoned. He was only one more thing to fret about and Jackie really should have come alone. At least when the pub came into view his brother slowed down. Then he stopped altogether. He took off his cap and started mincing about the pavement. He slapped it back on. '…I need a piss.'

'Ye might just find a toilet in the pub.'

He gazed towards it. 'Listen, man. That ned. Him with the ears. Any hassle, I ignore it. Aye?'

'Hassle fae him, I'll know what to do.'

'Cool.' Brendan nodded in front with a gulp. 'I'm right behind ye.'

Jackie swung open the door to an attack of roars and groans. Brendan had been right. Mobbed. Drinkers were three deep around the bar and huddled under TVs, they were crammed round tables and spilling out towards the exit. At the brothers' arrival, some customers made glances but returned to the screen as quick, although a few did blink back and possibly Jackie thought, sneer. He stepped for the bar, and saw the score on a screen and mouthed a *yes*. Coolly done, he was sure. Even cooler now would be a punch on Brendan's arm and a cheeky grin in return. But who was he kidding, he wasn't even sure Brendan had come in. He turned, saw his brother staring down at his trainers.

'Billy...? Drink?'

Brendan dared to lift his eyes. 'Nah.'

'No..? What do ye...?' He turned around again, at the same time taking a scan for any potential attackers. The crew-cut ned was on the same stool as before, in fact was now leering their way like he'd been waiting for their return. By a window, two middle-aged guys in golf jumpers seemed to be smirking across, then like piss-taking schoolboys muttered into their drinks. At a pillar towards the back, Jackie found a familiar-looking dark-haired woman who, caught by him staring, seemed to draw her eyes away in disgust. Jackie continued to squeeze his way to the bar, and once there fixed his eyes on a screen. He got served and grabbed the drinks.

Brendan took his pint, held it out like a live firework.

'Oh at least look like you've seen one before.'

'Heavy duty this, man.' His lips moved like he was some amateur ventriloquist. 'Major heavy duty.'

'Let's just find this guy and get out of here.'

'Canni...' Brendan pointed to his crotch. '...I'm...'

Jackie threw a finger towards the toilets. 'There.'

With a breath and a mutter and a pat at his hidden crucifix, Brendan set off on his trek, as Jackie peered around to the other side of the bar. No Wayne there either, he noticed, then it struck him that the guy might not even be here. Why must he? The shift he'd worked on earlier could have finished by now, it was likely that the guy went home occasionally. He stole more looks around, and as he did recognised the dark-haired woman as the lunchtime barmaid, now obviously off-duty. Their eyes met again but this time she nodded, and Jackie wondered if he'd imagined her previous scowl. The two golfers were now clapping at the telly and even the ned was cackling to himself. Whether they were in danger or not, the match was much more important.

Soon he'd scoured every inch of Crawford's except where Wayne had sat before. Blocking his view stood an army of drinkers, with only the blue sky of the mural visible behind them. The drinkers gazed at their screen, satisfied, edgy and perplexed, until a dodgy tackle on a player had them all pointing and pushing and screaming. Jackie shuddered. The fat baldies, the wiry teenagers, even the tomato-faced steamers, not a mob to piss off in their own house. With Brendan a liability, he headed towards the locals on his own.

Offering apologies, laughs and smiles, Jackie had a vague feeling of tightrope walking with his pint some useless prop. He caught glimpses into the back but nothing of Wayne, and decided to ask the barmaid a few steps away. Then he heard it ...*Fenian*... and he sensed the craning of necks. *Taig*... he heard after that and saw the nudging of shoulders. Feeling the heat of a hundred eyes Jackie stared ahead, steeling himself for a whack from any one of several directions. The word had been spreading since lunchtime, he guessed, was sweeping around the pub, the brothers of the Fenian thief had been in and asking a lot of questions. No slap came or any more names, instead there was a yelp. Jackie spun to the toilets, saw Brendan tumbling out before a skinny, shrieking figure. Wide-eyed and minus his cap, Brendan threw himself to the wall. Then he crouched down in front like a hunted goalie.

'Fucking TAAAIIIIIG!' The ned's mouth stretched wide and mad across his face, with the pub now nudged to silence. Across the bar a spiky, blonde-haired woman snarled the first threat at the impostor, elbowed her husband to sort him out. By a window a man with a swollen, purple nose rolled up his sleeves and pushed forward. Then others came, muttering and shouting, and Jackie was shoved by a tattooed fat-neck. He set off to his brother's defence, jumped on the fat guy who was now putting on a charge. As he fell, Jackie fell as well, crashed onto a table then toppled onto the floor. Among the flying glass and shouts, he saw a weapon and heard a roar.

'Fucking enough!'

Jackie jumped up, scrambled to the wall with Brendan. With his stick Wayne swiped away the attackers, then hobbled in front of the brothers. 'Leave it!'

The crowd backed-off and shouts fell to mumbles, under a foot a glass crunched and on the TVs a goal was scored. Wayne gave a sweeping glare of his regulars before he settled on the ned. He eyed up his terrified face, and sneering he drew back his free hand. But then he dropped it, turned to the rest. 'What's wrong with youse?'

'Tims!' shouted one. 'We're infested in here!'

'Look aboot ye!' called another. 'Pals of that Fenian thief! What's wrong with *you*, Wayne?'

'I'm no a *Fenian*!' Shouted by the guy now getting to his feet, the last word was spat, and Jackie near applauded his brother excelling in the role of the indignant Orangeman. But as Brendan stood shaking and wiping a tear, he saw it was no act. Even in this place, to call Brendan a Fenian was to cross a line. Before his brother might continue the arrangements for their joint funeral, Jackie stood up.

'Get something straight.' His voice quivered and his legs did too. 'We're no mates with that Catholic prick. Our sister's marrying him, that's it.'

Still sneering, Wayne flicked him a nod, Jackie not knowing if he was on their side or not. 'What else do ye want the troops to know?'

'We're Bears. Just like you. Want to be among our own.'

'Pish!' came a scream.

Wheezing, Wayne raised a hand for quiet. He got it and both hands again gripped the stick. 'How many of youse have been lumbered with Tims in your family? ...Eh?' He took the silence for embarrassment and nodded satisfied. 'Blame yourselves, dae youse? When your mad auntie bagged the mutant beggar up the Savoy, that was aw your fault, aye?' There was laughter now but the barman's face stayed straight. 'And how many of youse are related to Tims like the arsehole we kicked oot of here? ...Naebdy? Lying fucking arses. Bobby, there? We aw know Bobby you've got a *John Paul* in your family. A John fucking Paul with a season ticket for the Tims.'

The owner of the purple nose huffed. 'No my fault. The guy's a prick.'

'No saying that when you're pulling his cracker at Christmas, are ye?'

More laughing as Wayne shook his head. 'Spare a thought for these boys, that's aw I'm saying.' He headed back through the bar. 'Karen, get them a drink.'

The crowd backed off. The brothers got pats and smiles as well as lingering stares. But for the most part they were now ignored. There was a replay to catch.

As Jackie approached, Wayne passed over a pint. 'Don't mind our boys. Loyal, nothing more than that.'

Jackie shrugged. 'I get it. It's cool.'

He gestured with the second pint, but as Jackie leaned over he grabbed his arm.

'What ye doing?

The barman leaned in close, their faces now inches apart. He nodded through the window behind his visitor towards a brightly lit kebab shop. 'Doner Spectacular, ya Fenian prick. Half-time.'

12

Jackie kept his eyes on the TV screen in front. 'Three minutes,' he muttered between sips to his brother. 'Keep yir kecks on.'

Chalk-white and with a mouth like an open goal, Brendan had first tried getting his brother's attention by kicking at his foot. By now though he was mincing about and whimpering like a dog about to have a crap on a carpet. 'Fuck half-time, Jackie,' he groaned. 'Let's go now.'

But Jackie wasn't having it, they needed to look to be *into* this, like Scottish football wasn't every bit as crap as the last time he'd caught it on the telly. As customers headed to the toilets and outside for a smoke, Jackie had another scan around. He was caught by Skin who immediately raised a pint, and he gave a warm grin in return. With the floor now starting to clear he recognised a couple more faces. In the same seat as earlier sat the big guy in the stripy t-shirt, he had Unionist tattoos, Jackie noticed, and still looked pissed-off. Half-behind a pillar was the woman with the paperback, now in an orange top and groaning at a near miss. 'A few more seconds,' Jackie muttered.

Brendan braved a glance of his own. He shot back a yelp.

'What's wrong?'

He stared down, breathed hard. 'Come on, let's just…'

Jackie looked across. The blonde woman by the pillar was now gazing over, appeared to be smiling at Brendan. '…No way.'

Another yelp as Brendan tried to move, found himself blocked by bodies. 'Excuse me, I…'

'That's what's up with ye!'

'No, I just...'

'She's quite nice-looking,' Jackie said. 'What do ye think? Ye can still go for it.'

The whistle blew and the huddle of regulars dispersed, leaving the brothers to make for the door. Others followed and the blonde woman, mobile at her ear, was one. Seeing her, Brendan put on a march, although her path was clearer so she was behind him quick. At the exit she mouthed a *Hi* and flashed a shy smile, and Brendan thought Jackie, *appeared* to smile back. But then she spoke into her phone and all was revealed. 'Not around?' she said in a thick Northern Irish accent. 'I'll try later. Aye, it's Britt.' Brendan tripped over his feet and onto the pavement.

Donner Spectacular faced the side of Crawford's across a square patch of waste ground. By the wide street-lit road, Brendan remained some hesitant steps behind Jackie, but at least for now he'd stopped whimpering. Seconds from the shop's flashing green and red neon, the two customers were visible to the brothers, both were male and on the big side but neither of them were Wayne. Brendan called on his brother, suggested they just do one, and Jackie rubbed his brow and gave a solemn shake of the head. 'Shaun's been missing nearly three days and we're finally getting a head's up. And you want to chuck it?'

His lip trembled. 'Jackie...'

'What...?'

'This place, man...'

'Hey!'

The brothers peered up the street to find Wayne standing at a corner. He nodded into a side-street and disappeared.

The brothers started to follow. At the corner they saw Wayne now waiting further ahead, gesturing into an alleyway and moving towards it. Again they followed, finally found him behind a row of wheelie bins lighting a fag.

Wayne nodded like he was offering them a seat, and Brendan even looked around. He drew on his cigarette, exhaled into the air. 'Some goal, eh?'

'Aye,' Jackie snapped. 'Cracker. So? The truth?'

'Truth?' Wayne gazed at the night sky and chuckled. 'Talk to Daryl, aye?'

'Hardly had to. We know Shaun well enough. Know he widni just walk in there for a job.'

Wayne turned to them, the lamppost yellow lighting his flabby, pock-marked face. 'See the first time I saw that Shaun of yours? Know what he wore?'

'What?' Jackie asked with an impatient shrug.

'A fucking bright green bubble jacket. Like a giant snotter, he was. Seriously, enough to gie ye the bolk. But that's the thing with addiction.' The barman sneered at them like they could never know the pain. 'A massive leveller. When you're about to crawl with somebody oot a mountain of shite, ye don't ask if they've washed their hands, know what I mean?' He coughed then, spat on the ground. 'Two months ago that meeting was but it wisni his first, he'd heard me talk a couple of years back and thought we might hit it aff. Turned oot he was right, I actually liked

Shaun.' He paused for a moment, gazed at his cigarette. 'For a problem gambler he didni expect somebody to lick away his tears, know what I mean? We went for a drink and talked about our demons. Tell ye, was the first time I ever laughed mine right back into their box.'

Jackie kept his eyes on Wayne as Brendan gazed into a puddle. Jackie nodded for more.

'So he had cash issues. Fucking obviously. Kind of happens with us gamblers, canni work it oot.' He pondered his next thought, flicked ash to the ground. 'So I did the decent thing.'

'Gave him a job? Why?'

'Ye no listening?'

'Why there? Shaun could have worked in a load of pubs. Crawford's makes no sense.'

A mobile vibrated in the back of Wayne's denims and he pulled it out. The wrong one. He pulled out another, hit *ignore*. 'Suppose it suited him. He was after cash for a flat or some fucking thing, so I gave him shifts on a Saturday and Sunday for four or five weeks. Tax free as well. I'm owed a few favours by that failed apprentice hairdresser in there, but any longer would have been taking the piss.'

'Shaun wisni up for paying tax?'

'Who am I? Columbo? I'm guessing he wisni keen on writing down his Catholic name on official forms in front of somebody that wisni me.' He flicked his fag in the air and watched it cartwheel onto the cobbles. 'Anyway, for my good turn I got a fucking slap in the face, know what I mean? So how about youse show a wee bit of appreciation and…piss off?' He lifted his stick to move.

'Hold on,' Jackie said. 'Did ye ask what he was playing at? Letting his guard down in there?'

'Ask? I told him to sort it oot. He said they just wirni used to his patter and he'd win them over. I suppose he forgot to mention he was also a tea leaf.'

'Are ye sure nobody followed him on Sunday?'

'Sort it oot. If there'd been shite from a regular, I'd know. Hardest man in there's probably the Weapon, and he *took* the kicks, no the other way aboot.'

'The Weapon?'

About to head away, a faint smile now curled in Wayne. 'Ye don't know…?'

Brendan glanced at his brother, then the barman. 'Andy West,' he muttered.

'Andy West.' Wayne grinned. 'And here I was thinking you were just a sad Tim, Jackie. But you're what? Klingon?' He tapped the ground, nodded at Brendan. 'Wee man, fill your brother in on the Weapon.'

'Played for Rangers…For years.'

He rolled his eyes. 'Only 518 times, son. Only 209 goals.'

Brendan murmured what sounded like an apology.

'How did Andy West feel about Shaun?' Jackie asked. 'Did he have issues with him?'

At the idea of the two men being on level terms, Wayne sniggered. 'Came in on Sunday first time in weeks, as usual couldni get a minute's peace. Some of the punters told him aboot your pal and the missing collection tin. He was already raging about some other thing but he loves that pub, our club, our forces, so it set him off, know what I mean? He told Daryl to get Shaun to fuck and Daryl told me. An act of kindness on everybody's part or The Weapon really would have sorted him oot. By the way, he sometimes turns up midweek for a match. Fancy going back in? He's the *real* owner of Crawford's, could empty the place with a snap of his fingers. *And* he's the wan guy my daft rules don't apply to.' He spat again, hobbled off. 'Anyway, been shite talking. Ya pair of dicks.'

*

Thursday, 21ˢᵗ February (cont'd)

Sorry, mate, I...I didn't want to interrupt ye there.

I'm no sure if ye remember me. I remember you. A couple of years ago, it was. Aye, was in May nearly two years back. It was my first meeting and before it started ye spoke to me. See what you said? Some of those words, honestly, they've never left me.

Not that I took many on board at the time. Believe me, I wish I did. But I have now and I'm all the better for it. Listen, I'm sorry. What you're going through sounds tough. This secret ye know about, somebody in your family and how...Well, whatever it is, whatever the issue, I understand the temptation. To try to cash in. To try and use it. To try and make your break from here.

But maybe your words can help you now.

'Your family are like fitba fans. No matter how much ye let them down, they'll always be there.'

That's what ye said.

It's Wayne, intit it?

I'm Shaun.

Don't do anything drastic.

Just don't, man.

Talk later if ye want.

13

The brothers neared Crawford's again, and Brendan spied a black cab and waved.

Jackie swiped down his arm. 'What ye playing at? We're not going home yet.'

'I thought…'

'We've got zilch to go home *with*. We go back in there, we've got to get something.'

The stragglers strode back for the pub, and Brendan stood frozen until they'd all passed. He straightened up, turned and eyed his older brother. 'I'm done with that shitehole.'

Jackie was about to bark back but instead he sighed. 'Brendan, listen. Do ye no get it? After what he's confessed to us? That prick's screwed. He looks after us or we ruin him.'

'And Andy West? We gonni chin him, aye?'

'If he wants to come clean, I'm all ears. What do ye know about him anyway?'

'Told ye.' Brendan had come back down to size. 'Retired about five years ago.'

'Hard man?'

'Had his moments. Ugly bastard.'

Jackie huffed. 'Ye surprise me.'

'Straight up. Big and baldy. Eyes like pissholes in the snow. Good player but, man. Canni believe ye don't know him.'

'Has he ever been in the news for anything, like, dodgy? Gangster pals or-?'

'Excuse me?'

A breeze of sweet perfume hit them as they turned, and at who was smiling back Brendan jumped. Slipping her mobile into her pocket, the woman in the orange t-shirt smiled wider and giggled. 'Sorry, don't mean to interrupt. Just saying hi. Haven't seen you in Crawford's before.' She was looking mostly at Brendan, his face now angled like the visor of his cap was a forcefield. Silence followed. 'Sorry for…'

'Not at all.' Jackie put out his hand. 'I'm Jackie.'

Her eyes brightened again. 'Good to meet you. Britt.'

'Aye, we're new to Crawford's. This is my brother, Billy.'

Brendan edged his eyes upwards, nodded like he was pleading guilty to some stitch-up in court. He shook her hand, drew his own back quick.

'You enjoying the game?'

Brendan started patting about his body like he was after a gun to end it all. He glanced twice at Jackie but there'd be no bail out there. 'Ehm…aye, man… Cracking…'

Jackie grinned at Brendan's mangled tongue and fixation with the pavement. Then before she changed her mind, he made a move. 'You? Regular?' He glanced at the crest on her t-shirt, an embroidered Union Jack with a three-word slogan. Brendan did the same. It wasn't of a flute band or supporter's club, but a sports company.

Britt frowned. 'Nah.'

'Just over from, ehm, Ulster, then?'

She fixed back a strand of straight, shoulder-length hair, a hooped earring dangled. 'No. I'm in Glasgow six years now.'

'Right.'

'Not much of a football fan really.'

Jackie glanced at his brother, now daring to lift his eyes again. 'Okay…'

'Sorry. I'm confusing you.'

'Aye. So what is it about there? The cuisine?'

She laughed. 'No. But I'm going back in if you are.'

Jackie pointed pistol-style back to the pub. 'Sure.'

Britt collected her drink and the three stood by the bar, the other eyes again were all on the screens. 'Ye seen Andy West here the night?' Jackie asked. '…Ye know who he is, right?'

Britt grimaced. 'I…'

'No?' he laughed. 'Makes two of us.'

She sipped at her coke. 'My brother, he was the regular.'

'Your brother?'

'James.'

'Oh, right. Not here?'

'No.'

'Right.'

'He died.'

'Oh, I'm sorry. Really.' Jackie put his hand to his chest, Brendan stumbled over his lips.

'Yeah, six months ago. A massive Rangers fan, he was. Would get the ferry over every fortnight and stay at mine, come here after the match.' She lowered her voice and with a secretive smile inched closer. 'I lost count of the times he'd try and coax me in. But this isn't...*wasn't*...my kind of place.' With an appreciative shrug she raised her glass. 'But now? Here I am.'

'Ye come to, sort of, remember him?'

'I see the colours, hear the singing.' Her eyes welled, she took a breath and smiled. 'I even find myself getting involved. Crazy, eh? My God, even crazier is that I'm telling you this. I'm so sorry.'

'No, God.' Jackie held up his hands. 'Don't be.'

'Is this a new spot to watch your team?'

'No exactly. Did ye not see the fight half an hour ago?'

'Fight? I arrived late, I...'

'We're no Rangers fans either, are we, ehm, Bill?' Brendan gave a panicky shake of the head. 'Nah, we're looking for our sister's boyfriend. He's a Celtic fan but worked in here, was keeping that part of his life secret but got found out. Hisni been seen since Sunday and, I don't know, it's all just dead weird.'

'You're worried?'

'Our sister is especially.'

'I don't know if, I mean I *do* come...Do you have a photo?'

Brendan took out his mobile, showed a picture and at last spoke. 'That's him.'

'What's his name?'

'Shaun. John in here. It's quite a story.'

She nodded. 'I think I saw him a couple of Sundays ago.'

'Anybody threaten him?' Jackie asked. 'I mean, did ye see anybody hostile in any way?'

'I'm sorry, I keep myself to myself, not really too keen on my own story getting out. But I'm in touch with a couple of James's friends. I don't see them in tonight but I can ask.'

'Great. Would ye mind even phoning them now, Britt? Amy's losing her mind.'

'Sure, send me the photo.' Britt gave her number and she received the picture. 'Give me a few minutes.' She headed outside.

Jackie winked at his brother who was now dipping in and out of his pint. 'See where one chat gets us? No everyone will be as cool as her but let's see what else turns up. And,' he added as Brendan came up from his drink for air. 'When this is all sorted, ye can give her a call.'

Brendan pulled at his cap like it might just magic him away. 'I just want oot of here.'

Jackie peered down the bar to the barfly slumped on the stool. He raised his glass, and when the guy didn't see he did it again. This time he was noticed, the regular shooting back a glazed but delighted grin. Jackie nodded in his direction. 'The action never stops round here, Brendan. Next stop, the shortarse.'

14

Skin held up his pint. 'Good evening, detective!'

'Jackie.'

The barfly smirked like he'd known the name for months.

'Can I get ye a drink?' Jackie asked.

He nodded at his near-empty pint and Jackie ordered. As the barmaid poured, Skin beamed like he was collecting some sort of award, while Jackie gazed at the others on the row of nearby stools. The ned sat frowning like he'd been gagged, drugged and caged, while the rest to various degrees of engagement, sat gazing at the screens.

Part of the memorabilia on the royal blue wall behind Skin was a framed forty-year-old pendant. Jackie nodded. 'You'll be due one of them, eh?'

'Of what?' Skin lifted himself around.

'A testimonial. Like Sandy. How long ye drunk here for?'

He turned back and glared at Jackie like the whole world knew the answer, then he sat cross-eyed trying to work it out. Jackie checked him out. The guy's jeans had been made for a kid, his arms were bone thin and his eyelids looked set to collapse. With the answer clearly beyond him, he eventually sighed. 'Ach, you'd have been in nappies when I started.'

Jackie forced an impressed laugh, then found himself staring at a figure emerging from inside the bar. The snarling guy in the stripy t-shirt. As unlikely as it might be for a customer to step out like that, Jackie might not even have noticed if...Had the guy been staring at him again? ...And spun away like he'd been caught? Maybe. But for all that's happened why wouldn't he?

'Wisni Crawford's then either, let me tell ye.' Skin continued.

'Oh, right. What was it?'

Skin examined the idiot in front of him. 'The Admiral!'

'Aye, I think I remember. Anyway, mate? Ye know why we're here? The main reason?'

'Same as yesterday.'

'Shaun. He's a dick. But we need to find him.'

The ex-barman's new name lodged in Skin's head like an arrow. He glared around. 'Hey boys…Do youse know the-?'

'-Look, mate. It's Skin, intit? Skin, I'm no gonni explain myself again. I'm guessing ye were here over the weekend. Is there any chance ye can help us?'

'Who told ye?'

'That ye were here?' Jackie asked.

'My name.'

'The chief, Daryl.'

Skin sneered, crumbs visible among the strands of his parting, greying moustache. 'What did he say?'

'I canni remember, nothing really…'

'*Daryl*,' Skin spat. 'Couldni spell Gers if ye put a gun to his heid.'

'Watch it.' The barmaid shot Skin a look and he muttered into his pint.

'Fair enough, I'm new. But about-'

The barfly sat back up. '-Thought this would be a normal Bear's shop, dint ye? Boof!' He threw both hands up like his head had exploded and cackled, tiny shoulders shuddering. 'Blows yir mind, so it does.'

'Sunday night,' said Jackie.

'What's it like?'

'What's *what* like?'

'The Middle-East? Wayne says ye were there.'

'It's fine,' Jackie said. 'I...'

'I thought we'd finished with aw that shite. Where are ye stationed? Iraq?'

'What? No, I'm no a...'

'Thanks for yir service by the way.'

'...Whatever,' said Jackie. 'Look...'

'Didni agree wi it, myself.'

'My sister's boyfriend...'

'...Thought it was a lot of shite.'

'The *Celtic* fan...'

Skin thought for a moment, tapping at his small, yellowing teeth. Then he delved into his denim jacket and grabbed a pack of tobacco. A glance at the screen and he climbed off his stool. 'Mon.'

Jackie followed him towards the door. Brendan was no longer where he'd left him and Jackie doubted he'd risked another trip to the toilets, and when he couldn't spy him outside either he knew he was on his own. Starting to whistle, Skin leaned back against the pub wall, swiped out a cigarette paper and sprinkled in tobacco. He lit up and drew, gazed at the fag like it was a decent last request and stared out across the road. Jackie stood by a bus shelter with an urge to chuck him back into the pub. 'Ye were *saying*. Sunday.'

'Aye,' Skin said.

'*What?*'

He glanced up from his roll-up and sighed. 'The Proddie Pyramids.'

'The…eh?'

He gestured behind. 'The treasures. Priceless, so they are. Who do ye think's responsible for it aw? Who's the Crawford's hingmy…Indiana Jones?'

'Not got a…'

'No Daryl, I'll tell ye that for fuck all.' He shook his head. 'A snake. No, worse. He's that bird that nicks other birds' nests. What's that again? Ye know the fucking…'

'Cuckoo.'

'Cuckoo?' Skin glared back. '*Cuck*-?' He glanced to his side as if to spread this ridiculous answer, then remembered where he was. 'No, it's ehm…They come here from all over the world, the punters. Tumble in, eyes like fucking *that* so they are, greeting some of them. And who do they suck up to? The guy that started it? Nah. They near pish themselves over the wan who makes sure his coupon's aw over the website.'

'So who did-?'

'-Wayne,' Skin said. 'Back when he owned it.'

'Wayne owned it but now he disni. I sympathise.'

'Co-owned it. The two of them hingmy, inherited this place fae their uncle. Was always a Bears' shop but Wayne went the full nine yards. That photo of Gazza above the bar? That's how it started. Then he put up more stuff and a few of the boys helped oot. The treble scarf fae 93?' He sucked on his fag, winked. 'That was mine.'

'Look...'

'What was the name of that wee...the wee king in the pyramids...' Skin snapped at his fingers. '...Fucking...'

'Tutank-'

'-Aye!' He jabbed a finger, almost throwing himself to the ground in the process. 'Imagine hingmy, Tutan-fucking-khamen standing in his pyramid showing ye aboot? Ye widni get over it, neither ye would. Well, that's what we've got. Andy, wee Sergio, Davie Broon, legends everywhere. Started four, five year ago when he came doon for a Q and A, the Weapon. His da and Wayne's da were mates fae the shipyards, and Andy had no long retired and was on a right downer. Nae wonder, eh? How do ye follow banging in goals for the Gers half your life? What a night. The Weapon couldni get enough, told every player he knew that Crawford's was the place to be. Of course Billy Big Time stepped in after that but Wayne was the wan that got Crawford's the rep. Tragic he's just a barman now. Could have walked away but he'd never dae that.'

'Am I wasting my time?'

'He's got it *here*.' Skin punched his chest, fell back to the wall. 'His cousin, but?' he said, stepping forward again. 'Withoot Wayne, withoot what Wayne *built*, he'd be nothing. So on Sunday, right? On Sunday? I was watching the guy.'

'Daryl?'

'The barman! Fuck's sake, ye listening? I'd clocked him fae the start, so I had. The crew were getting wound up cos he didni look happy at the goals, but I'd seen something worse, caught him badmouthing us under his breath. I had a word with Wayne, private an that, wisni gonni embarrass the guy in case I'd made a hingmy, mistake. Anyway, turned oot Wayne didni sort your pal oot after all.'

Jackie waved at Britt along the pavement. 'Wrong. He sacked him. See ye.'

'I'm no talking about gieing him the boot. I'm talking aboot sorting him oot! That was Daryl.'

Jackie stopped. 'What do ye mean?'

'Had to prove himself, show he meant business. Player of the Year dance in three weeks and the biggest legend of the lot might no even turn up.'

'West?'

'Who else? Pansy-features likes to think they're best mates but it's no like that, the Weapon just uses him for the private lock-ins. Anyway West, aye, he told Daryl to get your pal to fuck. Raging he was, and Daryl got feart that he might no come back. So after Wayne gave your mate the hook, Daryl made a wee hingmy, gesture.' He nodded, and Jackie followed his line of sight in the darkness to parked cars and shuttered shops.

'What am I looking at?'

He nodded again. Not across the road but just in front of Jackie.

The bus shelter.

Jackie checked the grazed Perspex. Graffiti and fag burns and hardened bird crap. He shrugged.

'Here.' Skin stepped forward, shone the light of his mobile.

'I don't...What...?'

Skin stepped back to the pub door. Jackie thought he was heading inside and was about to shout him back, but instead he turned and ran, and head-first mock-hit the wall. 'Bam!' he laughed, wheezing as he staggered away again. 'Hey, Daryl did what he had to dae, nothing more. What happened after that, but?' With a cackle he put the fag again to his mouth. 'I'm guessing The Weapon followed up. He was magic at that. Following up.'

Then Jackie saw it.

The head-high smear of congealed, darkened red.

Skin smiled and winked like it was all his own work. 'Fenian Blood.'

15

'*Blood?*'

'Could be anybody's, and could have been there for weeks as far as we know.' Jackie took out the milk and bread from the carrier bag. 'It's the middle of Ibrox, for God's sake. It was dark and I was being shown it by Lieutenant Blotto, it could have just *looked* like blood. I thought it was best not to freak ye out.'

A red hairband between her fingers, Amy stood by the kitchen door open-mouthed. 'I'm just finding this a bit hard to process. Last night ye told me ye got the truth out that barman and met a lassie who's going to help. And now this?'

'It's just…'

'How much *look like* blood are we talking?'

'I suppose…' Jackie said.

'A lot?'

'…I'm sorry.'

'You're sorry?'

'Having slept on it, I should have said.'

'And this…' Amy threw up a hand in disgust, her hairband dropping onto the kitchen floor. '…Andy West? My God,' she said, swiping it back up. 'Even I've heard that name. Is he like untouchable or something? And if it is our brother's blood on that bus stop, shouldn't we be doing something right *now*?'

'Let's see what Britt finds out. She'll call Brendan today.'

'*Brendan,*' she sighed then, snapping the band around her ponytail.

'Come on, Amy. He calls in sick to that dump again, they stop calling *him.*'

'I know, I know,' she muttered, leaving for the living room. She grabbed a hoodie and her trainers. 'I've got to see this for myself.'

'The bus stop? Ye don't need...'

'Please don't tell me what I don't need to do, Jackie.' She nodded outside. 'What if it rains and whatever that is disappears? The police need to see it. I've at least got to get it recorded.'

This time Amy was out the door not caring if Jackie followed or not. Apart from anything else, she needed space. Last night someone had answered Shaun's phone again, and *again* they kept quiet, a hopeful sign the first time but pretty worrying the next. What could it mean? Was he being *tortured* or something? Something else to tell the police, due at lunchtime but might well turn up early. She hurried outside.

Jackie caught up with her at the top of the avenue and he peered up at the puffy white sky, it hadn't rained overnight and wasn't about to either. But aye, it had been dark, could that blood be even *worse* than he thought? They jumped into a taxi, and for the journey they sat in silence.

It wasn't worse. After they'd got out and marched down the pavement, he saw the same dozen lumpen strands and few inches-wide smear through the middle. For several seconds Amy peered, then crouched down and examined the ground.

'When did it last rain?' she muttered, sweeping her fingers across the scattering of grit. A passer-by slowed down to stare and another craned her neck as she passed.

'Sunday morning, I think.'

She took out her phone and made a recording of the blood, and Jackie watched her turn to Crawford's then check the time. Whatever was on her mind, it was shut for another hour. 'Now do ye get why I didni say anything?' he asked.

She didn't answer, just turned back for the road.

At around twelve the police called, and an hour and a half later a PC Caldwell pressed the flat buzzer. Amy jumped to let her in, brought her into the living room and offered her a seat. The thin-faced, red-haired officer looked young to them both, and when she opened her notebook with a confident smile Amy felt a touch relieved. 'I understand your brother Shaun has been missing for over seventy-hours,' she started.

'That's right,' Amy said. She was handling turquois beads that Jackie had last seen when their mum had been dying.

'And since you reported him missing there's been no communication?'

'Not a thing. Someone's answered his phone twice now, but I don't think it's him.'

'Someone?'

'Refusing to speak.'

The police officer nodded and wrote. 'How did he appear recently? 'Did you see any kind of change?' She addressed them both now. 'Did Shaun express any fears?'

Amy shrugged.

'Disappointments?'

'Not at all.'

'The last time you spoke, everything seemed fine?'

'We were supposed to be having lunch on Monday so on Sunday night I called his work. I can be a bit overprotective I suppose so he wasn't happy at being reminded, but it wasn't exactly a falling out.' If Officer Caldwell was unconvinced she gave nothing away, and Amy nodded at Jackie. 'His brother's home from Egypt, so the last week or two and before it as well, he's been on great form. Tired but nothing more. He's got two jobs, you see. Lives with me because he's saving up for a deposit on a mortgage.'

The policewoman went to speak but Amy hadn't finished. 'But we found out some things that he'd kept hidden from us, and to be honest that's what's making me think the worst.' She swallowed, looked around for a glass of water and Jackie jumped for the kitchen. 'He'd been working in a pub, Crawford's in the southside, but he's a Celtic fan and that's a Rangers pub, ye probably know yourself it's a *big* Rangers pub. The locals, apparently they got suspicious and he ended up being sacked. And...' She took the glass from her brother and drank, and Jackie took over the story. At the mention of blood, Officer Caldwell raised her head.

'How much did you see?'

'I've got it here.' Amy stood.

A few seconds of the film was enough for the policewoman to give a polite nod and return the phone. She turned back to Jackie. 'The name of the man who pointed this out to you?'

'Skin. That's all I know.'

'He thinks it's Shaun's, is sure of it.'

'But he didn't say he witnessed it,' Jackie said. 'He implied that it was Daryl, that's the owner. Said he was under a bit of pressure from another guy. An ex-Rangers player, Andy West.'

From a fleeting moment the policewoman stopped writing, it was obvious to Jackie she was taking in the name. Then she continued and offered a sympathetic smile. 'When you reported Shaun missing, Miss O'Leary, you said he'd done something similar before.'

Amy shifted on the couch, wiped her sweating hands. 'Two years ago. He had a gambling problem. It was a terrible time for everybody but especially Shaun. Our mum had just died and he felt really guilty.'

'Did you report him missing?'

'No, it was different then. He packed a bag and headed off without saying. We knew he was sorting himself out, I mean obviously we were worried but...' PC Caldwell's tilt of the head felt like a punch in the stomach. 'Ye have to understand, officer. We're talking about a different Shaun now. He's turned his life around, doesn't gamble or go anywhere near those bookies or websites.' She felt her voice quiver but couldn't stop. 'He just wants what everyone else has got.' She wiped her eyes, fumbled at the beads. 'And he was getting there.'

'Did he get in touch?'

'After a week. He was in London.'

'And does Shaun have any debts that you know of? From his time gambling?'

'No.'

'You're certain.'

'Aye.' She threw up her arms, the beads falling onto her lap. 'I'm *almost* certain.'

Jackie gave a powerless shrug. 'As far as we know.'

The policewoman put away her notebook and addressed them both. 'Since Shaun has been missing for seventy-two hours, it's the standard procedure for the Missing Person's Bureau to be notified.'

Amy rubbed at her face. 'Right.'

'A risk assessment of your brother has been carried out, and since his mental state hasn't given you cause for concern, and also because he's gone missing before and returned safely, there's no reason to change it from its current category. That's low-risk.'

'So, what next?' Jackie asked. 'You're gonni help us, aye? We're not on our own, are we?'

'You're not on our own. We'll take this a step at a time, first by making basic enquiries.'

'You'll go to that pub?' Amy asked. 'See the owner? And this Andy West? They know something in there. Someone does.'

Officer Caldwell stood up. 'We'll make enquiries in Crawford's. And when we find out anything that could lead to your brother's whereabouts, we'll of course let you know.'

'You'll go today?'

'Miss O'Leary.' The policewoman gave a warm smile, appearing for the briefest moment now to be as young as she perhaps was. 'We'll go as soon as time allows. Good afternoon to you both.'

'Bollocks,' Amy snapped as they watched her from the window. 'Did she even listen?'

Jackie put a hand on her shoulder. 'Hard as it is to believe, I suppose low priority means there's not a lot to worry about.'

'Aye right. It means a thousand people disappear every day and they can't deal with them all.'

'Maybe that as well. Ye got a text, by the way.'

Amy marched to the coffee table and swiped up her phone. 'Brendan. *I gave the lassie your number in case she calls and I miss it.*' 'You have her number, right? We should call her.'

Jackie twisted at his earring. 'Maybe give her more time.'

'Jackie...'

'Okay.' He dialled Britt's number, and right away she answered.

'I'm sorry, Jackie, I didn't mean to keep you waiting. Just that I wanted something concrete before...'

'Okay,' Jackie replied. 'That's fine...'

'Well, I spoke to an old mate of my brother's, Alan, he's been sick and didn't know much. But he asked around. Right enough your brother working there had got under some people's skins. And something went missing? A collection tin? On Sunday night a few guys were heard making threats, not to Shaun's face I don't think. But one guy was fuming.'

'Did ye get a name?'

'That's why I didn't call, Alan was funny about saying. He said he had to be sure and would let me know. I'm sorry, it's a bit useless at the moment.'

'No, it's great. Thanks, Britt. Just keep at him, eh?'

'I will. Stay positive.'

Amy gazed red-eyed at her brother. 'Later,' Jackie said.

She jumped up and grabbed her phone.

'Ye calling Daryl? All ye'll get is more smarm.'

'I'm not calling the pub, Jackie. We're *going*.' She flashed her brother a picture of a jubilant, fat-necked footballer. 'I'm not leaving until we talk to this prick.'

16

Jackie threw open the door to Crawford's and felt like he'd stepped in on a minute's silence, although one for a tragedy the regulars didn't particularly care about. He got a nod from the old boy in the taped-up glasses and he gave one back, just as Daryl appeared singing with a nod of his own. 'Wayne's day off, I'm afraid. Best chance of catching him is up the park.' He grinned like this was a sight worth seeing but he failed to lift their frowns. 'Ach to be honest, if he's filled you in already I wouldn't hold out much hope.'

Amy stepped closer. 'You and Andy West.'

'Sorry?'

'What did youse got up to on Sunday night?'

The owner waved away an old guy rattling a coin on the bar and chuckled, then nodded to his visitors, fairly impressed. 'Having suspicions about yours truly? Hey, I even doubt myself at times. But did you say Andy West?' He pointed to the big framed picture hanging in the centre of the bar. The stocky, bald striker, fists clenched in full scream. '*That* Andy West?'

'The very one,' Jackie said, not looking round. 'He calls the shots in here, seems obvious. He was raging about Shaun doing a few shifts. So are ye gonni fill us in?'

'On his whereabouts on Sunday? Seriously?' The owner stood staring at his visitors, then stepped away to serve the old guy. Slamming the till, he returned and glared at them again. 'To get this straight so I don't act somewhat rashly. Andy West and *me* attacked, then I'm assuming possibly did away with, your boyfriend?'

Amy felt her insides begin to cave. 'Maybe ye can just tell us what ye know. Did ye hit him?'

He placed down his dishtowel, scratched at his stubble. 'Did I...? Look, I'm a big boy and I can these take silly accusations. But since Andy's not here it's my duty to defend him. Did you ever see him on the pitch?'

Jackie's nod was unconvincing and Daryl leaned towards him. 'Barely a bone in his body they didn't break. Barely an insult he didn't hear. But in fifteen years how many times did he get sent off? Any ideas, fellow Bear?'

'No exactly.' Jackie said.

Daryl laughed, grabbed the towel again and spun a glass in the air. 'Once. Any frustrations, he channelled them. No just a great player but a great captain.'

'Still barking out orders in his retirement, is he?'

Daryl stopped polishing, put the glass down. Then, drumming his fingers on the bar, he nodded to the door. 'On you go.'

'What?'

'You're barred.'

Amy spluttered a laugh, folded her arms. 'Are you serious?'

'I'm very serious.'

'We're not going anywhere.'

He placed both hands on the bar. 'These are my premises. I'm asking you to leave.'

Jackie frowned. 'Disni exactly make us less suspicious, mate.'

'Oh for…' Daryl spluttered a laugh and started to wipe the bar. A middle-aged customer waddled inside, and he winked and grabbed a glass.

'The police are coming,' Amy called as they backed further away. 'We'll get the truth.'

He sighed, started pouring a pint. 'I wish you all the best in your search.'

Outside Crawford's, the two headed back down the pavement towards the subway. 'That guy,' Amy groaned, skipping round a man carrying a crate of vegetables. 'I find it impossible to believe him.'

Jackie raised his voice above the snap and hiss of a departing bus, shrank back at the burst of black smoke. 'But between him and Skin? I'd probably choose him.'

'I'm not sure. The way he talked about his cousin?'

'They don't get on, that's for sure. Skin was right about that.'

'He lost his half of the business, that Wayne guy,' said Amy. 'Through gambling, wouldn't you think? Maybe if we tried talking to Wayne about his cousin. Or if *I* tried from a different…' She stopped, got her ringing phone out from her pocket. 'Hello?'

'I was looking for Jackie,' said a woman's voice. 'Is this…?'

'I'm Amy. Britt?'

'Yeah. Amy, hi. Look, I talked again to my brother's pal. He said that the guy making the threats was someone called Andy West. The thing is, he's not just a regular but an old player. Really popular one. Famous. But…'

'Uh-huh?'

'Alan said he's got history. Not to be messed with.'

'Right.' Amy shot a concerned look to her brother. 'Did he say what he's done?'

'No, but I've looked online. ...Ye should maybe check.'

'Okay, Britt. Thanks.'

They walked a few steps past the subway, leaned by iron railings of a beige-coloured tenement. A door slammed behind them as two excited kids scurried ahead of their mum. Amy swiped at her phone and searched. They read.

Ex-Rangers star cleared of attack on own fan

...West, who has since retired, was acquitted of the serious assault which left the 19 year-old unconscious and with severe internal injuries...had denied attacking the fan after a remark made about an on-field incident...West's plea of self-defence and claim that Peterson fell due to being intoxicated was accepted...Mr Gardner and Mr Marshall were also acquitted...

'Five years ago,' Amy muttered. 'Ye know, I remember this. It was in the news for ages.'

'Hey.' Jackie nodded at a photo of two bulky, grim-faced middle-aged men leaving the court-building. 'Gardner and Marshall.'

'You've seen them before?'

'Last night. They were in Crawford's giving us the eye.'

'More than anyone else?'

'They clocked us from the start, I thought I'd imagined it at first. Aye, they were wearing golf jumpers, it's definitely them. What else have we got?'

Amy scrolled further through the entries, clicking onto a fan's forum. '*Player of the Year Award's night,*' she read. '*...Callum Peterson, drunk at the top of stairs...Asked West about a penalty miss...Ends up bottom of a fire exit...*' There are a lot of comments that have been deleted, maybe liable since he was acquitted. But check these out. '*...a disappointment to put it mildly... a hero in the colours, arsehole in life...Nearly ripped a boy up my street... Shouldn't have asked for his autograph when he was having a piss...*' Not happy, some of them. And these are Rangers fans.'

'Okay,' Jackie said. 'We chin the barman again, find out what we can. Or you do this time.'

'No.'

'No? Then what?'

Amy looked up from her phone. 'We find West.'

'Find him?' Jackie stood back. 'How? Apart from Crawford's, we've no idea where the guy hangs out.'

'Then we'll just have to try his house.' She showed her screen. 'A building dispute with his neighbours two years ago. Unless he's moved since then, that's his place right there.'

17

Amy marched to the roadside and flagged down a taxi, leaving Jackie trying to get to grips with the day's next move. Chinning this ex-footballer on his front door? What did they hope to get from this? An invite inside and a confession over coffee? What was it driven by anyway but their own frustration? Maybe, Jackie now wondered, both those cousins were right, Shaun had left that pub for the last time and none of them had a clue what had happened after. An accident maybe or an escape, neither were less likely anyway than the claim of the resident jakey. Jackie also knew right enough that Amy had made up her mind, and he'd have to go with her to see this out. West's village was fifteen miles south-east of the city, and after spitting out his frustrations Jackie hurried for the road. His sister leaned forward and instructed the driver. Jackie shut the door and smiled.

Speeding past warehouses five minutes south, Jackie mentioned Brendan. He hadn't said anything about West's time in court so he must have just forgotten, Jackie took Amy's mobile and fired off a text. Work or no work he was sure he'd get a reply quick, Brendan had boasted to him that he could practically text from his pocket. Ten minutes later Jackie had got no response and he laughed out an excuse, their brother had probably sent a text alright but to his boss instead. The taxi had stopped at lights and Amy didn't seem to hear, she was gazing out at a scrapyard and its twists of rusted metal. Then she muttered that she too had sent a text to Brendan. But he hadn't replied to hers either.

Soon the brother and sister were staring across fifteen metres of curved drive and freshly manicured lawn, to the modern, red-bricked two-floored home. Again Jackie checked out the photo then peered through silver railings. No doubt about it, this was the place. West had certainly made a mint, Jackie saw, the parked black Jaguar in front of them was just more evidence. Amy eyed up the intercom on the pillar ahead, then nearly jumped as she noticed a man at her back. Having spied the potential intruders from his garden further up, Andy West's elderly neighbour had removed his gloves and taken his phone from his pocket. He'd then followed them in silence to the bottom of the expansive cul-de-sac, and now stared expressionless through his raised and glimmering phone.

Jackie had already clocked him and cupped his hand to whisper. 'He's got a trowel in his overalls. Gonni carve *Daily Mail Ya Bass* on our foreheads.'

The neighbour continued to film as Amy ignored him and read the engraving on the pillar. *The Armoury.* Jackie nodded. 'There we go, then.'

'What?'

'His nickname was the Weapon.'

Amy took a step to the buzzer, gave a long and silent push. They both peered down the drive at the oak front door, then at the large but darkened windows and the opened but still curtains. She was about to press again, when from a burst of static came the voice of a woman. It was crisp and indignant. 'Can I help you?'

'Andy West,' Amy almost blurted. 'I... I'd like to speak to him please.'

'I'm sure ye would, honey. He's done all his signing for today. Goodbye.'

'I'm not going.'

'...I'm sorry?'

'I'm not going anywhere.' Amy glanced at her brother before speaking again. 'My boyfriend's missing. I need to talk to your husband.'

There was a pause and even Amy and Jackie thought, a stammer. '...I have absolutely no idea...'

The static died.

Amy pressed the buzzer again and this time her finger didn't leave. Finally Jackie lifted it away. 'Keep it together, we're no done yet.' Jackie got ready to speak but the voice didn't return. Behind him meanwhile, the cameraman continued recording and Amy gave the gate a once-over. She stepped back, rolled up her sleeves. 'What ye doing? Ye canni...'

'Enough pissing about.' She gripped the bars.

She lifted one foot then the other, as the silent neighbour took a step closer.

The woman's voice returned. 'Never mind damage. If you so much as leave a smell on my gate, you'll be paying for it until you die. ...One minute.'

The last two words had sounded like a threat but could well have been a request. A one-minute warning or a one-minute wait? Amy had no idea, even remained hanging there until her brother gestured at her to get down. As she did the front door opened, and in a grey and pink jogging suit out walked the owner of the voice. Had they known no better, Amy and Jackie would have thought the full-figured, full-blonde woman was unaware they were outside, she strolled straight up the drive and flashed a grin at her neighbour. The filmmaker waved and pointed a finger as the woman stopped by the inside of the gate. At the source of the disruption, the large, mascaraed eyes of Melissa West glared.

Stepping back, Amy attempted an apologetic smile. 'I'm sorry about that, I'm just losing my mind a bit. Can we speak to your husband, please?'

Bangles clashed as Melissa West folded her arms. 'I doubt it very much. What do you want, anyway?''

'Answers, really. The police aren't helping us so…'

'So what…?' the woman shrugged, eyeing them both now. 'My husband's an agony aunt?'

From the road the neighbour waved his mobile. 'Police?'

Melissa beamed. 'Thanks, Harvey. I've got this.' She held her smile until her neighbour saw she was serious and retreated up the cul-de-sac. She turned again. 'Who are you?

'My name's Amy O'Leary. I'm a librarian. A university librarian. What I mean is…'

'And *you*?' She flicked a nod at Jackie.

'Amy's my sister. So Shaun's well, family.'

The woman stood, her tongue pressed firm against her front teeth. 'Autograph hunters aren't what they used to be, you know,' she said. 'Half an hour after whatever Andy's signed, it's up on E-bay. Not right that, is it? I mean, it's not *fair*.' She flashed another smile, kinder now, it took them both by surprise. 'I'll give you two minutes.'

Melissa and Andy West's living room was a spacious area with a high-pile carpet and purple velvet walls. As they entered, the house owner glimpsed at the shoes of her guests, and Amy noticed and stopped, waited for an instruction. But instead she and her brother were pointed to a grey, crescent-shaped sofa and asked to sit, then with no other word Melissa West left the room. As Radio 2 played quietly elsewhere, both Amy and Jackie sat on the sofa's edge, Amy's stomach churning like *she* was about to be asked questions, and Jackie half-convinced he'd soon be accused of stealing. After a few minutes a Simply Red song was the only sound to be heard, and Amy wondered aloud if the woman had somehow forgotten about them. Jackie said nothing, sat back and scanned the room, took in two mounted portraits directly ahead. One, veins bulging in ecstatic fury, was the blue-shirted West at his peak. The other showed the couple in evening dress, like the owners of a country estate.

With the clink of tall glasses, Melissa West returned, placing orange juices on the coffee table in front of her guests. She left again for a drink of her own, coming back with a half-full glass of red wine, and sat on the arm of a chair opposite. 'So…' she started. But then she yelped, bounced up to swipe a magazine from the table in front. With a laugh she tossed it back again, rolling her eyes at her own lack of stability. Jackie had been feeling self-conscious since he'd noticed a growing rip in his jeans, but their host was clearly a rocket and he held up his juice. 'Thanks.'

The glaze in Melissa's eyes hadn't been noticed until then, but it was now clear to Jackie and Amy that she was drunk. 'I'm not in the habit of inviting in complete strangers,' she said, stern-faced again. 'But you're upset. More to the point if someone in that den is starting rumours about Andy, I need to know *who* and *what*.' She swiped up her drink and took a gulp, a dribble escaping her mouth and down her chin. She dabbed with a finger. 'What happened in Crawford's?'

Amy cleared her throat, rubbed her hands. 'Shaun was a barman. Until Sunday, he was. We haven't heard from him since, and we've asked around and your husband's name has come up more than once. That's why…'

'How many times?' Melissa's painted eyebrows were raised, her mouth open.

'I….'

'Has his name come up?'

'From two different people,' Jackie said. 'So far.'

'Regulars,' Amy said.

'Uh-huh. Who?'

'Skin, one is called.'

'*Skin*?'

Amy had no idea if the woman's sneer was for the name or the man, but she felt the weight of her stare. She sat up to meet it. 'Yeah. The other guy's called Alan.'

'Alan…?'

'Not important.'

'But that's it?'

'It's enough to bring us here.'

Melissa West beamed, gold falling up her arm as she gestured around her room. 'The words of a…a *skin*head and a mystery man are enough to bring you here?'

Jackie put down his drink. 'Is he in or what?'

'Afraid not, no.'

'Got a reputation, your husband.'

'I'm aware of that, yes.' She gave a mischievous raise of the eyebrows, took another drink.

'He's a Celtic fan, Shaun,' Jackie continued. 'A major brass neck for that whole pub. So maybe Andy set about him, or somebody else did it *for* Andy. Like the owner.'

Melissa spluttered a laugh. 'The owner? Daryl?'

'Will he be long?'

'You won't be speaking to my husband. But please tell me how the *owner* could...' Then she sighed, shook her head. 'No, I can't help you.'

'Gardner and Marshall?'

'I'm sorry?'

'If we said Gardner and Marshall were involved, could ye help us then?'

The woman stood up and headed for the kitchen. With her glass topped-up she reappeared by the door. 'You saw my husband on the park, I take it?'

'No much, to be honest.'

'Hard as nails, he was. Oh yes,' she laughed. 'But off it? A teddy bear. It might help you to understand that footballers like Andy are never ready for retirement. Oh, they get professional advice about investments, the media, but really they're on their own, told to settle down to a life of golf and after-dinner speeches. Not easy going from forty-thousand people screaming your name to spending every day in the house, even this one.' She shut her eyes, gripped her glass and groaned. 'Andy missed that adulation and Crawford's was a good substitute, up until certain assholes expected him to *stay* that hard man. So he puts an act on now and then because it keeps those clowns happy, and in return that adulation, it never goes away. That trial? You really want to know?'

'No. We're here…'

'He was strung up before it had started,' she snapped. 'Every second of it was a farce. Gardner and Marshall? They might have attacked…they could have a-… Oh, I don't know. Look, if I'm going to be completely honest?' But Melissa West paused and sighed, looking for the first time like she had strangers in her house. 'I'm sorry about your brother.' She stepped forward and took the unfinished glasses from the table. 'But you won't find any answers here.'

'The fuck…' Jackie's mutter at the gate had been the only words to leave either of them for two minutes. Neither were up for talking, never mind camera-wielding neighbours, there could well be microphones in the grass. They retreated up the cul-de-sac then the winding, tree-lined road. With the houses now far behind, Amy was about to speak. Then she heard the approaching roar of a hurtling SUV.

As the navy blue vehicle sped past she spun to watch it go. 'Was that him?' she asked like it was all too late anyway.

Jackie shook his head. 'Don't think so.'

'So you heard her, right?' she said, turning again as they continued to walk. 'Before we left? Sorry about your brother. *Brother*. We said *boyfriend*.'

'I know.'

'She knew about us. Even before we turned up, she knew.'

Jackie frowned. 'Possible.'

'Only possible?'

'She was pished.'

'That barman told her husband. Her husband told her.'

'Maybe...'

'The whole sketch, Jackie. Oh my God, it was batshit. We try to break in and what does she do? Invite us in for a bloody drink? If I'd put a brick through her window would she have taken me on holiday? And what was the pantomime with the magazine?'

'That *was* weird. A property magazine?'

'Spain or Greece or somewhere. She was freaked out, that's for sure.'

'Until she heard about our witnesses.'

Amy shook her head. 'I thought she'd ditch that wine for champagne when she heard the names. Or the fact that there were only two. I don't know, it's like she just sits there worrying about her husband hurting somebody. Hey…'

At their backs, the SUV had returned and was accelerating towards them, roaring through the gears and showing no sign of keeping clear. Jackie and Amy backed into the hedgerow before it thundered past, the driver and passenger staring calmly ahead. It reached the end of the wooded road and headed west for the city.

'Too fast, creep!'

Jackie nodded into the distance. 'That was them.'

'Who…?'

'Gardner and Marshall.'

'Ye sure?'

'Same hair. Same ages. Same jumpers.'

'They've been following us?'

'Bit late if they are. Did you notice that car on the way?'

Amy shrugged.

'So, what? They came down to see their mate? Exact same time as us?'

'Or their mate's wife,' Amy said. 'Hey, to warn her, do ye think? About us?'

Jackie reached up, grabbed a leaf from a hanging branch. 'To get her to lay off the Vimto, maybe. Keep her mouth shut before we chinned her.' The leaf snapped free and he crunched it in his hand. 'Or maybe they're just sightseeing.'

*

Monday, 25th February

Hi, I'm Shaun.

I'm a problem gambler.

I'm here to talk about…well, youse know about my da and my ma… But really, I'm here to talk about what I did last year.

In London. I just need to get it out, that's all.

Just…

Then I can put it behind me.

The thing is, see after my ma died? …I hated youse. All of youse. Not anybody personally obviously, but for what my life had become I hated gamblers. Full stop. Way I saw it, with those guys in my da's work I'd been too understanding. I mean they could have just let him sit there with his wee book of equations but they didni, they hassled him until he broke. More than them though, I've got to say I hated all the people in this room the night my ma died. Far as I was concerned, if it wisni for your tears and back-slapping, I'd have got to say goodbye to her. She widni have left this world convinced I was scum.

Well, that's what I told myself, I'm sure at least part of it was an excuse. I needed one, I know that, I needed an excuse to get away from here. Get away from anybody who'd look at me and judge.

London, that sounded far enough.

I borrowed cash from Amy and was off.

Revenge I was after, nothing more and nothing less, I thought somehow that would make me feel fulfilled. I got a job in computing and settled down in Hackney, went clubbing for a bit and even got a girlfriend. My ma's inheritance was due so I'd no money worries, and I worked day and night on my system, improved it bit by bit. When I started the gambling again there was one change from up here, rather than bet in my room I hung about the bookies. I just wanted to win while being around losers, see them pinning tails on donkeys when I was dealing in the truth. See, that's how I saw myself, not a gambler but a mathematician, with my wee book of formulae they'd never understand. But before long man just winning wisni enough. The gamblers would have to lose.

London, not hard to stay anonymous, must be a thousand betting shops and that suited me fine. What I'd do was in one place I'd make a few bets, and when I pocketed my winnings I'd make sure I was seen. At some point some sad case would notice and we'd have a wee chat, and sooner or later he'd ask me for a tip. So I'd chuck one his way, a first goalscorer or something, and if it came up trumps he'd be there for me the next time. Now but I'd break the news that I was just passing through, this next tip would be the last but they were lucky cos it was a cracker. So what does a gambler do but put half his house on it. Then sit there greeting when the house disappears. My tip was a dud, of course, what a shame, eh? I'd move on to the next bookies, wait for the next sucker.

But then of course my discipline goes, my self-control slips right through my fingers. The cash from my ma comes through and I'm cocky and careless, then I'm anxious then desperate and it all goes to shit. My girlfriend gets spooked man, does a runner, and by this point I'm like deranged because I barely even notice. I lose my job as well, was hardly turning up, I manage to get another but I know it willni last. Of course, as far as my family know everything's fine, I call Amy the odd time but I tell her no to visit. Then I suppose the worst thing happens. I win again. And I keep winning and keep winning and I claw back some cash. It's the system, it's a winner, it's finally paying out. No, it won't come through every time but more often than not it's a cash machine. Of course luck's involved as well but all that matters is I'm flying. Anyway I'm back at the bookies and I spy this loser.

Or he spies me I should say, I wish I'd never... Anyway, a wee guy he is, pointy nose and jerky head, looks a bit like a chicken, that was the first thing I thought. Well, he noticed me ages before apparently, has even been following me about, says he's no interested in my tips, wants to know if I'll work for him. Greg, his name is. A pain in the arse. I tell him where to go but I keep bumping into him, he keeps just strutting up to me like we're a couple of kindred spirits. Anyway he tells me he's got a brother, really bigs him up, a major player he says and canni believe I don't know him. Sure enough I google the guy and he's some kind of gangster, no doubt a professional gambler who thinks I'll fall at his feet. Well I think, how about I step it up here and go the full nine yards? How about I rip that fucker off as well?

Sorry, I need to...

...get some water.

...Aye.

I'll be back in a minute.

18

'We go to the park, he'll be walking his dog there. His cousin said, remember.'

Amy left Jackie behind on the underground escalator and marched her way to the top, she slipped her ticket into the machine and walked on to the exit. Her brother didn't move, before he caught up with his sister he needed a moment to himself, to decide if what Amy had suggested now made more or less sense than earlier. The trip to West's place had only confused things. The ex-footballer *could* be having them watched, just as likely though it was his wife he was keeping tabs on. So maybe Amy had a point about talking to this Wayne again, a friendlier approach might well manage to open him up. It'd do no harm, that was for sure, and besides Jackie thought, there was still a chance Shaun would turn up anyway. When he reached the exit, Amy stood waiting. She nodded across to a cafe. 'Starving.'

At a table by the window, the soup and roll inside Amy seemed only to exhaust her, propped up by an elbow she closed her eyes for a few seconds. The kitchen radio blared out a report of a recently-found body and she jerked up, the spoon clattering around the empty bowl. His coffee mug raised, Jackie didn't blink. He'd heard this story enough times to know the victim was a mother from Motherwell, and enough times to be sure that Amy had known it too. Amy gave herself a shake and sat back on her seat. Jackie smiled, then swiped up the phone and called Brendan. Their brother picked up right away.

'Sorry, Amy, just starting my break. Any news?'

'It's Jackie. Not much. We found Andy West's house, had a word with his wife.'

'Andy West's gaff…? Ye were inside? Gen up?'

'He was up for a serious assault some years back, ye know that?'

'I think so, man. Let aff, I'm sure. How did…? What did his wife…?'

'Their taste is in their arse if their living room's anything to go by.' Amy yawned and raised a hand. 'Here's sis.'

Jackie passed the phone and strode down to the toilet, expecting Brendan to get the heads-up he couldn't be bothered delivering himself. Brendan would likely get a lecture as well for not pulling his weight, maybe even the third degree on what he was possibly holding back. But as Jackie returned, Amy had put away her mobile and was now taking out her purse.

'Is he meeting us after his work?' Jackie asked, buttoning up his jacket.

'No idea.' She headed for the counter.

'He didni say?'

Taking the receipt, she smiled at the waitress. 'Yeah, he did. But for all that means, eh?' She paid the bill and turned, forced through a smile. 'So, Wayne?'

Amy got out the taxi at lights and jogged towards the park, and Jackie paid the driver and caught up with her at the side-gate. This was daft, Jackie knew, and not just because the size of this park could leave them searching the rest of the day, the hint from the bar owner had come hours ago, a fat chance Wayne would be here now. In the cab Amy had barely acknowledged Jackie's doubts, only muttered that Wayne could go there a lot. 'Fat guy with a walking stick,' she'd reminded him as she'd opened the door. 'And a weird-looking dog.'

On a path metres from the gate, the brother and sister took in their surroundings. A whitewashed public toilet, artificial football pitches, a wide sloping hill and woodland beyond. There were few people around and even fewer with dogs, so they headed for the hill for a better view. Once at the top they gazed around. Further ahead the park rolled onto a wide, flat expanse, and there were more than a few people out and about with dogs. They jogged down and got close to some, and for others they split up and ran in different directions. They could have continued on but they'd need to meet this guy together, so soon they were on the hill again, scrutinising figures on the other side. On the edge of the woodland several dogs were out, its owners either running, chucking stuff or sitting on benches. The brother and sister headed down, and finding their path blocked by the football pitches, peered through the wall of mesh. No limping dog-owner or possibly mad-looking dog anywhere. Forehead against the wire, Jackie groaned, they'd need an hour to comb this place then they'd have to start again. As he straightened up, his sister still hung onto the mesh like a broken prisoner. 'By the way.'

Amy didn't reply.

'He said *the* park.'

'Aye.'

'There's another one, about the same distance from Crawford's.'

'He meant this one.'

'Maybe. Then again, maybe not. It's smaller.'

Amy nodded, to herself it seemed. Then she pushed herself from the wire. 'So let's go.'

With Wayne being a local they might even bump into him on the way, Jackie thought, and if neither the walk or search turned him up, they could head back to Crawford's and try for his number. After ten minutes the pub was in Jackie and Amy's sights, and in the vague hope of catching a friendly face they slowed to close to a crawl. Too soon though they reached the front door and as a stranger pushed it open, Jackie peaked in. The barmaid called Maureen was gazing up at a TV, and the ned was slumped asleep at the far end of the bar. By a window a fruit machine gurgled and out of sight an old man coughed. There were a couple of others maybe. But no barman.

From the outside Festival Park seemed to be empty of not just funny-looking dogs but normal-looking ones too, not to mention funny-looking and normal-looking people. The place was so empty that Amy even wondered if it had been closed, it had been a magnet for nutters years ago and there'd been talk of it being padlocked for good. But the main gate was opened so they headed inside, followed an overgrown path twisting into wood. Arriving at a crescent-shaped pond strewn with crisp packets and cans, they were eyed up by a group of schoolboys. They ignored their insults and continued on, past bushes and benches and flower beds. Coming through a thin line of trees they arrived at a clearing, where a couple of women were chucking a tennis ball over two yelping dogs. On the other side a family messed about in a swing park, and an old woman fed squawking pigeons from a bench. But there was nobody else around. The brother and sister sat at a picnic table.

In seconds Jackie was on his feet again, wanting to scream but instead fuming in silence. A joke of a place, this was. A joke of a move. Did someone know something? *Did* they? Then they should be in that shithole now threatening to burn it to the ground. He turned his back on his sister, bit into his fist. Was it obvious? Could she tell? That he was missing his home every bit as much as his brother? He turned around, saw Amy wipe a tear. He saw her tremble, then he saw her laugh.

He smiled. 'What's funny?'

'Snow White.'

'Eh?'

'Shaun and Brendan, they played dwarves in a school play. Do you remember? God, yeah. Got into a fight backstage over who was to be Sneezy. Both came on minus their beards, the *two* of them sneezing so...' Amy's eyes widened. 'Look.'

Jackie spun around, saw across the clearing a bulky figure limp into view. He dropped himself onto a bench, got out some earphones and stretched his gammy leg. In front of Wayne sat a squat, black and white dog. 'That's him,' Amy said, getting to her feet. Before the earphones went in, she brought her hands up to shout.

'Hold on.' Jackie pointed towards the mutt, at its owner's feet now squealing and tearing up grass. 'Fancy that's jaws sinking into ye?'

Her arms fell. 'Not much.'

'A pit-bull. A holocaust-denying pit bull, by the looks of things. Let's just wander up, make it look like a coincidence.'

They started along the path that circled the clearing, the barman now chucking a stick and his dog scrambling off. Jackie couldn't help but slow down. He tilted his head. 'That dog…? Is it *skipping*?'

Amy stopped. 'No…I think it's hopping.'

The barman's dog had set off in the direction of the stick but started to drift away, missing it completely then coming back in one entire loop. Closer this time, it began its journey again, but once more missed its target and once more returned. The next time it started closer still and the next time nearer again, and all the while it was barking like the stick was taking the piss.

'How many legs has it got?'

'Three…no, two.'

Amy shook her head. 'Two and a half.'

The dog finally reached its prize and started whimpering and circling back. Wayne stood up, limped towards it and pulled the stick from its slabbering jaws. What Daryl found funny raised not even a smile in Jackie or Amy. Instead, Jackie stepped back from the path into bushes. 'Amy, give me your phone.'

'To record him? No, let's just do this.'

'No, I need...' He gestured at her to join him, and Amy stepped past branches into the bushes. Her white trainers half-sinking into mud, Jackie took the mobile and hit a key. He put the phone to his ear.

'What's the point in calling him? We'll-'

'-A minute.'

'And how did his number get on my phone?'

'It'll be nothing,' Jackie muttered. 'Wait.'

The barman stretched back to throw the stick again, and at the interruption he paused. Then he chucked it for the sky and pulled the phone from his back pocket. He stared, stabbed and put it to his ear.

After a few seconds he hung up.

Jackie dropped his arm, glared at the sky.

'Am I missing something? What was that about?'

'I didni call him, Amy.'

'Ye didn't…What…? Then…?' Amy's eyes widened, her jaw dropped. 'Did you…?'

'Aye. I called Shaun.'

19

Staring open-mouthed through the branches, Amy peeled her brother's fingers one by one from her arm. *Last night...* he was explaining *...the alley... ...He pulled out two phones... ...didni seem the type....* She let out a shout and made a lunge to get out, but Jackie swung her back and they both splattered into the mud. Jackie jumped to his feet again as his sister glared in the direction of the barman, muck smeared over her denim skirt.

'What the hell are ye...?'

'We need to think about this,' he said, pulling her to her feet.

'He's been lying through his teeth!'

'Wait. Just...' Jackie peered out. The barman hadn't heard, was halfway across the grass still gazing at the mobile. 'All we've had from him is shit, why will now be different?'

She grabbed back her phone. 'Then the police.'

'Alright, but how about we follow him first. See what he's up to.'

Watching Wayne approach, Amy hung up on her call. She checked the state of her skirt. '...Fine. Better not lose him.'

The barman roared and swiped at his dog with the stick, and Jackie and Amy started to follow. Once outside the gate he picked up his mutt and struggled across the road, the dog scanned around and spied their pursuers. It growled at first then wriggled and spat, and Wayne dropped it on the lip of a hill. The dog bit its owner's ankle then and turned with a howl, and the barman peered back towards Jackie and Amy. They jumped behind a parked car, not sure if they'd been spied, and by the time they came out again Wayne was gone. The top of the hill led to a quiet residential street with scaffolding, skips, a few cars. Figuring the barman had gone in an entrance, Amy grabbed at her hair to scream. Then from behind a skip he reappeared, limped into a tenement.

Amy marched down. Under scaffolding and dust sheets she peered at the names on an intercom, then took steps back to check up at windows. Then from inside there was a slam and the turn of a lock, and she darted behind the skip. The front door creaked open and without his dog Wayne hobbled out, continuing down for the main road. As he turned for the short walk to Crawford's, Amy stamped her foot. 'Not there!'

Still watching, Jackie shook his head. 'Check it out.'

The barman had taken a few steps but stopped at a bus shelter. Staring at a coming bus, he got out his wallet.

'He's going into town. Mon.'

They grabbed a taxi, and were soon peering through the windscreen of a red single-decker at the back of Wayne's head. They instructed the driver to hang back so they could watch for him getting off, but with every stop the bus got busier until they could no longer tell. They tailed it across the river into the centre of the city, Wayne would surely be bailing at one of the next few stops. When the bus pulled ahead at traffic lights they got out and followed on foot, caught up as it hissed and opened its doors. By the entrance of a Tapas bar, Jackie and Amy watched its passengers pile out.

With a nod to the driver, Wayne stepped off the single-decker, headed for then leaned against the bus shelter. He placed his stick to the side and sighed in what Jackie thought was relief, and he wondered if even the guy's disability was bollocks. But the sun had made an appearance and

Wayne was just tying his jacket round his waist, then with a grimace he started uphill among the crowds. As the street levelled out he turned onto a precinct, continued to a side-street then stopped. On railings hung a shrine of football scarves and flowers, and behind it sat an old pub. From a disused phone box Jackie and Amy watched, the door half-open to expel the stench of pish. 'A boy got stabbed there last month,' Amy groaned. 'Was on the news.'

The barman didn't go in. He leaned against the wall of the pub, lit up a fag and rested his eyes on the shrine. Jackie and Amy scanned the area but Wayne could be waiting for anybody, in fact he'd now turned his attention to the approach of an old woman. His mum? Wife? Shaun's frigging captor? They watched as Wayne continued to glare, then he shouted and pointed at the woman's shopping bag. The pensioner stopped, rearranged her overflowing bag and with a smile continued past. Wayne wasn't waiting for anybody, Jackie realised, he'd finish that cigarette and head into the pub. But on the barman's far side a short guy in a red baseball cap appeared, called out Wayne's name. They shook hands and went inside.

Amy pushed open the phone box door. 'Now what? We just let him get steaming?'

'Ye see that?'

Amy shrugged. 'What?'

'I don't think...'

The pub door opened again, Wayne and the other guy stepped out.

Jackie raised his eyebrows. '...Here we go.'

The two men crossed the side-street and too quickly were out of sight, Jackie and Amy darted to the precinct corner and peered around. 'No smiles, Amy.' Jackie continued. 'Barely a word between them. Who knows the real script but I don't think they're pals.'

The two men headed diagonally opposite for a multi-storey hotel, the short guy in quite a rush and the barman struggling to keep up. They disappeared through sliding doors, and a minute later Jackie and Amy did the same. The other side was a high-ceilinged, beige-coloured lobby, and there were gushes and calls of a rainforest. A mum signed her name at the reception and a group of suits chuckled on sofas. Head bowed, Jackie moved beyond the reception to lifts, and at a corridor he turned for the bars and restaurants. Directly to his right was a dimly-lit, lattice-bordered lounge. He peered in. Then he marched back to Amy.

He flicked her a nod. 'Let's go.'

She stepped forward, but only to grab her brother's arm. 'I've seen him before.'

'The other guy? In Crawford's?'

She frowned. 'I suppose so. Have you?'

'Not seen his face.'

'I'm sure of it.'

They headed back round the corridor, strode past the lounge door to gaze through a gap in the partition. The two were at a far table, the short guy with his back to them. As Lionel Ritchie sung and the bow-tied barman whistled, Wayne rung an invisible neck. His pal threw himself back on the couch and rubbed at his temple. Between a pint and a coke sat a phone. They looked at it. They moaned.

'Is that Shaun's?' Jackie whispered.

'Looks like it.'

Jackie called the number again, and the mobile on the table burst into life. With a glance at his pal, Wayne grabbed it and hit *answer*. Glaring ahead, he growled *Hello…?* As Jackie kept quiet, Wayne chucked down the phone. The other guy slammed his fist on his chair.

'They're both into it,' Jackie said. 'Let's move.'

'No. Look.'

The stranger got up from the couch and turned for the exit, and the brother and sister scrambled back up the corridor and waited. The man's steps got quieter and Amy stole a peek around, saw him disappear round a bend towards the toilets. Jackie's rage almost carried him in with him. He stopped to take a breath. 'The minute he's back it's war.'

After two minutes he didn't come back. Three and four, nothing. Five minutes and Amy was checking that Wayne was still there. Then seven and Jackie was in the toilet. He came back out throwing up his arms. 'They barely spoke, didn't look like he was bolting anywhere. Where…?' At the words above Amy, just under *Toilets*, his mouth dropped. 'Fuck…'

Amy turned and read. 'Car park.'

'Gone,' Jackie said.

'But the barman's not.'

They rounded the corner, Amy almost colliding with a receptionist who'd been staring at her skirt. At the corridor they stopped to watch Wayne drain his pint then grab Shaun's phone and stand. When he made to leave, Jackie and Amy retreated up the corridor, then once again began to follow. Not far this time, only until he looked like he was going home, then they'd pounce. He left the hotel and hobbled for the precinct, stopped to grab something to eat then continued towards the bus stop. After a few minutes Wayne arrived, leaned on the window of a newsagents and unwrapped his burger. Across the road Jackie called Shaun's phone again. When it rang, he and Amy crossed.

The barman brought out the mobile, hit *ignore*. Then on the kerb in front of him Jackie said, 'No gonni answer? Might be important.'

The barman looked up, jolted back against the window. 'Fucking following me?' His eyes jumped several times between the brother and sister. They settled on Jackie.

'We were following your dog. That's how we're late.'

Amy held out a trembling palm. 'Now.'

The barman sniggered, looked away. 'Sure.'

'You're in enough shit. Give...'

He took the phone from his pocket, and with a wink slapped it into her hand. 'Just keeping it safe.' He peered past Jackie at an approaching cluster of buses, pulled out his wallet. 'Anything else?'

Jackie took a step to the side. 'Where's Shaun?'

Wayne sneered. 'I found that in the staff room, awright? Waiting for him to call. I'm nice that way.'

Jackie was inches from his face. 'What's *happened* to him?'

'Fucking told ye last night. The fuck should I know?' A bus trundled past and Wayne moaned. Leaning back against the window, he sunk his teeth into the burger.

'We've seen the blood,' Amy said.

Crumbs spat out. 'What blood?'

'Police have as well. So what's going on?'

Wayne smiled, licked ketchup from his mouth. 'Told ye, I was waiting.'

'Waiting?'

'Oh fucking hell, I feel responsible, awright?' He wiped his mouth with a hand, glowered at his accusers, then he swept a wary glance past the other queuers. 'Disni matter who it is, I've got my job to dae. Youse got a taste of Crawford's last night, no exactly a coffee lounge, eh? And that was they boys behaving themselves.' He ripped another couple of bites from his burger and nodded at Amy. 'He's a dick, your boyfriend, insulting everybody with his lying pish. But the thing is I need to know he's alright, and *that* might come when he calls to find out where his phone is, know what I mean?' He bit again, and again.

'Lies,' Amy whispered.

'If you say so, doll.' He stuffed the rest of the burger into his mouth, scrunched the wrapper into his fist. 'Anyway, things to dae.' He tried to step around Jackie but Jackie stepped with him.

'Off to work?' he asked. 'I might nip in with ye, tell all those fans about your employment policy. A bit on the tolerant side, do ye not think?'

The barman muttered, gripped his stick, looking for a second like it might become a weapon. But instead he gazed at the sky and groaned like he was stuck in a lift with halfwits. 'For fuck's sake,' he sighed. 'This is oor culture, awright? We don't hassle anybody, don't chuck it in people's faces, we keep oorselves to oorselves and bring a mint into the city. But the council? The polis? Dae we get any respect? Dae we fuck. Canni sing this. Canni march there…Trying to destroy us, so they are. So it's my job to keep they boys in line, give the authorities no excuse. Over the piece I'd say I dae a good job, but sometimes?' he shrugged. 'Things sort of run away.' He turned to Amy, unmoved by her now flaring eyes. 'You're right.

I don't give a fuck about your boyfriend, just that him lying in a ditch someplace is bad for business. The minute I know he's alright, I can chill.'

'So somebody *has* attacked Shaun?' Jackie said, rising over him. 'Taken ye three days to tell us?'

'That's no…'

Jackie lunged, grabbed the guy's neck. He stumbled against the window, stick clattering to the pavement. His wallet fell next, his bus pass and assorted cards scattering around the ground. 'Ya fucking…'

'Less of that!' A shout in his ear and crumbs on his cheek, and Jackie turned to see two office-workers in his face. The young men weren't alone in stopping. An old woman pulled at her husband's arm, and two teenage boys stopped and grinned. A group of schoolgirls rushed across, picked up Wayne's things. Taking in the audience, Jackie stepped back.

Wayne fixed his t-shirt over his flab, then patted down his bomber and collected his cards from the schoolgirls. Silent now and face flushed, he pushed between the brother and sister, then he made for a newly-arrived bus. Without looking back he stepped on, limped down the aisle.

'Tell me where he is!' Amy shouted as Wayne sat, took out his earphones. 'Tell me!'

On Jackie's shoulder she collapsed into tears, as the young team chuckled at the wrecks caked in mud. 'Pair of mad junkies, man,' one said. 'State of them.'

20

Amy lifted a leaking silver carton and dropped it onto a plate. Grabbing a dishcloth, she wiped up a thick, golden drip. 'You being around just might have helped, Brendan. It's all I'm saying.'

'Sorry.'

'Forget it.'

'It's that job.'

'I know. Oh, look,' Amy smiled at her brother, rubbed his shoulder. 'It probably would have made no difference. I can't place that guy, he could live upstairs for all I know.'

With their takeaways the three slumped down in the living room, and Jackie grabbed the remote. On blinked the news, and soon a smiling man in a suit was administering an evening dose of football. He and Brendan zoned in, and like she'd been given no choice Amy again swiped up Shaun's phone. But she'd have grabbed it soon enough anyway, Brendan turning up had been a relief but her insides were churning once more. She stroked the phone, turned it over. A wreck. The screen so badly shattered it was a kaleidoscope of crystal, and the casing so full of cracks it barely fitted on. The thing hadn't been so much dropped from a height as attacked with a hammer, and this had happened *after* Sunday not before, Shaun would have mentioned it otherwise. Of course Amy had noticed the damage the second Wayne had handed it over, and again she cursed herself for not demanding to know what had happened.

Still, it worked, and with Jackie and then Brendan she'd read its web history. At first they'd gleaned nothing of importance, flats for sale, football stuff, a bit of news, but then they came across something that had sunk Amy's heart. Taken on Sunday hours before Shaun had vanished, a screenshot of football games and odds, with around ten of the fixtures marked with asterisks. Of course maybe it had just been a temptation and he'd gone on to change his mind, or the list had been snapped by Wayne while Shaun had been working. But if Shaun *was* gambling again, had Amy driven him to it? Had that argument on Sunday somehow pushed him over? As for the log of calls, zero made since Sunday and just their own received or missed. Before that, and no real surprise, quite a lot of contact with Wayne. Then there were the photos, downloads, emails… but not the vaguest hint of what was to come. She chucked it back on the couch, ran her hands down her face. She started to pick at her vegetable curry.

Rangers' suspensions and Celtic's injuries, or maybe the other way round, Jackie hadn't taken in very much. *That guy*, he was thinking. *That bar*. Did he really leave the hotel for the car park? Could he have gone somewhere else? Like…? He placed his plate on the coffee table, about to ask his sister, when her phone burst into song and she grabbed it, her dinner almost toppling. From her silence Jackie knew it was the police. She stood there motionless and he tried to read her face, until she hung up and explained that Officer Caldwell would be visiting. She started darting about then scooping up glasses and plates, like a tidy room might convince the officer to treat Shaun as a priority. There'd been no developments, Amy said, grabbing Brendan's empty dish, but she'd hardly be turning up for tea and a cameral wafer. She appeared to not notice Brendan's hands

134

clasped on his head like the officer was an old pal. But Jackie did, just like he'd noticed him turn back to the TV well before the call had ended. Just like he noticed him now, glued to the frigging *golf*. He stood over him. '…What ye thinking, Brendan?'

'Hmm?' His brother nodded, forehead knitting a worried brow. 'Nothing, man. Fingers crossed, eh?'

Still holding his gaze, Jackie teased out a smile. 'Fingers crossed.'

Amy stepped past them both to the window, pressed her forehead against the glass.

She opened the door to not one but two police officers. PC Caldwell's smile was sympathetic but a smile nonetheless, and with a sigh of relief Amy stepped back. The officer sat down on the couch and introduced her colleague, a tall and attractive woman who Jackie could see behind a perfume counter rather than working for the police. Officer Caldwell brought out her notebook. 'So we've been to Crawford's and spoken to staff and customers from Sunday night,' she said as Amy gripped the arm of her chair. 'The owner, a Mr Daryl Russell, stated that Shaun was dismissed when his shift ended at midnight for as he put it, failing to match the needs of the customers. He didn't dismiss Shaun personally, that was done by the head barman, a Mr Wayne.'

Amy rubbed her sweating palms. 'That's what we know.'

'We got in touch with Mr Wayne. He told us that their conversation was brief but not unfriendly, and immediately afterwards Shaun left the pub. This was past closing time and all the customers had gone, but one man stated he saw Shaun outside heading alone towards town. This sighting was confirmed by the man's friend.'

Amy nodded like this was all good news, and Jackie bit at his lip. Brendan observed his brother and sister like he wasn't sure what any of it might mean. 'First we've heard this,' Jackie said. 'Who told ye?'

'A Mr Charles Small,' the second officer answered. 'He said he'd gone for something to eat, then with others doubled back past the entrance.'

'We haven't heard of...' Amy shrugged. '...Charles Small?'

Officer Caldwell flipped back on her notebook. 'You referred to him as Skin.'

'Skin?' Jackie scowled. 'He said nothing about that to me. It was him who showed me the blood.'

'Mr. Small stated that he might have mislead you,' the other officer said again. 'He blamed the amount of alcohol he'd drunk.'

'Okay,' Amy said. 'But the blood? Ye saw it?'

'There appears to be blood stains on the bus shelter, yes,' Officer Caldwell answered. 'But it's worth bearing in mind that the area around Crawford's can be very lively at the weekends. Disturbances are common.'

Amy slapped her hands to her face. 'I don't know what to think anymore... I...' Her head fell back on the chair. 'But this is good, right?' she said, upright again and palms raised. 'They saw him walk away.'

Jackie said nothing, handed over Shaun's phone. 'What about this?'

'This is Shaun's?' PC Caldwell inspected the damage.

'That Wayne had it,' Amy said, jabbing a finger outside. 'He lied to us for days. Practically had to prise it out his hands and we get it back like that? He's an animal.'

With her colleague Officer Caldwell studied it a moment longer, then she handed it back. 'Mr Wayne Boyd stated that he found Shaun's phone in the staff room, and given the circumstances of Shaun's departure he panicked when he realised Shaun had gone missing. He said he wanted to-'

'-We know,' Amy groaned. 'Total crap.'

'Shaun left other items on the premises, is that right?'

'Aye.'

'A jacket?'

She nodded.

'Miss O'Leary...'

'Doesn't mean he's not lying. What about Andy West and his pals? Gardner and Marshall? Ye talk to any of them? Ye know they've all got a history of...well, they got off with it, but...Look, people are talking. Maybe not to you but they're *talking*.'

The policewoman nodded but she closed her book. 'With the results of our enquiries and Shaun's recent history, there's no evidence to suggest your brother has or will come to any harm.'

Amy started to tremble like she'd just heard the worst. Brendan scratched at his head and looked at Jackie, still holding the phone. 'Wayne's hiding something,' Jackie said with a nod. 'Youse really don't think so?'

'We've got no reason to believe a crime has been committed,' the officer said, standing up. 'Now I can imagine this must be a really difficult time for you all, and should you discover anything you feel might be important, please tell us. But unless circumstances change we won't be carrying out further enquiries.' The policewomen moved to the front door. 'Try to see this as a reason to stay positive,' PC Caldwell continued. 'In the meantime

Shaun's details will be passed on to Missing People. It's an organisation that offers support for people who've gone missing and their families. They're very helpful.'

Amy grabbed a cushion and with a scream tossed it across the room. 'So, what? Are they right? Is Shaun just selfish?' With a reddening, teary glare she dared her brothers to say aye, to say *anything*. Brendan flopped onto couch and Jackie sighed.

'Starting to look like it,' he said.

'But Wayne, what's he called? Boyd? He's lying, we know he is.' She threw another cushion and it slapped against the window. *'Don't* we?'

'Maybe he just nicked the phone,' Jackie shrugged. 'Answered it cos he's a weirdo. There's a lot of weirdos around.'

'No. Jumping up and down on a phone until it's practically destroyed is a lot more than weird.' She fixed her glare on her younger brother, messing with the zipper of his trackie. 'Brendan?'

He shrugged. 'Out of ideas, man.'

'Well, you were fucking flatmates in mum's *womb*. What's your gut?'

He blinked back, dazed. Then he stood up, found his cap and slapped it on. 'Just know I'm no use sitting here.' He patted down his pockets. The clunk of a phone, the jingle of keys.

'Where are ye going?' Amy asked, softer.

'Do some digging.'

'But ye talked to his pals.'

'No Mince.'

'Who?'

'Boy from school, works in Finnegan's in the town. Plus Shaun was never away from there back in the day. Maybe there's pals I don't know about.'

'Let us know what ye hear,' Jackie said, not getting up.

'Defo, man.' His sister approached and he let her kiss his cheek.

Then he left, the door slamming shut.

Alone and turning on the tap, Jackie couldn't help it, and like the water flooded into the kettle thoughts of home flooded into his mind. Was it selfish? To miss his life? To even steal these seconds to cherish what he loved? Because he did, he missed and loved all of it. His wife. His friends. The heat. God, he even missed the heat. Well, it only seemed clearer now, whether Shaun returned or not he'd soon be going home, three or four days and he'd be out of here. *No evidence he's come to harm*, that was it in black and white. No story, nothing to fear, just a grown adult who'd made his own decision. Amy might have seen the truth by then and if not she'd understand. It was harder to know with Brendan but whatever, he was no longer a boy. He placed the teapot on the tray and searched for a biscuit. In the next room a text alert rang.

Four seconds of silence.

'Oh my God!'

He ran in.

His sister was staring open-mouthed at her screen.

'Amy?'

She whimpered then turned, an astonished smile lighting up her face.

'Amy, what is it?'

'It's Shaun. Shaun!'

Jackie vaulted the couch and checked the message.

Sorry, Amy. Can't explain now but no worries, It's cool, back in the morning.

He shook his fists and screamed, hugged and sat down with his sister. They scanned and rescanned the text, and Amy sobbed and Jackie groaned. Their brother was fine, home tomorrow, they'd see him and hug him, and kick his fucking arse. Amy's cries grew loud and he wiped from her a falling tear. He thought she whispered ...*no*... like it was just too good to be true. So he went to bring her close and whisper that it wasn't.

She didn't budge. 'Amy..?'

She mouthed each word of the message like it was a final note of goodbye.

'Amy? What...? What is it?'

The phone fell onto her lap, and she collapsed into deep sobs.

'Amy! Everything's alright. We'll see him in the morning.'

He could barely hear her next as sadness choked her throat. 'No.'

'No? What do ye mean? What are you saying?'

'I'm saying that's not from Shaun.'

21

Sorry, Amy. Can't explain now but no worries. It's cool, back in the morning.

Jackie shook possibilities from his mind and threw himself back on the couch.

Head buried in her hands, Amy barely whispered. 'Believe me. It's not him.'

'Okay,' he huffed. 'I get it. It canni be our brother because he disni like writing texts.'

Amy's gaze at the floor was a whirling violet and blue. '*That's* what we'd argued about. I knew he'd be busy so I just wanted a text. But his dyslexia, he's so insecure, Jackie. If I'm lucky I get an *OK* and a frazzled smiley. Then that comes, a frigging letter practically. With no mistakes.'

'Auto-correct.'

She looked up now. 'Still too perfect. Anyway, it's four days. He'd call.'

'Ye think?' Jackie asked. 'Amy, that'd mean questions. What if he disni want that? No yet? It's a private number as well. This makes sense, don't analyse it. He's coming home.'

'No name.'

'What?'

'No *Shaun*.'

'That's…'

'There's no *Shaun* because whoever wrote it doesn't know how Shaun *spells* it. It could be the other way.'

Jackie slapped a thigh, and with an exhausted sigh sat up. 'Okay, say you're right, somebody else wrote it. But *back in the morning*? What sort of pishy lie is that? Why not *I've got a ticket to Australia and might turn up in five years*?'

'Who have I given my number to?'

'In Crawford's? The owner.'

'Anyone else?'

'Don't think so.'

'I wrote it on a bit of paper. Did he put it his pocket or…?'

Jackie bounced to his feet and grabbed Amy's hoodie. He chucked it at her. 'Let's get out.'

'He could have stuck it on a wall. For everyone to see.'

'I'm serious. Let's go.' Jackie nodded towards the door like on the other side was freedom. 'Gonni be murder waiting until tomorrow to see that big stupid prize walk in the door.' He clapped his hands. 'Come on.' To his surprise his sister got up and trudged half-dazed to her room, but then after a minute he assumed she was crying out this latest headfuck in the solitude of her bed. But she returned, her stained skirt replaced by fresh jeans. Jackie smiled but got nothing back. He grabbed the phone. 'I'll tell Brendan.'

Amy started to zip up her hoodie. But she stopped and lifted her head, mouth dropping open, green eyes widening. 'That's it.'

Jackie shrugged.

'Where I saw him.'

'Saw…?'

'Him in the hotel. I knew it wasn't the pub, Jackie.'

'Where then?'

'It was *outside* it. Yesterday.'

'Passing by?'

'No.' She thrust her zip to the top. 'He clattered into Brendan when he ran out.' She nodded. 'It was definitely him.'

'Local guy, then. Mates with Wayne Boyd right enough.' Jackie grabbed his sister's keys, chucked them and smiled. 'Maybe Shaun can fill us in.'

By the time the subway escalator was carrying them upwards Jackie had given up rhyming off his favourite teenage haunts, and not just because Amy had barely been listening. It wasn't only her he'd been trying to distract. She'd had a point with that text, it *was* weird, longer than half of Shaun's emails and maybe he *would* be more likely to call. But for God's sake it was still a breakthrough. It was *something*. He took his sister's phone again and swiped and stabbed and listened, depending on how Brendan saw this, Amy might just be persuaded. But like just before they'd stepped onto the subway, there was no answer. He sighed, thrust the phone back in his pocket.

As an unexpected shower battered the underground's glass exit, Jackie stood wondering whether to stay sheltered or bolt. Amy hung behind so he guessed she was up for waiting, but with the sky mostly clear and an urge for loud music, he stepped out anyway. His sister tugged at his sleeve and he turned around. 'Come on. It won't last.'

'That guy in the hotel.' She pulled him close. 'He was a *guest*, Jackie.'

'Shit, ye know that crossed my mind earlier. I forgot to say.'

'Maybe he didn't leave. Maybe he went to a room.'

Stepping away from the shake of a brolly, Jackie wiped his cheek. 'But if he's local...'

'No. Let's get up there, ask at reception. Come on, we might even see him.' She still held Jackie's sleeve, and he knew she wouldn't be letting go. He nodded, and Amy smiled a thanks. Then she marched out into the rain.

In minutes they arrived at the hotel entrance, but even before the doors had opened Amy felt doomed. They had a vague description and no name, or even a plausible reason to ask in the first place. They strode past the lifts and checked out the lounge, a Whitney Houston ballad wafted out as couples chatted over wine. In an Irish Bar then a Thai restaurant they found similar stories, and after getting no luck in an Italian restaurant they took the lift to the twelfth floor. The sister and brother skulked its corridors then each of the floors below, before they finally trudged their way back to reception. Amy slumped onto the desk as a Pakistani-Scottish guy approached with a smile.

'...Aye, that's it,' she finished with a sigh. 'Quite small, baseball cap.'

'And this gentleman's not a friend?'

'It's complicated.'

The guy spun his pen in his fingers. 'I'm afraid I...'

'Your colleagues?'

With an obliging smile, he turned to the other receptionists. One woman was on the phone, another had retreated into an office. 'I'm sorry, but without a name...'

144

Jackie stepped forward. 'Thing is mate, in our world real names, well, they aren't allowed.'

The understanding smile drained away. 'I see.'

'Ye know why?'

'I…'

'Well, we wear blindfolds.'

The receptionist stuttered, even appeared to fumble for some sort of panic button. Jackie folded his arms, maybe now they'd get somewhere. But when he turned for Amy, he saw she was no longer by his side. He gave the receptionist a solemn nod and marched off.

He found his sister by the entrance. 'What *was* that?' she laughed, shoving him in the chest. 'Ye could have warned me.'

'It's a five-star hotel, probably full of perverts. Surprised he even blinked.'

Hands on hips, she gazed at the darkening sky. 'What are we doing, Jackie?'

'I've been trying to…'

She threw up her hands. 'Come on. Let's get a drink.'

'I know the place. Finnegan's.'

'Where Brendan was heading? Nah, was ages ago.'

'But I know why his phone's off.' He nodded back at the hotel. 'Celtic are on the telly, he's in there watching.'

A march back across the precinct then down several streets, to an alleyway and an oak door, flanked by two green lanterns. It sounded dead from the outside, Finnegan's, seemed dead on the inside as well, then Amy pulled open the second door and saw the silence was just tension. No face turned to her, all attention was on the screens, then a penalty was scored and met with roars and jumps and punches. The sudden celebrations had Amy almost off her feet, through a parting among the crowd she jostled for the bar. Turning round, she saw Jackie in a hug of a stranger and eyeing up the replay. He finally caught up. 'You get the drinks,' she said. 'I'll try and find him.'

Arriving at the bar, Jackie stepped onto the foot-railing, craned his neck for a look. No Brendan so far, maybe Amy will have better luck, and he peeled a note from his pocket, gave a wave to the barman. But the barman served only the telly and soon Jackie was watching as well. Minutes later Amy gave him a nudge, and he turned from the TV.

She shook her head.

'No?'

'Unless he's in the toilet.'

'So what about, what was his name? Mince?'

'No idea who he is.' Amy nodded at the absorbed barman. 'Ask.'

Jackie took the guy in for the first time. He was around Brendan's age and had blotched and podgy skin. Jackie felt a bit bad for assuming he was Shaun's old pal, but between him and the other two further down, he was the most likely.

Jackie made his way into the guy's earshot. 'Mince?'

The barman didn't look round. 'No kidding. McNally should have been strung up after his testimonial.'

'No, I mean are you Mince?'

He stole a glance.

'Just that we're…'

He'd already spun back to the screen, and now slapped a fist into a palm. 'Mince left two years ago, mate.' He threw a tea towel to the floor. 'Lives in Aberdeen. Probably shagging a sheep as we speak.'

22

When Jackie got out of his bed after eight, Amy was already up, and it looked like she'd been awake for hours. The coffee pot was near cold and the dishes had all been washed, and the living room had been swept and the couch cushions rearranged. It looked in fact like Amy was expecting a visitor, and watching her hold back the curtain and peer outside, one who was already late. Amy felt his presence and turned and braved a smile, he forced one back and went to put on fresh coffee. What could he say? He'd gone on enough about that text and how everything would be cool. He hadn't convinced her of anything but still felt like crap for trying, now he even tip-toed about the kitchen like he might remind her of his assurances. It was still early but he knew Shaun wouldn't be back, Amy had been right and games were being played. Why so sure? Because Brendan had now disappeared as well? Probably, he was hiding something, Jackie knew that. He'd been up half the night wondering what.

He brought his coffee into the living room, eyed Shaun's demolished phone on the table. In a minute he'd call Brendan but this time he'd do it from the bathroom, Amy didn't need reminding of something else to freak out about. He'd actually planned to head to Brendan's first, demand answers face-to-face, but he couldn't leave Amy alone, this morning she'd need him here. His sister turned with a half-hearted smile like she'd just given up on a bus, then sat on a chair opposite and gave a loud yawn. An act, Jackie knew, not even for him but herself, coming down gently from a place she'd never quite been. 'We'll give it until after twelve,' he said. 'Then plan our next step.'

A visit to the bathroom found Brendan's phone still off, and returning to the living room Jackie killed the silence with the radio. Whether Amy had any idea of what he was doing, she asked if there was news, and Jackie couldn't quite meet her gaze when he shook his head. For much of the morning, Amy sighed that waiting was pointless while praying it wouldn't be, and Jackie muttered at her not to give in while hoping that she would. A few more trips to the toilet to get a hold of Brendan, and a few more times he was back cursing him under his breath. Later there was a clatter on the door and only Jackie sprung up, Amy had already seen the guy with leaflets enter the building. He stayed on his feet and joined her at the window, but unlike her he barely looked out.

An old Hipsway tune came on the radio, and when Jackie realised he was singing he almost bit his own tongue off. A surprise and a relief to see Amy laugh, a short burst of life that then left her red with shame. She groaned, pulled at her unwashed hair and marched away, and Jackie wondered if she'd now start to break down. But from the kitchen there was a clattering of plates and she returned with sandwiches, she slammed them on the table and stood back, arms folded. 'The way I see it, Jackie, we've got a lead,' she said. 'Whoever sent that text knows we're onto them. We need to keep pushing.'

Jackie glanced at the time, five minutes to twelve. 'We'll start with Brendan.'

Amy didn't hesitate as her tenement door slammed behind, and as she and Jackie marched for the main road she barely glanced back up her street. Jackie admitted that he'd tried but had failed to talk to Brendan, and felt a hint of relief as Amy barely blinked. His phone still being off, she explained as she slipped him a subway ticket, didn't have to mean the worst, if it rang in Brendan's work he could end up with the sack. A train rumbled below and they rushed for it, and within fifteen minutes they were heading down an escalator to blinding lights and manic techno. As Jackie stepped into Brendan's sports shop, he noticed everyone around was young, staff were marching about in headsets and a few shoppers were even strutting. The workers wore white trackies as well, Jackie noticed, so Brendan even wore that gear *in his work*. He half-expected a tap on the shoulder and a word in his ear to leave, when Amy rushed to a young woman with tattoos and bleached hair.

'I'm looking for Brendan?'

She glanced up from a rack of t-shirts, went back to them with a mutter.

'I'm sorry?'

'No seen him.' She swiped at a price tag with a marker.

'Well,' Amy said, voice rising. 'Could you maybe look?'

Like the woman had had her fill for the day of freaked-out relatives, she shut her eyes for a second. Then she pressed a switch by her ear. 'Brendan? Aye? Is he on?.... Thought so. Ta.' She grabbed another label. 'Off sick,' she said with a sing to her voice, like she was handing a customer their change. 'No been in since Monday.'

Amy stormed up the escalator with a scream, stumbled and fell and stormed up again. Onto the precinct she raced, her face reddening and wetting as she stopped and pulled at her hair. Jackie ran to her, placed his hands on her shoulders, but he had nothing worth saying now except her name. Standing there and hugging her until her shrieks became sobs, he pointed out a bench and took her phone from the pocket of her top. They sat down, and as Amy gazed into the cracked and gum-splattered ground, Jackie shook his head and hit *dial*. There wasn't much point in this, who knew what he was up to. But Brendan answered and Jackie jumped to his feet.

'Alright, Amy. That's me on my tea break.'

'Tea break?'

'…Jackie? Aye, man, just sat down. I've…'

Amy jumped. 'Is that him? Brendan! Brendan!'

Jackie nodded. 'Ye sure you're in the right shop? Your pals hivni seen ye in days.'

'What…? I…'

'You're lying.'

'No, I'm…Alright. Jackie, don't say to Amy, eh? I'll explain, it's…'

'Amy's here.'

'Where is he?' she said, grabbing for the phone. 'Let me talk to him.'

'I'll put ye onto her.'

'No! I'll come round tonight.'

'Are ye in town somewhere?' Jackie asked. 'We'll meet now.'

'I canni, man. Just…busy, ye know?'

'Brendan?' Jackie asked. 'Are you drunk?'

151

'What? Course no..'

'Ye sound it. Sounds like you're in a pub.'

'Oh for fuck's sake. He's my twin, Jackie. This is hitting me hard.' He burst into tears. '*Really* hard.'

'Come on, then. We should be together. Sort this out as a family.'

'Together? Jackie, youse hivni listened to a word I've said, youse think I'm some mad bigot cos I know Shaun would only work in that place if they put a gun to his heid.'

'What? No, that's-'

'-Ye know what, man? While youse are taking selfies wi they scumbags and are never out of hotels, I'm tracking down Shaun's old mates. A better chance of the truth from them than that shitehole of a pub.'

'You're not being fair, we've not stopped looking since Tuesday, Amy's not slept a wink. So, what? You're making progress? Let's hear it, then. Let's hear about these mates you've tracked down that didni even exist before.'

Brendan sighed. 'I'll fill youse in tonight,' he said. 'Just give us until then.'

He hung up.

'Brendan!'

Amy stood open-mouthed, needing the right words from Jackie to keep her sane. He passed back the phone. 'Independent wee shite.'

More than that, both of them knew, much more. But what could they do but take him at his word and let him go for now. On the bench Amy fired off a text, groaned in relief when Brendan sent one back. 'Okay,' she whispered, like she was re-entering a marathon. 'That pub.'

152

That pub. That owner. That barman. Daryl had asked for Amy's number, aye, but Wayne Boyd could have taken it from Shaun's phone. They ran from the precinct and bolted for a taxi, weaving through shoppers and dodging bins and traffic. While Amy was spurred by knowing only Shaun now was missing, for Jackie it was a resolve to shake growing doubts. And he was losing. What could be ahead of them here but more sneers and lies? Or what if both of those guys were telling the truth? Could this mean Brendan *did* have something? Could this be even deeper and murkier than they'd imagined? There was no queue at the rank, and they jumped in a taxi and told the driver to get to Crawford's. Through his mirror the young guy beamed and pumped a fist. A pleasure, he declared. No, a *joy*. Crawford's. It was the greatest pub in Scotland.

A smattering of late lunchtime customers and two staff behind the bar. The scowling, jaundiced Maureen stepped onto the floor with plates of fish and chips, and a skinny blonde guy, fringe over one eye, was finishing pouring a pint. 'I'll ask to see their phone,' Amy said approaching him. 'They don't hand it over, we know they're up to something.'

Desperate, Jackie knew, and knew Amy thought the same, but he gave a nod of agreement and waited for the barman to look round. After a moment he did, but from the opposite side of the bar the old guy in the taped glasses called him over. The barman stepped across and there was a hushed conversation. Then he turned, collecting cash from a customer. 'Youse need to leave.'

'It's alright mate, I'm no here for the craic.'

The barman rolled his eyes. 'Never have guessed ye wirni a Bear. You, Eric?'

The old man held his nose, wafted the air.

'I'm looking for your boss. Or the head barman. Either will do.'

He nodded behind them. 'Door.'

'Just a word,' Jackie said. 'And we'll be on our way.'

He picked up a spill-tray. 'They're no here.'

Maureen reappeared, with a scowl Amy thought was reserved for them alone. She swiped a glass at Amy's side and continued to the back.

'Mon,' Jackie said. 'We've got Daryl's number, Wayne's address.'

To cackles and groans they left the pub, and started to trudge up the road. Amy didn't get her phone out to call the owner, and neither suggested heading to the barman's. They continued for the subway in silence, the only thing they could face now was home.

'Hey!'

They turned around. The barmaid was hurrying their way, a phone in one hand and a packet of cigarettes in the other. Amy and Jackie stepped towards her and she stopped, then after a contemptuous glance back at the pub she raised her phone. Jackie thought she'd got hold of the owner or the barman and would now hand the mobile over. And for a heart-thumping, dizzying moment, Amy wondered if Shaun was on the other end. 'Take this number,' Maureen said.

'What...?'

'*0 7 9...*'

'Okay. Wait, wait.' Amy got out her phone. 'Right...'

With a roll of the eyes, Maureen started the number again and Amy swiped and stabbed. 'Margaret's her name,' she said with another look behind. 'Got news for youse.' Bony, Indian-ink stained fingers pulled a fag from the packet as she stared at Amy hard. 'But this didni come from me, awright?' Amy nodded and she flicked at her lighter, sucked the life out the start of her cigarette. Then she turned and left.

'Okay, but…but…who's Margaret?' Amy shouted after her.

The reply came under a short cloud of smoke. 'The cleaner.'

23

Margaret would rather meet than talk on the phone. She was apologetic about this but wouldn't budge, she needed to say this right so it wouldn't come back to bite her. She also wasn't free until five, she explained so Jackie and Amy headed home, Jackie chucked on some pasta and they pretended to watch TV. As Amy cleared things to the kitchen and Jackie sat by the computer, Britt called. She was sorry for the intrusion and no, had nothing new to give, but she couldn't get them out of her mind and had there been any developments? Amy filled her in on Melissa and getting the phone back from Boyd. But she was short, Jackie thought, hung up pretty quick. The lassie had deserved a bit more.

Jackie checked out the Crawford's website, it wasn't his first time having a look but it was his first time scouring the gallery. Mostly it was photos from parties, fans hugging their heroes or standing by them all cool, in some Jackie had no idea which one was even the star. There were familiar faces as well, Skin gazing at the camera like it was some baffling new invention, and Wayne Boyd snarling into it with a Rangers badge crunched in his fist. Going back what looked like years were pics of the West's, the husband all sturdy and stern and the wife with a grin or a pout. And in almost every other photo was Daryl. If an arm wasn't around a player's shoulder, it was round a woman's waist.

But there were no clues, and soon Jackie and Amy were outside again heading for the subway. Down by the Clyde, Margaret had said, right opposite the courts, she'd have finished her other job by then and be waiting on a bench. The cleaner had managed to sound both confident and worried they'd find her, so Jackie and Amy set off early in case she bailed out. Once out of the station they headed towards the river, and when they reached the bank they followed it down. Striding past cyclists and walkers and mostly empty benches, soon they stood opposite the three-storey court. Amy sat down and Jackie leaned on the railings, and ten minutes passed before two women approached from the road behind. At first Jackie didn't notice one was Maureen, her hair was down, and in joggers and pink trainers she looked younger and healthier. She nudged at her pal, a stout, glum woman in greying curls and blue overalls. The woman gave a nervy glance their way, coughed into a tissue.

On the walkway Maureen introduced her friend, and with a wheeze Margaret nodded and sat down on the bench. The woman's swollen calves, Jackie and Amy noticed, were scorched with twists of purple, she stuffed away her tissue and took a couple of sharp breaths. 'This goes no further, hen,' she said to Amy before glancing back again at Maureen. 'Just want it aff my chest.'

Amy nodded. 'We just need to know what's happened.'

Pulling out a fresh tissue from her overalls, Margaret gazed out at the dull, rippling water and coughed again. 'Well,' she started. 'I'm in Crawford's four mornings a week, so I am, right? Friday to Monday, half-six to half-nine. Got my own key, so Monday as usual I finish my fag and step in. I go right up the back, that's what I usually dae, and I see the light's on, in Daryl's office I mean.' She shrugged at Amy and carried on. 'Daryl likes his wee after-hours doos so that isni a big deal. But I hear him as well, and he's frantic like he's trying to shut somebody up.' She coughed a few more times, her pale eyes now starting to water. 'So I make a bit of noise so he knows I'm in, no exactly hard with that buffer I've got to lug about. Well, he pops his heid oot, dint he?' She glanced at Jackie now. 'All smiles so he is but I can tell he's jumpy, asks me to leave the rooms and start on the floor instead, I'm guessing he's got company if ye know what I mean.' She looked at her pal again, got back a subtle nod. 'I widni have anything to tell youse at aw if I hadni notice it when I'd finished my shift.'

'What?' Amy asked.

'Blood, hen.'

'On the bus stop?'

'Aye. Well, no. No just the bus stop. My cagoule. I'd taken it aff, hung it up inside then picked it up again. A smear right across the hood. I'd only had that hood up when I was leaning on the bus shelter, finishing my fag before my shift. Well, the next day I checked and sure enough, blood over the bus stop.' Jackie and Amy exchanged looks. 'Youse get what I'm saying, aye...? I'm not sure if youse...The blood was *fresh*, spilt no long before I'd started my shift. I'd never have cracked a light aboot it, then Charles told me that a boy behind the bar had gone missing over the long weekend. A boy nobody liked, supposedly.'

'Charles?' Jackie asked. 'Skin?'

'My husband,' Margaret muttered, with an almost embarrassed glance at her pal like a warning had been issued years ago. 'I tell that waster about my cagoule and ye know the rest, suddenly he's a pishy-drawered Sherlock Holmes.'

Maureen broke into mischievous laughter. 'Aye. And the mystery of the Shite in the Washing Basket.'

Margaret beamed back, but then frowned an apology to the brother and sister. 'But no,' she said. 'I told him to lay aff talking to the polis cos I didni know for sure. Maybe Daryl or wan of his pals smacked your boyfriend then for some reason hid in that office. But at the same time it might be nothing. Like I say I don't want involved, just wanted to fill youse in.'

Jackie smiled. 'A big help, Margaret. We appreciate it.'

Maureen checked the time then slapped the thigh of her friend. 'Weans' dinner to get on.'

Gazing blankly out at the river, hands in her hoodie pockets, Amy slid down the bench. Jackie gestured for her phone and at first she ignored him. Then with a huff she passed it over, stuffed her hands back inside.

'What's his number?' Jackie asked.

She pointed to the call she'd made two days before, and he put the phone to his ear.

A moment passed. 'Stranger! How's things?'

There were seconds of silence. 'Who are you?'

'Ye know, mate. Have a think back.'

Daryl sighed. '…Oh. Yeah, listen. I've got no time for your crap.'

'No…don't hang up. How about we meet? Aye, ye can tell us all about how ye smacked Shaun outside your pub on Monday morning.'

'How I…? What…?'

'Were ye so wasted it's just no come back? Don't worry, we've spoken to somebody who saw the whole thing. He's a bit shy, no too up for chatting, but if ye have trouble piecing it together he'll be happy to tell the polis. What do ye think? ...Daryl?'

'You really need a hobby.'

'You're right,' Jackie said. 'A movie to watch. Got anything worth checking out? Like some CCTV of Monday morning?'

'I've asked you already, buddy. Believe me, this is us being nice.'

'Aye, I understand. So will ye be alright with me and my sister checking out the film for ourselves? We'll bring the pizza.'

'Oh for fuck's sake. Look, I'll show you the CCTV if you then piss off back to your East End hole.'

'Excellent. We'll be up in ten minutes.'

'I'm out of town. Come tonight.'

'Right. Is that an *I need to get time to wipe the tape* out of town? Cos that might be a be a bit of a problem.'

'No, buddy. It's an *I'm a bit fucking busy to deal with requests from delusional victims* out of town. If wanted to wipe my CCTV I could do it on my app right now. Half-past seven or not at all.'

At the news Amy nodded, and sat up with a hopeful shrug. Just like his cousin, she remarked to Jackie, the owner had lied, and there was surely no way that they could both be innocent. Of course if Daryl was hiding something he'd hardly show them the tape, unless that threat of the police was a bit too much to handle. Or maybe he wasn't in danger, Jackie wondered aloud, maybe he was protecting someone else, the contents of the CCTV might well present them with another surprise. There was an hour and a half to wait until they might get closer to the truth, and Jackie suggested killing time in a pub. Aye, they were sick of them by now but at least one round the corner was supposed to be friendly.

It was a Scottish folk pub, and under a string of flags from around the globe they ordered two soft drinks. The traditional tunes playing on CD seemed a world away from those in Crawford's, while the scattering of early evening drinkers acknowledged their presence with smiles and nods. Jackie jokingly cursed Shaun for not going missing from here instead, then he grabbed an entertainment guide and thumbed his way through it. As Amy swiped around her phone, the barman wiping a table beside them tried to catch her eye. When he did, he asked if she'd just been to a funeral. He apologised quickly when he saw her reaction, he only meant it as a joke. He said sorry to Jackie as well, as he hurried outside after his sister.

24

The bar owner led the two through the back of the pub, a bright and noisy kitchen was on the right and steps descended into darkness on the left. Ahead was another set of steps and they climbed behind Daryl, then found themselves in single file in a narrow, creaking corridor. At the first door they reached, Daryl took out a key and unlocked, then swung it open and nodded for Jackie and Amy to enter. Behind them Daryl hit the light switch of his box-sized office and gestured at a blue two-seater couch. As his guests sat down he smiled, rubbed the back of his head. 'No, it's not much. But more than enough to make an escape now and again. So, a peace offering. Drink?'

Amy could barely keep down herself never mind a drink, but Jackie nodded, it'd give them time to take this all in. 'Tea would be good.'

'Coming right up.'

The owner left and they gazed around at the cramped furniture: the desk with the chair and the PC, the sink and the mini-drinks cupboard, the safe and the filing cabinet. Around twenty framed letters hung on the wall opposite and Jackie stood up for a look. An ex-soldiers' hospital, a kids' home, a hospice... all charities thanking the pub for its donations. Peppered between the letters were at least as many photos, similar or identical to some of those on the website. Except one. Kilted in front of a castle by the sea, stood the bar owner and Andy West.

Daryl returned and placed a tray on the desk. 'Yeah, we do a lot of work for *chari-dee* but don't really like to talk about it.' He continued to stand there, eyebrows raised, but then at Amy's unimpressed glare he shrugged. 'Nah, our community's everything to us, giving a bit back is the least we can do.' He sat on his swivel chair and scratched through his denim shirt. 'But if only all the correspondence was positive.' Opening a drawer he pulled out a small, white envelope, slid it across the desk.

Jackie picked it up. 'What's this?'

'Take a look.'

He unfolded a single page with four typed lines. With Amy he read them then slid it back. 'Nice.'

Daryl hit the mouse and the computer screen was brought to life. 'Touching, isn't it?'

Amy folded her arms. 'Irrelevant.'

Daryl clasped his hands round his head. 'Not really, Amy. It's tough to take sometimes. I'm not sure if Gregg's next door gets threats that it'll be burnt down *from the inside out*. And have ye ever tried their cheesy bakes?' At the silence he breathed a sigh, placed the envelope back in the drawer. 'No worries, I'll show it to the police, Just like the one I showed a couple of months ago. And they'll tell me how they're taking this all very seriously indeed.'

Amy nodded at the screen. 'CCTV, please.'

'Coming,' he said, scrolling down for some seconds. He pushed the screen around. 'This is what you wanted. Monday morning.'

The black and white screen was split in two, one part showed the road to the west and the other towards town. Daryl sat back, and Jackie and Amy leaned forward.

163

0620. A car passes…A second car…A Hackney…After that, from the distance emerges a figure, a guy in jeans and a t-shirt stumbling one way then the other. The average height, the slim build, the receding fair hair, Jackie and Amy know it's Shaun. He walks into a wheelie bin and bounces back again. He reaches the pub. Eyes it up. He turns the corner and disappears.

Daryl pressed *pause*.

'The only camera we have is this one at the front door, and seeing as we're short on sound effects I'll do my best to fill you in. First it was one bang then another, bricks bouncing off our reinforced windows. Then it was the shouts. *Orange bastard. Loyalist scum.* All that. But unlike the regular Nobel Prize nominees we get round here, I recognised the voice. Then it went quiet.' He took the mouse, span the film forward.

0623. Shaun's round the front again and banging the door, then stepping back and peering up at all the windows. One eye is discoloured and swollen, his mouth is twisted in a sneer. He lunges for those windows but falls hard, tries again and lands on his back. The third time he really goes for it and again hits the deck, and lies there grimacing holding his head.

Another pause.

'I know who's outside and I'm hoping he'll see sense, we're having a poker night you see and I'm well, on fire. But if I don't show my face, both my buddies will. And they've been losing all night if you get what I'm saying.'

0625. The door opens, Daryl appears and shouts. Shaun's up again and tries to get in the pub, and Daryl steps about from one side to the other. An exchange of words and Shaun gives Daryl a push, and when Daryl pushes back Shaun falls towards the bus stop. Shaun steadies himself and spits an insult, and Daryl appears to ask him to repeat it. Shaun's having none of it and makes a charge, so Daryl gets ready, holds up his fists. His punch isn't strong but it's on the money, and Shaun staggers back, head hitting the bus shelter. Leaning against the perspex, he chucks one last insult, then stumbles back the way he came. Daryl watches him leave and goes back inside.

Again Daryl pressed *pause*.

'Totally steaming. Seriously, I'd not seen anyone that drunk for about a week. Anyway, ...*jacket...jacket...*, that was the one word I could make out, and he'd have got it as well if he'd stood back and kept his mouth shut. So as you will see I acted in self-defence, and the blood on the bus stop wasn't from his collision with my fist. But the pavement.'

Without waiting for an answer, he ran the CCTV to *0628*, to Margaret plodding into view and leaning against the bus stop. She took two draws of her cigarette and stepped to the door, and Daryl pressed *pause* again and smiled.

'Your witness?' He waved away any coming answer. 'It's okay, was a weird time all round. I was in uncharted territory with my Royal Flushes, then after our incident it threatened to go a bit pear-shaped. She'd have noticed I wasn't happy.'

'Two mates ye were with?' Jackie asked, putting down his mug of tea.

'Who?'

He smiled, clicked off the CCTV. 'Strangers to you.'

'Gardner and Marshall?'

'Gardner and...?' He sat back and glared at his visitor, not just insulted but even a bit hurt. 'Believe it or not, my whole life doesn't revolve around Crawford's and its regulars. But okay, yeah, I apologise, I can only imagine what you're going through and I wished I'd been straight sooner. But you understand, surely. I tell you that I saw Shaun then I also tell the police. Fine, happy to help, but how long before it becomes common knowledge for the whole city? You saw that letter, and we all know how our rivals like a wee conspiracy now and then to help them get up in the mornings. To survive, I'd need this place bomb-proofed and the Terminator put on the door. *Or*,' he said, leaning forward now and lowering his voice. 'I could just change the name to Finbar's and win Pub of the Year for the *craic*.'

Amy wanted to lift herself but could barely lift her gaze.

'Go back,' Jackie said.

'What?'

He flicked a nod at the screen. 'Six hours. To closing time.'

Daryl checked his watch and sighed. 'No problem, I've got all night.' Again he clicked the mouse and soon the screen read *0011*.

He scrambled it to *0014*.

> Dark. A dozen or so ex-drinkers are scattered outside the pub.
> Three older beerbellies around the entrance laugh as they puff
> on fags, and staggering by the roadside are a group of young

166

guys, chanting. A lassie in a short skirt is dragging her boyfriend from an old rockabilly, and between them on the ground lies a barely-touched kebab. Most people leave and others come in their place, Skin is one, and finally at *0018* there's Shaun. In a t-shirt he's scowling, starts to walk towards town, and no one around seems to take any notice. Thirty seconds later Wayne Boyd appears, marches in the same direction.

'There.'

With a roll of the eyes Daryl pressed *pause*. 'Our barman lives two minutes that way.'

'Back again.'

Daryl huffed, rewound to Boyd leaving.

'*There*. Pause.'

Daryl clicked. 'You know buddy, I'm beginning to think that showing the police my right hook might be an idea, I'm giving you my time so you could at least listen. The only part of my fat cousin's behaviour worth any comment at all is that he hasn't turned right for Doner Spectacular. But that's only because he's going to Tikka Treat.'

'No. *Them*.' Now Jackie was off his seat, pointing not at the barman but two jumper-wearing middle-aged men on the edge of the east-showing screen. Standing by the front of the pub, they're muttering and nodding towards Shaun. Then they're off in his direction, crossing the road and out of shot.

'Where are they going?'

'Home, I imagine. Speaking of which…' He stood up, winked.

167

Amy turned to Jackie. 'They were following him. That's...'

'Gardner and Marshall, as you know them. Duncan and Keith for the rest of us. They're your suspects?' He grimaced. 'No offence, but you should probably discuss this wee *development* on your own.' He gestured at the door.

Jackie and Amy got to their feet, but Amy didn't turn around. 'You won't have any problem showing us your phone, will ye?'

'Showing you...?'

'Texts you sent last night.'

Daryl spluttered a laugh. 'Yeah, I do have a problem.' He picked his mobile up and slipped it into his pocket. 'I've been hell of a patient, invited you into my office and given you the truth, I must say that's a good deal more than what you've given me.' He drew his eyes up and down Amy. '*Girlfriend?*' he sneered. 'You sure about that? And....' He tilted his head at Jackie, giving him a chance to come clean. '...One of *us*?...Oh look,' he finally said. 'Some friendly advice. With the state of your brother on Monday morning? Maybe just wait till he sobers up.'

The owner left them at the stairs and signalled to the barmaid, and Amy and Jackie walked through to the floor. The place wasn't yet half-full but already had an edge, ABBA would soon be struggling for attention under the rising shouts and laughs. Jackie thought he heard his name but continued for the door, and when a guy in a paint-splashed t-shirt scowled he continued to stare in front. He had to get out, had to think. Then Amy waved towards a figure sat behind a pillar. 'Britt!'

At a table with an orange juice, Britt smiled back, put down her paperback.

Amy marched across. 'Britt!' she said, as loud as before.

The woman blinked at what sounded like hostility, even shrunk back an inch. 'Hi!'

Amy folded her arms. 'On your own?'

'Yeah, I...' She gestured to her book. 'Just finished work.'

'Where *do* ye work, by the way? You've never said.'

'In-'

'-And no sign of...what was his name again?' She turned to her brother. 'Andy...?'

'I'm always on my own here, I just like to...'

'Alan,' she said, snapping her fingers. 'That's it.'

'He's not well, recovering from an operation. A hernia.'

'Of course.'

'Amy,' Jackie muttered. 'What are ye...?'

'Just talking,' she said, eyes still on the woman. 'Wondering how Britt seems to have as many friends here as we do.'

'I told you, I... What's wrong, Amy?'

Amy grabbed Britt's leather bag from her chair, thrust in a hand. 'Got a wee problem. Someone sent me a text. Said he or *she* was my brother and it threw me. Made me vomit, actually. You had my number, didn't you?'

'What...? Well yeah, I...'

Jackie grabbed his sister's arm. 'Amy, have you lost it? Put it down...'

'Let go.' She shoved him away. 'So let's...'

Amy grabbed out the phone and threw Britt back her bag, then stepped back from her brother and stared and swiped. She trembled, eyes reddening as she struggled to find the icon.

'Hey, hey…' Jackie placed one hand on her shoulder and the other under the mobile. 'Let's keep it together, Amy. Britt's been an amazing help.' She started to shudder, stabbed harder. Her face crumpled and the phone fell from her grip.

Britt jumped up, grabbed a seat and helped Amy down to it, and with a groan she collapsed on the table. 'It's okay,' Britt said. 'I'll show you, Amy. Look.'

Jackie waved a hand, returned the mobile. 'Don't. Please, just forget this happened.' He felt the weight of stares and stole a glance behind. Curious but not unkind, and there were looks of what appeared to be sympathy.

Britt slid the phone under Amy's bleary gaze. 'Here's my history.'

Eyes closed, Amy gave a defeated nod. 'I'm so sorry…' she whispered.

'No, *look*.' She slid it to Jackie and he did. Four texts sent the day before, none to Amy or her number.

'It's just a pretty tough time,' Jackie said, arm on his slouched and now sobbing sister's shoulder. 'That message was brutal.'

'Amy?' Britt touched her arm. 'Listen, I understand. 'My God, when James died I wanted to kick the shit out of strangers for *smiling*. But you've got every reason to be positive. Shaun wasn't troubled, right? James? He was…' She gave a helpless shrug then sat back, forced through a smile. '…If there's anything I can do.'

The last place Jackie wanted to talk was here, and his heart sank as he realised he'd probably have to get drinks. Skin shuffled to the toilet so he took his chance and moved for the bar. In the mirror opposite he noticed behind him the big guy in the stripy t-shirt. Still glaring, he was. Then looking away. Was Jackie going mad or did he have something to hide?

He got back to the table as Amy and Britt released themselves from a hug. 'Britt?' He gestured to the guy now gazing again at his phone. 'What do ye know about him?'

She gave a sad smile. 'I only hope I look miserable, not downright hostile like him. But I've never seen him before. Sorry.'

Jackie leaned forward. 'Okay, so Daryl,' he started. 'What do we think? Amy?'

She gave a faint shrug. 'Telling the truth, probably.'

'I'm not so sure. But Andy West and his mates? We chin them.'

'For what? More crap?'

'What else can we do?'

'Spy?' Britt said.

'How do we do that?' asked Amy.

'Don't know. Record their conversation?' Britt picked up her phone. 'You've got mobiles. An obnoxious pair of pricks, those two by the way, their leers and comments.'

'Ye think they'll be there this weekend?' Jackie asked.

'They come regular.'

'You could be onto something. Oh, by the way...'

'Yeah?'

'Do you maybe...kind of like our wee brother?'

Britt almost spat a mouthful of juice. 'What?'

Jackie grinned. 'Thought we might have detected something. He could do with some company.'

'Oh my God.'

Amy gave her biggest smile of the week and Britt threw her hands to her face. 'I *did* think…the first time…well, he seemed uncomfortable in here and it was sort of endearing. But no, he's a bit young for me…' She smiled. 'He's off the hook.'

'We should get back actually,' Amy said, taking her first and last sip of coke. 'Brendan's been…Oh God, one worry at a time…difficult.' She got to her feet. 'I'll be in touch, Britt. And again, sorry.'

Britt took her hand. 'Just remember I'm here.'

Outside the door, Amy jabbed at her phone and waited but got no response from Brendan. *Tonight*, he'd said, *still plenty of time.* She moved for the subway. 'Let's just get back.'

Jackie grabbed her arm. 'No.'

Amy was done. 'What do ye mean *no*?'

The thought had been on Jackie's mind for hours but only now had the time come to say. 'I might know where he is.'

'Brendan? Where?'

'Come on.'

Twenty minutes later the brother and sister rode up the same escalator in the same station as the night before. Hearing Jackie out on the train, Amy had just gazed at the floor like there was nothing she could any longer take in. Jackie wasn't even sure himself, only that what Brendan had said to him was weird. *While you're never out of hotels, I'm trying to find Shaun's pals.* They'd explained how they'd followed Boyd to the hotel but not that they'd gone *back*, they just hadn't seen Brendan to go into any details.

Aye, Jackie could be wrong, but when they'd returned there last night Brendan might have been there too.

After heading through the slide doors, they gave an immediate scan of the lobby. Amy made for the reception until she saw Jackie march up to the back, followed him past the lifts and round to the open lounge. As two pairs of suits and cocktail dresses strolled in ahead of them, Jackie slowed down like the absurdity was hitting home. Amy overtook, marched straight through the entrance, Brendan sitting here would be no madder than Shaun working in Crawford's. As glasses clinked to laughter under gentle piano jazz, she took in the groups and couples around the softly-lit room. Then she peered into a corner. And at the lone, white track-suited figure slumped over an untouched pint, she gasped.

*

Monday 25th February (cont'd)

Aye...

No, I'm fine honest... Just need to say this.

So aye, Will Stark, the brother's name was. Fat and miserable, loads of tattoos. According to the papers he'd done time for serious assault, fraud as well and been cleared of attempted murder. That was all I needed to know and I got Greg to set up a meeting, and next thing I knew man I was in the guy's office. Stark was a case, he wore this...sneer, it was like he saw me coming from a mile away and couldni wait to rip me off. There was an Irish guy as well and he looked even worse. Jimmy, his name was. Cheap suit, ginger tash. He put me on edge, this Jimmy, the sort who'd stamp on someone's head then go nuts about the blood, and it bothered me as well how he kept disappearing into the next room. No enough but, obviously. The worse I found these guys, the more I wanted in. We struck a deal right away.

For a couple of grand I'd teach Greg my system, then hand over a file with all my data and formulae. Except of course there was no way on earth I'd be giving them my work. Inside the file would be a file-destroying program, and within a week of me saying goodbye the whole lot would vanish. No, no exactly Bill Gates but it gave me a buzz, and I couldni wait to sit down with this Greg and shaft them. We met in a café and things went fine, I once even bluetoothed all his files when he went to the toilet. But then for the last session he didni turn up, a bit of a worry cos I hadni been paid, and although Greg had warned me against going to the office, I had no choice man, I headed right there. The door was open and the office was empty but in the other room I heard voices. Lassies' voices, Italian or something, and they wirni so much talking as...greeting and pleading. The Irish guy was there, I heard him shout, 'Elena!' Then there was a punch. Then thuds and yelps. Next thing I just heard this...this...splutter.

25

Brendan's name was called and at first he didn't flinch. Then it was called a second time and he still sat there dazed. But he'd heard, alright, and sensed the two figures standing in front of him. He wasn't actually surprised that his brother and sister had turned up, and Amy and Jackie both detected what sounded like a groan of relief. Across Brendan's table Jackie crouched, tried to catch his brother's eye. 'What ye doing here, Brendan?'

Amy sat on the sofa next to him and took his hand. 'Tell us, Brendan. What's wrong?'

Brendan's voice was a whisper. 'Ye'll no see him.'

'Shaun?'

Gazing through the pint glass, he shook his head.

'Who?'

...

'*Who*, Brendan?'

'The guy that was here.'

'Wayne Boyd's pal?'

He nodded.

'Brendan do you *know* that guy?'

He lifted his head to his sister, showing exhausted, bloodshot eyes.

'Have you been looking for him?'

'...Aye.'

'Who is he...? How do ye...?'

No answer came. Brendan's gaze now hit the floor and Amy rubbed his hand. 'I think it's time, pal. Aye. I think it's time ye filled us in.'

The hour for casual dress had passed, and the bow-tied barman approached the table to ask Brendan to leave. It was clear to Jackie that the guy had asked before, and he persuaded him to let Brendan stay so long as he took off his cap. Jackie ordered drinks, and with a sigh and a hesitant nod Brendan lifted himself up.

Time, right enough.

'He's from London,' he said, a hand wrapped around his pint and giving his sister and brother a nervy glance. 'I saw him last year.'

'Okay.'

'Expecting me to get doon there and change Shaun's ways, that was never gonni happen, Amy. I'm no blaming ye, but soon as I set foot in that place I knew.' Brendan bit into a knuckle then and shook his head. 'Everywhere I looked man, exotic faces, I saw mine in a window and nearly turned round again. But I didni, I got to Shaun's place. Dead nice area and banging flat, and he was in this Ted Baker t-shirt and with a gorgeous lassie. Not to worry but, eh?', Brendan sneered back into his drink. 'Brendan will whisk him back to Glasgow on the next available Megabus. I just stood there man in the same trackie I'd worn for six months, stuttering everything was sound and it was just a flying visit. He got the lassie a taxi and asked us to spill the beans, I didni but he was fine with me spewing crap, barely even listened. Next night man his heid was still somewhere else and it clicked that he was thinking about that system. He seemed happy with life, Shaun, much more than I was, so I knew he should be the one to help *me*.' He took a gulp of his beer then looked Amy and Jackie in the eye. 'I tell him I want in,' he said, louder now, 'and he thinks this is why I'm doon in the first place, stays dead quiet. But then he knocks me back man, says he's been studying Maths for years, ye canni just pick it up, you've got to know it inside-oot. I keep on at him, ask for a crash course and I'll take it fae there, just after a bit of his time, man, nae big deal. So he gets oot his laptop and starts to explain, but he's practically talking Chinese and I hivni a clue. So he was bang on really and I feel like a clown, but at the same time man he could have chucked me a bone. So the next night in his local I ask if he can text me some tips, I'll just go to the bookies and take care of the rest. Oh it's no like that he says, even placing the bets takes skill, plus to win big ye need to risk big and he canni be responsible. Pure sounds like bullshit man and he's pissing me off, but then I notice a lassie looking my way and smiling. I know, shock of the century eh? But no way do I go and talk to her, Shaun bolts and I follow him back, get ready for my kip. But soon enough we're doing each other's heids in and he wants me gone by the morning. I'm too late for the bus but I'd rather kip in the station than there, so I shoot straight back to his local to hang oot for an hour or two. A bit stupid man thinking that lassie might still be there but she is, and waving at us noo to come over for a chat. I really want to go up to her but I crumple at aw that, then she just rocks up and buys me a drink.' He slapped his cap back on his head, scowled and took it off again. 'She's a wee lassie, brown eyes, massive smile. Claire, her name is and she's a stunner. I talk complete pish to her but she totally laps it up, although I think she's putting it on and will do a runner in seconds. But no, she loves my accent man, my patter as well, and eventually my heart stops racing and I start to chill. I suss it out, Jackie.

I'm exotic! I mean Shaun's got a gorgeous bird and he's a baldy bastard. So soon man I'm loving it, my best night in years, I'm even thinking aboot chucking it aw and moving doon for good. And this lassie's no just stunning but minted, drink after drink she's buying me, nae questions asked. You call Amy and I'm high as a kite, I almost put this lassie on the phone to ye, call her my bird. Anyway, I canni mind how it happens but we start talking about gambling, turns out she's a whizz and it runs in her family. I tell her Shaun's the same but he's a bit of a prick, and when I explain the rammy she's up for sorting it oot. She thinks there's a chance she can crack Shaun's codes, and she spews out some mumbo jumbo and asks to see the laptop. She's touching my hair man, hand on my knee, and I couldni care less about Shaun's system anymore. I know where he keeps his spare key right enough and that he went oot with his pals, so we get back to his flat and go right to his room. I open the laptop and we kiss, then just my luck there's a knock at the door. I tell her it's nothing but she practically pushes me out, and I walk down that hall and feel her behind us. I realise then, I just fucking *know*, and I open the door and I see this guy's face. Next thing man I'm punched in the back of the heid and I fall to my knees, and my face is on the carpet and the guy's stepping over us. Then my hands are tied and there's a bag over my heid, I feel a knife on the other side and I'm told to sit on my arse. They're calm, the two of them but they're no messing about, they turn Shaun's room upside doon and then they're away. I'm sitting greeting man, I want that bag to stay over us till the day I die. I need to get away but so I try to untie my hands, and it's actually pretty easy and I rush to the window. They're doon below, the lassie's got the laptop and the guy's got some books, and I boot the door to make it look like a break-in and I'm off as well. Sitting at the station man I almost phone Shaun, tell him I'd been shafted by somebody he must have pissed off. But no, I'd be a total sadcase, even bigger than I was already, I mean I'd have to explain this to youse, and honest I'd rather die. When Shaun comes back here I'm no that shocked, those two didni look like psychos but their boss might be. So I wait for Shaun to chin us, blow the whole game, he'd have seen they got in with his key and who knew aboot that but me. But no, not a peep, and for ages we're dead cagey, me waiting to be pulled up for lying, him waiting to be asked what he'd been up to. But it disni happen and after a couple of months we're talking again, meeting for the fitba, things almost normal. Then he just does one. First I'm jealous that his life's that mad, then my heid's scrambled cos of where he worked. Then I start to come round. Fair enough I think, widni be me, but maybe London's changed him and he just needs the extra dosh. In that pub man I'm getting freaked oot and I bolt, run into that guy. He's up again and marching aff, and I realise I've seen him before. He's the guy that tied me up. I know it is and I'm fucking all over the place, tell myself it was a coincidence, it's no like he was *in* the pub. But then you tell us that barman was with a pal in a hotel, and I think is it *him* and is he *staying* there? I've got no idea what they'd be up to or how they'd even be mates, but I know this can be heavy and I've got to check it oot. So the past two days man I'm here looking, was gonni give it until the night. Naebdy on reception coughs up and in the bars they're clueless, disni help right enough that I know almost nothing about the guy. Then half an hour ago a receptionist feels sorry for us, gives us the script. An English guy, she says, checked oot two days ago before dinner. Smiling, she was, thought it was pretty funny. Says I was right. He did look a bit like a chicken.

*

Monday, 25th February (cont'd)

Aye, ehm…

…Well, all the noise just stopped then and that chicken-face, he came up behind me. I swapped the file for the cash and I was out like a shot. But… and this is something I'll need to live with…I didni call the polis. I knew terrible things were happening to those lassies and I'd guessed that they'd been trafficked as well, but I didni get them rescued. Why not? Well, I told myself it'd be pointless, Greg knew I'd heard them screaming, he even made a joke, so it was guaranteed that those lassies would pretty soon be gone. But true or not, that was just an excuse, I was so precious about that system I couldni tell the polis a thing. So a week later I'm in the flat, a bit down because Brendan had turned up and we'd had a fight. I head out to a club and get back around three, find my room's been tanned, notebooks, electronic stuff, everything's gone. There hisni been a break-in so maybe Brendan had let them in by accident, then it hits me that the file-corrupter had gone off that day. They found me, Stark and that. They took away my system. That was bad enough, but maybe next time it'll be me.

I've barely got time to think, just pack my rucksack and get off my mark to an all-night café. My world's not collapsed completely, I'm backed up in cyberspace, but I'm spooked at how they found me cos I lied through my teeth. I just need to collect myself, think through my next move, so what I do is I pick up a paper, one of they… Anyway, I don't even open it. It's just there. Front page. Elena Adamescu, her name was. 22 years old. Found strangled in a park opposite Stark's office. What do I think? Well, I think it's somebody else, because I fancy the easy way out thanks very much. But no, I canni forget it, that face willni leave me, then I remember those files that I nicked from Greg. They're in cyberspace as well so I check them and I see it, the same photo that was in the paper. Elena. One of seventeen lassies from Eastern Europe. Thought they were gonni be waitresses.

I send the files to the polis totally anonymous, with Will Stark's address and the article of Elena's murder. I don't get in touch personally cos I just canni do it, face that lassie's family in court and admit I walked away. I know, cowardice, no other word for it, and the other thing is I just want to start again. I've realised now, it's finally sunk, how shitty and pointless my life is. And see returning to be that person for a second? It'd make me puke. Anyway there's tons of info on these files, the polis will surely find the bastards, and I catch a train up here and move in with my sister. For five months after that I'm watching the news, desperate to see an arrest. Then two weeks ago, just as I'm thinking about having to make a statement, there it is. The Irish guy, Jimmy, jailed for life for Elena's murder. Greg Stark, his case collapsed and there wisni a word about his brother. But one out of three, it's better than none.

So now...now I'm just putting it behind me, and I know it willni be easy. I've got no cash or degree or even come to that, mates, and of course that lassie's screams are never far from my head. But I've got my health and my family and a wee job in a supermarket, and I'm looking for a flat, just need cash for a deposit. So it's slow but I think my life might be starting to happen. I don't see myself gambling again, I feel like a different person.

But I know as well that it might creep up on me and then, well, I'll be screwed.

Aye.

So that's why I'm here.

I do feel…better.

Thanks for listening.

26

Amy swiped the bay curtains shut as Jackie carried in a tray of tea. Brendan sat slumped on the couch, his cap half-hiding the world. 'Sorry I didni say,' he muttered again. 'I just…'

'Cool it. You've said now.' Taking a seat next to him, Jackie patted a grass-stained knee of his trackie. There was mud around the legs as well, orange stains down the front. He might have made a joke if he didn't also notice a fraying and yellowing on the sleeves, the same gear Brendan had been embarrassed about months ago.

Amy pulled back the curtains for a final gaze, then with a yank unzipped her top. 'It changes everything,' she said, throwing it over the chair in front of her.

Re-fitting his cap, Brendan sat forward and from the coffee table grabbed a pen. He rattled it against his thigh. 'Narrows things down, Amy, right…?'

From having had her arms around him half an hour before, Amy now stared at the wall than have to look at her younger brother. He understood why as well, if he'd come clean earlier Shaun might even by now have been found. 'We know Boyd lied again, that's for sure,' Amy said, collapsing onto the chair. 'He didn't meet Shaun at a meeting.'

Jackie sighed, rubbed at his eyes. 'Nah, that's the only thing that makes sense.'

'Can't be. That guy was English, Brendan, yeah?'

At the acknowledgement, Brendan brightened. 'Hunner per cent,' he said, sitting up. 'Willni forget the voice.'

'So he lives down there, otherwise why stay in a hotel? Shaun met the guy in London, the guy must have introduced him to Boyd.'

'No,' Jackie said, shaking his head. 'There's no way Boyd would kick about down there, he'd need a Lonely Planet for an afternoon in Paisley. And I'm telling ye, their body language. They aren't mates.'

'Associates. Who cares, they're gamblers. What matters is Shaun must have known both of them before he came home.'

Jackie rubbed at his head, his hands fell down his face onto his thighs. 'Probably. But maybe Shaun and Boyd met at a meeting *before* he went to London. Maybe Boyd gave him that chicken face's number then.'

'One meeting he attended, Jackie. On the day mum died. *Okay*,' she added under her brother's dubious glare. 'As far as I know. But he must have known Boyd a while, this makes no sense otherwise.'

Jackie added a sugar to his mug, drops of tea dripped from the spoon as he raised a hand. 'So why chase Shaun here?'

'His system, man,' Brendan said, glancing at both. 'If that was what they were after when they stole Shaun's gear, maybe they didni find it. Or else couldni get into the laptop. I canni mind if there was a password.'

Amy frowned. 'Those *gangsters* found themselves locked out of a laptop? Don't see it, more likely they couldn't understand the system. Maybe…' Her eyes fell onto the coffee table. '…Here, maybe the system was on *that*.'

Jackie leaned forward, picked up what the three pairs of eyes were on, Shaun's battered mobile. 'Looks like they tortured the thing,' he said, inspecting it again then passing it to Amy. 'Well, if we're right,' he said with a hopeful shrug. 'This means they're looking for him but canni find him.'

Amy blinked up from the phone. 'He's hiding somewhere?'

'He disappeared on Sunday night, and that chicken was still in the hotel on Wednesday afternoon. Ye could argue he left because they'd found Shaun by then, but maybe Boyd had warned him we were on their tail.'

Amy sighed. 'You're wrong, Jackie.'

'Wednesday, we were in the hotel then.'

'About Shaun. Why would he hide somewhere? He'd just come home. Or at least get in touch.'

'No phone? No numbers?'

'For God's sake, there are ways. He could...Oh no...'

'What?'

'That CCTV. Oh my God, the state he was in. What if he just...fell into the Clyde or something?'

'He was ages from the river.'

'A half-hour walk.'

'The *other* direction.' Jackie gestured for the phone again as Amy hung back her head and groaned. 'There were no documents, were there?' he muttered as the mobile flickered to life. 'Hidden away or...'

'No, man. Hey,' Brendan asked. 'Did Boyd put up a fight?'

'For this? No really.'

'Deleted it, maybe.'

Jackie swiped the screen and the two of them stared. 'It sat between them on the table, I think they were waiting for Shaun to give it a call. Trick him into coming back or something.'

'He *wouldn't* do that alone,' Amy muttered through gritted teeth.

Brendan nodded at the one page to have shaken Amy, the list of match odds. 'Could they have been betting on those games?' Thumb hovering, Jackie could barely register a shrug, while Amy gazed scunnered at the ceiling. Brendan admonished himself with a shake of the head. 'Widni need Shaun's phone for that.'

Amy sprung up. 'Those games with the asterisks, when were they played?' Before either brother could read, she peered over their shoulders.

'Monday night was the first,' Brendan said. 'Then Tuesday, Wednesday, through to Saturday. Ten in total. From Spain, I think that one's Brazil, Argentina, Australia, Rangers Celtic. All over the world.'

'They were waiting,' Amy said. 'Jackie, you said yourself they were anxious.'

'Gamblers aren't worried about a few quid.'

'No, maybe it was more.' Amy bit at her lip. 'Maybe it was a lot more.'

'Shaun's system? Ye think it's actually better than we've given him credit for? Could they have put it to work?'

For seconds their sister could only gaze past them, open-mouthed, eyes welling. 'No. I...I mean, *yeah*. They're using it, they're maybe depending on it. But I think it's more than that. Look, if Shaun had run away he'd have been in touch by now, and you're right, if he'd come to any harm that guy would have left. What if they're not *looking* for Shaun? Not looking because they don't need to?' Amy turned towards the window as if Shaun was right outside. 'What if they've already got him?'

27

At Amy's insistence they were up and out early. Her brothers hadn't been sure about the next step, in fact they had major doubts, that system might have been profitable but surely nothing worth kidnapping for. More than that, on the off-chance that Shaun was being held prisoner, they had no clue where to even begin. Wayne Boyd's flat was the only place that came to mind and here all three had doubts, the barman ticked every box for living with his mum, hardly likely to have a hostage in his bedroom. Amy had insisted however, they'd never know what they might find out, even just seeing the place could lead to some random clue. Once more they headed down to the subway, and twenty minutes later stood by the buzzer for *Boyd*.

Amy jabbed, and after thirty seconds there was a crackle. She almost missed the buzz that came next, and Brendan nipped from behind and shoved open the door. The three entered the stairwell and heard an unlocking above, then they climbed for the second floor. A few steps from the landing a door lay ajar, and at the music wafting out the three of them tensed. Incredibly to Jackie, it was the same Loyalist stuff they heard each time in Crawford's, Boyd, it seemed, never had a minute off. The door creaked open further, releasing a waft of frying bacon. An unexpected figure stepped into view.

Mrs Boyd was small and round with rosy cheeks and bushy eyebrows. Wiping her hands on her apron she looked up and smiled. She took in her visitors. '…You're no Angie...'

'Ehm…' Amy started. '…no…'

'Has she got a day aff? Bill's ready for his dressing, he's…' She stepped back, wringing her hands. '…Youse urni fae the health centre...'

'Is Wayne around?' Amy asked without a smile.

'Ma Wayne…? He's…How…? Oh, whit's he done noo…? Bill…!' she shouted over the music. '…Bill…!'

A thud from a back room. Then, up the sunflower-papered hall with a trouser leg rolled, limped her husband. A dog followed, or tried to but ended up in the kitchen. Mr Boyd had thick white hair and a heavy wheeze, and eyes as angry as his exposed big toe.

'The polis…' Mrs Boyd quivered, '…they've come aboot Wayne…'

'Polis?' Mr Boyd scrutinised the three. With a cough he nodded at Brendan. 'That's no a polis, that's a fucking halfwit.' He held up a fist, his wife cowering at his side. Leave our boy alone! Debts, is it? *Debts?* Collect them oot my arse! Away youse go an…!'

'We're not-'

The door shut. Amy thumped on it but only got barks in return, and these became muffled under a din of rising flutes and snares. They headed back for the stairs. 'Got to hand it to their son,' Jackie said as they stepped outside. 'How did he turn out so nice?'

They trudged on to the pub, but when they arrived they agreed to keep moving. For Boyd's bottle to crash there'd need to be a lot of customers, not too likely at 11 o'clock. They headed instead to Bellahouston Park, sat on a bench by the all-weather football pitches. As Amy cast wary glances at the sky, Brendan found himself talking to Jackie about the Rangers Celtic match, how it was already controversial with Celtic playing twice in three days. Jackie asked where Celtic had gone wrong in the season, and as Brendan launched into an explanation Jackie heard Amy groan. Or maybe he imagined it but he stopped listening anyway, and Brendan muttered he probably wouldn't even watch the game. For a while after they just sat in silence. Then they headed back for Crawford's.

Jackie swung the door open to the blaring sports channel and a smell of fish and lemon. Had they only been coming here four days? Four years it felt like, although surely nothing compared to the punters sprawled around like abandoned puppets. Well, at least they were here. The old boy. The ned. The big guy. Purple nose. No Skin, but a pint sat in front of his stool said he wouldn't be far. About a dozen others were there as well, surely enough for Boyd to feel the heat. He was behind the bar, Boyd, listening to Maureen and jotting down stuff down in a notebook. At the sight of the newcomers, the ned shrieked and Boyd glanced up, but after he took in the arrivals he looked back down. Jabbing a bony finger now, the ned shrieked again, some voices murmured he was right and another warned him to *…shut it…*. A glare from Maureen sat the ned back onto his stool, and Boyd disappeared through the back.

As the barmaid approached, Jackie gestured behind her. 'We need to speak him.'

Maureen's voice was softer than expected. 'Youse shouldni be here. Youse'll have to leave.'

Amy dropped her fists on the bar. 'We're not going anywhere.'

'He's stocktaking. He'll be a while.'

'We'll wait.'

'Youse canni-'

'-We'll wait.'

Maureen huffed, swiped up a dishcloth and moved to the other side of the bar. They didn't move, the three of them, they just stood, waiting for a threat, a warning, an apology. They got nothing however and Maureen didn't come back, and they were either barred or they weren't so what was going on? Amy kicked at her older brother's ankle and Brendan stood with fists clenched, while Jackie turned and made a broad scan of their side of the pub. Between mouths of lasagne a middle-aged woman gave a sympathetic smile, and the old boy in the taped-up glasses made a mischievous wag of his finger. Then he noticed him once more half-behind a pillar. The fat guy was muttering into his mobile.

'Morning, detective!' Holding up his jeans with one hand, Skin made a pistol sign with the other. 'That boy turned up yet?'

'No, mate. Actually, do ye mind..?'

'Aye, he'll be licking his wounds somewhere. Guaranteed.' He climbed onto his stool like a bus driver starting a shift, and drew his drink towards him. Then, pointing to a poster behind the bar, he asked. 'What do ye make of that? Always on the lookout for new blood, so we are.'

Quiz Night

Every Friday 8.00 pm.

'Not interested. Sorry.'

'Military History? Aw that?' Skin rubbed his stubbly chin. 'That's a gap in our knowledge right there son, don't mind admitting it.'

'Alright mate. Whatever.'

Jackie turned to his brother and sister. 'Okay, so one minute and I'm following-'

'-Hey!'

Jackie turned again.

'It's Billy, intit? Billy, aye?' Skin was calling for Brendan who now stared frozen across the bar. Jackie and Amy eyed her brother, looking like his name had been called out in a gunfight. 'He's fae generation hingmy, int he?' Skin said to Amy now. '...What's it...? Fuck, canni mind. Anyway, they've got it sorted oot, with the internet and that. Billy! Youse...'

Still staring ahead, Brendan gulped. 'I'm shite at quizzes...'

'You're what? No! *Me*, on the other hand...' He glared at his pint, gave it a disappointed shake of the head. 'Sozzled cos of *that*. But you've got it, Billy. Ye could-'

'-No!'

'Billy boy...'

'Stop calling us...!'

'Aaah...!' Skin yelped like he was falling out of a rollercoaster. His barstool toppled and Jackie threw out his arms, guided him back as the stool steadied itself. Then they both stared at who had opened the hatch behind him and with a roar charged into the bar area. As the big guy disappeared through the door, Skin drained his pint and wiped his moustache. 'Nae bother, son.'

Jackie looked around, saw every face was watching. This *wasn't* normal. He gestured after the guy. 'What's going on with him, Skin?'

Skin shrugged. 'Ach, I'm just a foot soldier in here.'

'But ye know him, right? Ye know everybody.'

'Wayne's mate. Bluenose. That's all ye need to know, it's aw anybody needs to know.' He gulped at his pint.

'But ye don't know his name or…?'

He resurfaced, glared like he'd been asked to state the guy's blood group. 'How am I supposed to know?' He wiped his mouth. 'Old pals, that's it.'

'Fair enough, I'm just…Hang on. All three, even Brendan, stared back at the barfly. 'Did you say *old* pals?'

He nodded. 'Turned up start of the week, so he did. After a ticket, probably. Wayne will see him awright. Like I say, I'm a foot soldier.'

'Skin,' Amy started. 'This could be…Do ye know where he came from?'

The barfly's head was sozzled, right enough. Too many questions had him fall into a daze.

'*Skin*! Where is he from?'

He swotted the question with a hand, sighed into his pint. 'Chelsea. If that's a place. Going by his tattoos, aye. Chelsea.'

'Right.' Jackie stepped by Skin and opened the bar hatch. He entered, Amy and Brendan followed.

'Now, that's a court-martial if ever I've seen wan,' Skin chuckled.

Maureen marched across. 'This area's private. Ye canni…!'

The brothers and sister ignored her, opened the door to the back, Maureen grabbed it before it shut. 'I'm telling ye! Wayne!'

They stepped across the corridor and up the stairs. Jackie was about to open the door of the office when the barman burst out the one before it. '…The fuck's going on?'

Jackie pointed at the office. 'Let us in there!'

'…Are youse for real?'

Amy made a move but the door was covered by Wayne Boyd's bulk. He jabbed at her with his stick. '*Get*. Or it's the polis.'

She took out her phone, thrust it at him. 'We've got an officer on speed dial. You'll be doing us a favour.'

'*What*...? Oh just get down the stair.'

Brendan squeezed past his brother and sister. 'Your pal done wan, aye?'

'My pal? He's having a rest, son. That alright, Inspector Beanpole? Your final warning. Oot.'

Jackie folded his arms. 'All we've had is lies from this place. So how about this? You open these doors. Or that wee secret of yours? It stops being a secret.'

The barman glared back at his blackmailer.

Then he shook his head and turned around.

'Lunatics.'

He opened the office door.

28

Boyd entered the office, and shut and locked the door.

Murmurs and growls. Bangs and boots.

For about a minute.

Then the door re-opened.

Boyd emerged, followed by the other guy. He looked furious, the other one, his blazing eyes alone forcing Jackie and Brendan further up the corridor. With the floorboards creaking under everyone's weight, the stranger continued to the steps and down, muttering and barging past Amy to the bar area. Amy climbed back up.

Boyd shrugged. 'Ye might have guessed that he disni take to being disturbed.'

'Who is he?'

He smirked. 'A pal.' With a hand on the office door, the barman pushed it open.

The nearest to the door, Jackie poked his head inside. There'd be no sign of his brother, he knew that, and sure enough apart from the half-empty mugs and plates and pastry crumbs, it was the same as the day before. Without waiting, the barman yanked open the second door and pulled at a cord. The toilet, Amy saw, no bigger than a mop cupboard and no need to inspect it. She nodded at Boyd but he nodded towards the pan, with a sneer he insisted that she take a good look. He turned away then and opened the door nearest the stairs, this time Brendan entered, clattering into a plastic chair half-under a plastic table. A fridge and a sink sat at one end and a tatty armchair was by the other, and there was a noticeboard of takeaway menus and a handful of party photos. By the time Brendan had turned round, the barman was already down the steps.

The three followed, saw him next opening the door to the entrance of the bar. Like some underpaid tour guide he huffed until all three were in front of him, then he stepped into the kitchen. Placing pies on a tray, the red-haired cook didn't hear the barman's shout over the radio. He tried again. '*Chas…!*'

The cook looked round.

'Any dead bodies in here?'

He laughed, killed the music. 'Ye know what that sounded like, Wayne…?'

'Nae time for small talk, we need to check the freezer, mate.'

'What?'

The barman gave an apologetic shrug. 'Is there anything ye want to tell us?'

'Ehm…' The cook nodded at the visitors at the barman's back. '…Who's…?'

'Oh, aye. They're pals with that Tim we binned. They think…'

Chas took his hat off, gave his head a scratch. '…That he's in my freezer?'

Boyd turned to the family, eyebrows raised in the hope of an explanation for his mate. He didn't get one. Since the opening of that first door, they'd all felt like they were the butt of a joke, a joke of their own making maybe but still. Each of them now actually felt like leaving, never mind the chances of Shaun being in there, this was the *kitchen*, the last place they'd want to find him. Still, turning around would feel even more humiliating than staying where they were.

The kitchen was no bigger than Amy's living room. An oven and a dishwasher, a fridge and a freezer, a couple of sinks and some low-lying cupboards. There was a storeroom as well, and it was to there Amy marched first, taking a breath and throwing open the door. Faced with shelves crammed of tins and boxes she shut it again quick, turned and met the eyes of the speechless cook. Clasping his hands and with a solemn nod, Boyd asked Chas to lift the lid of the freezer, by this time Jackie had entered and he gave a glance inside. He did the same with the fridge, and when he and the others then made to leave, the barman didn't look impressed. 'Youse willni get another chance. Sure youse don't want to check the pies? Ah well,' he said, ushering the three out and winking at the cook. 'Wan more stop. Then exit through the gift shop.'

Amy and her brothers moved back up the corridor, the barman now hurrying behind. With a shout he squeezed past and limped down bare, rickety steps, and opened one of two doors. 'Cellar,' he grunted, hanging back, and as Brendan stepped behind him Jackie and Amy entered. It was low and musty and dim, where along two walls sat several gurgling barrels with boxes of spirits piled between. Jackie checked behind some boxes and Amy even opened the wall-hatch. But it was obvious. There was no one and there was nothing. No sign there had been either.

After they stepped back out, Boyd locked the cellar door. 'Tour's over. Oot.'

Brendan nodded behind him. 'What about that?'

Pocketing the key, the barman glanced at the other door. Its wood was faded and warped and its hinges were rough and reddened. 'Aye, very good.'

'No.' Amy stepped forward. 'Show us. Open it.'

He glared back. 'How? That's been shut for as long as the average Tim washes his green and grey hoops.'

Brendan stepped across, turned the corroded knob.

The door didn't move.

Amy thumped. 'Shaun…? Shaun…? Are ye there…? Shaun!'

Boyd nodded at Jackie. 'Is she on something? It *was* a cellar. Now it's fuck all. Look.' He kicked at a hinge. Specks of red dust blew up. 'Let's go.'

Amy crouched, peered through the keyhole. 'Okay, is there….? *Hey…!*' Her eyes widened and she gasped. 'Hey! Shaun!' She sprung to her feet, stared open-mouthed at her brothers. 'I saw something!' She yanked at the doorknob. 'I *saw*…There's someone…!'

She pulled again as Brendan leapt forward to help, fumbled for a grip on the underside. '…I canni…It's…'

Jackie felt for space between the frame and the sill. He pulled as Amy did, but the door barely moved.

'I'll be billing youse for that, ya fucking clowns,' Boyd sneered. 'Enough.'

Amy pulled again and again. 'Shaun! *Shaun!*' she shouted as her brothers took steps back. Once more she peered inside.

'*You*,' said the barman, jabbing a finger. 'Need a lie down.'

She turned to Jackie, gestured at the keyhole. He got down to look but saw only a blur of blackness.

'A flash…' she shrugged. '…A light. Ye don't…?'

He stood back up. 'No. We need a key.'

'No,' Boyd nodded back. 'Youse *need* oot.'

'Key.'

'There isni wan. Show's over.' The barman turned away.

'He's in there. I *know*…' Amy pulled and thumped. 'Shaun! She peered again, then in the silence pressed her ear to the wood. Brendan had a go next, came back up with an apologetic shrug. 'Okay,' Amy said, taking a breath and nodding. 'We'll talk to the owner.'

'Youse do that,' Boyd said with a sarcastic smile. He pointed up the steps.

Amy and her brothers trudged back through to the bar. There was no final threat from Boyd or lingering insult, he didn't even follow them out, just carried on to the office. They continued past the regulars and out the door, stepping into the noisy afternoon. Amy took no more than a few paces before stopping again, for a second looking like she'd turn back to the pub. '…I really did…I *mean*…I…' Her voice creaked under the weight of her anguish. '…Youse have got to believe me. I *saw* something.'

Jackie shrugged. 'What?'

'…I don't know. A flash. Like a torch or something.'

'Okay, but…'

'But what?'

'Just does that have to be Shaun? Not, I don't know, a reflection? We need to get this right.'

'A reflection of what Jackie, if there's nothing in there? It moved!' She snapped a finger. 'Like *that*.'

'Fair enough. But...'

'I *know*. It can't be his bloody phone because he's not got it.' She stormed off, leaving her brothers by the bus shelter. 'And hey!' she shouted, startling an old woman crossing the road. 'Why wouldn't he *say* something!'

'Ehm, Jackie,' Brendan said, as his brother again started up the pavement.

He didn't answer so Brendan gave him a nudge.

When Jackie turned, he opened his hand. 'What are these, man?'

Half a dozen round white tablets.

Jackie stopped. 'I don't...' He took one. 'Amy...! Where did ye get these? Amy, come here...!'

Brendan shrugged. 'They were scattered down the stairs,' he said as Amy hurried back. 'I just picked my moment and grabbed them.'

Jackie read. 'Zop...'

Amy came back. She took one and examined it. '...These are Z drugs.'

'Z drugs?'

'Sleeping tablets. You found them by the cellar?'

'Aye, man. The stairs.'

'God,' Amy whimpered, shaking the thought from her mind. 'One way to keep Shaun quiet.'

Jackie bit at his lip. 'Not finished in there, then.'

29

Jackie tried the TV and it was off again in seconds. Then he threw on the radio and stared out the window. He switched on the computer after that, messed around on Facebook. Then he grabbed a hardback from Amy's shelf and collapsed onto the couch. Four lines of the book he read before he chucked it to the side, then wondered about waking his sister, knocked-out in the room next door. He'd thought Amy was joking when she said she'd downed one of those tablets, then her eyelids had started to drop and he practically carried her to bed. He guessed she'd been more than exhausted as well, Officer Caldwell's rebuke had been a setback. Not that Amy had expected the woman to run round and smash down the cellar door, but neither had she thought *she* could be arrested, for threatening to blackmail Wayne.

Still, Jackie knew his sister would wake up feeling no less certain than the second before she'd crashed out. The gambling. The cellar. The pills. The flash. Shaun was in there so they *get him out*. As for Jackie, he'd been far from convinced three hours ago and was only further away now. How Boyd and the chicken guy had got acquainted still messed with his head. They were mates before Shaun had gone to London? Okay, but how could they have met? And why would Shaun escape from one to walk right into the other? What Jackie did know, standing up and stepping for the window, was that they both were gamblers, and since one was an addict and the other a thief, they *could* be keeping Shaun prisoner. Hands clasped behind his head, he took a deep breath. So what if Shaun's system stops paying out? And what if it was never that great anyway? *What*, he wondered, shutting his eyes, if all it was built on was his brother's bullshit? There was nothing else for it. They had to find out at least. They had to get in that cellar.

It wasn't Jackie who woke his sister up but a phone call. Britt. She was in the West End and didn't want to be a hassle, but if Amy fancied company she'd be happy to pop up. Each call to Amy brought hope and dread, so a stranger offering sympathy almost threw her back onto her pillow. But she did want company, even a chance to nearly forget, so she gave Amy her address and splashed herself awake. Britt had been closer than Amy had assumed, as she was collecting mugs from the coffee table the intercom buzzed.

Standing at the door with a bag of filled croissants, Britt grinned. 'I know,' she said, wiping her feet and entering. 'Too late for lunch and too early for dinner. Forever between worlds, me.'

Amy smiled. 'You're a star. I was about to send Jackie on a mission.'

'Vegetarian,' Britt said. Hope that's alright.'

Amy collected plates and they sat in the living room. After she gave out the food, one croissant remained in the bag. 'For Brendan?' Amy asked. 'I'll keep it for him.'

'What he doesn't know…' Jackie said, dragging his own plate towards him.

'He's working?' Britt asked.

Jackie hesitated, his sister did too. 'Putting in a shift,' he said.

Amy tried a smile. 'Trying to find Shaun.'

'Oh, of course, I...I'm sorry.'

'Don't be.'

'Is there anything at all?'

Amy pondered the question then frowned. 'We know that pub is, *ach*...there's just nothing right about it. We're starting to think...' She glanced at her brother like she'd be giving away a secret.

'It's okay,' Britt said. 'If ye don't...'

'No.' Amy wiped her hands and sat back, then recounted their reasons for believing why Shaun might be in that cellar. As she finished she didn't ask for Britt's opinion, she hadn't exactly prepared herself for the hesitant doubts of a stranger. Instead she studied her, and a reaction wasn't hard to find.

'My God.' Britt stared at Amy then her Jackie. 'That's unbelievable. But how are you going to get in?'

'Giving it a go tonight,' Jackie said. 'Still working out how.'

'Well,' Britt said. 'If I can help, just shout. I'm here.'

Britt's eyes welled then and she looked Jackie thought, like she was about to ask for the bathroom. But she swiped her glass, took a sip. Then she put it down and muttered an apology.

Amy got to her feet, put an arm around her. 'What was his name?'

She breathed in a sob. 'James.'

'Ye must really miss him.'

Squeezing Amy's hand, Britt shrugged out a laugh. 'Yeah. Ye know I should have been at work today, I'm a nursery teacher but I've barely been in all week. Sometimes those kids are all that keeps me going but other times, even after a year I can't handle them.'

'How did he die, your brother?' Jackie asked.

'Suicide.'

'Shit, I'm sorry.'

'Yeah he just...' Britt bit at her knuckle, shook her head. '...I suppose he had a problem he didn't think he could talk about. I found out too late. And the worst thing is it would have been so easy to...' She shut her eyes, squeezed the napkin in her fist. 'God, I came here to see how *you* were getting on...But I suppose he's why I'm here really, if you know what I mean.' She gave a sad smile. 'I'm sorry.'

Amy smiled back. 'I really appreciate you coming, Britt. And you're welcome anytime.'

'That's good of you. Thanks.'

Inside the bus shelter across the road from Crawford's, Brendan stood with his hands thrust into his pockets. One hour down and three to go, ages before Jackie would come and take over. Stakeouts, Brendan spat, no wonder the American polis hated them, and at least they had donuts and coffee to batter into. At the paucity of the newsagent's behind he rolled his eyes, took another swig of Lucozade and scoffed another handful of Monster Munch. He sighed then because this plan of theirs, there was a problem. If Shaun really *was* in that cellar, he might be moved out, so aye it was a good idea to watch the exit. But neither Amy or Jackie had been right about the other door, the kitchen fire-exit that opened out to the back. They thought they knew the lot those two, but that could screw things up.

Amy had made out she was sure Shaun was being kept in there but still hoped he might turn up at her door, that was why she'd insisted on going straight back up the road. As for Jackie, he and Brendan taking separate breaks had been his idea, and since a kidnapped Shaun would likely get piled into some kind of vehicle, Brendan was to watch for any driving round the back. Anything dodgy, he was to call. Anything super-dodgy, he was to get the polis. Aye, very good, Brendan thought, but what if Wayne and those other pricks were a step ahead? What if Wayne knew they'd be watched and had made other plans? He slipped the bottle into his pocket and threw the packet into the bin. Then, pulling his cap further down his face, he stepped across the road.

Brendan strode past the Crawford's main entrance and turned around the side. He carried on to the back, a patch of weed-strewn gravel as wide and deep as the building. A four-wheeled bin sat in one corner and on the edge grew a line of bushes, behind them snaked a faint track round to the nearby square of wasteground. On the wall was some arty but fading graffiti and there were three narrow windows and the door. After Brendan eyed up the bin, he got out his phone and sent a text- *running low on juice, phone off now*. Then he stabbed on the camera and marched across. Placing the phone in a groove on the top, he focused the screen on the fire-exit, when it kept falling he scanned his surroundings and grabbed a leaking can of vegetable oil. He heaved it up and leaned the phone against it, then pressed *record*. Finally he stepped out again, took a sniff of his fingers. *Not* vegetable oil, he realised with a grimace, wiping it down his jeans. He strutted back across the road.

Three hours later Jackie arrived at the bus shelter. Brendan sat gazing dead-eyed at the screen, and when his brother touched his shoulder he jumped and grabbed at his heart. With a muffled clang, Jackie dumped on the ground a small rucksack.

'Tooled up, then?' Brendan said, swiping out his earphones. 'Sound.'

Jackie gestured at his brother's phone. 'Thought that was dead.'

'No, man,' Brendan said with a rub at his eyes. 'Just couldni be bothered explaining. It was round the back for a couple of hours recording the door.'

'Good thinking. So?'

'Waste. Of. Time. Here *and* there.'

'No a bad thing.'

'Suppose. He's still inside, by the way. Wayne, I mean.'

'What about the other guy?'

'The fat yin?' He scowled. 'Did wan a couple of hours ago, walked towards town.'

'Alone?'

'Aye. Fucking hell but…' Brendan shook his head. 'I'll tell ye…'

'What?'

'…It disni matter.' He looked away, took a stretch of each leg.

'No. It does.'

'…There's…'

'*What?*'

'There's a fair amount of ugly bastards in there, Jackie.'

Jackie sighed. 'Right.'

'I'm no being a bigot. It's true.'

'Well, shoot,' his brother said. 'Ye earned your rest.'

Brendan drew back an inch, scanned him up and down. 'Ye want my earphones? This'll be a test of your sanity here. Seriously, that bus to Paisley will look like a life-saver.'

'I'll be fine. See ye at eight.'

Brendan removed his cap, slapped it back on. 'Any more thoughts on how we'll get in?'

'No yet.'

'Same here.' He turned to head off. 'Half eight, then.'

Pushing the rucksack with his foot, Jackie planked himself on the shelter bench, as a departing bus farted then near crapped itself in front of him. He told himself there was a point to waiting, Shaun might well be in there and he could still get shipped out. Plus at least he was on his own, the recent absence of solitude had been something else to bug him. In Cairo it was the cafés, their sights, sounds and smells, even when he had company he could sit for hours in near silence. Here? Not a lot to admire in Glasgow's southside. Not in the miserable, balloon-shaped citizens, that was for sure. Or the food, the cafes or weather. Except after a few minutes, Jackie was hit with a realisation. It didn't matter that he didn't love this place. He only had to *feel* it. And he did. Right now he did. Shit. The sooner he got out, the better.

As the minutes crept to the first hour he rubbed at his eyes, then walked across the road and round the back of Crawford's. Nothing to see there and no point hanging about, he was back at the shelter in seconds, eyes again fixed on the pub. By half-six there were more people entering Crawford's than leaving. One of these was Skin, stopping to comb his hair then shuffling through the door. A lot of the regulars, the tanned women and the tattooed men, Jackie recognised, some had been alright as well and he might just need their support. At a quarter-past eight the Londoner reappeared. Then from the same street, Boyd. At first Jackie thought nothing then he blinked back and groaned. Brendan had said Boyd was *inside*. So what about the others? What about the owner? And *Shaun*? And where was Brendan, anyway? Typical, of all the nights to be late, he chose this one. Finally, peering along the pavement he saw a dawdling white figure.

'Got held up, man,' Brendan said, putting away his phone and reaching the shelter.

'Doing what?'

'Ach, I was busy.'

'I called Amy half an hour ago, she said you were on that phone since the minute ye stepped in. Is there something I should know?'

'No man, it's cool.'

'No more secrets, Brendan.'

'I'm telling ye.'

Jackie slung the rucksack over his shoulder. 'Ye missed Boyd leaving, by the way.'

'No way, man…'

'Did ye have your nose out that phone for a minute?'

'No, I'm…'

'Forget it.' Jackie stepped for the road. 'Let's go.'

30

'Hey! You two!'

The shout went up as they found their way through the throng to the bar. It was as Jackie had hoped. If he and Brendan were to last the night, they'd need a pal like Skin.

'Ya pair of...!'

Jackie ignored the barfly for now at least, but when he scanned his side of the horseshoe bar he saw him at a table. He was off his seat as well, yelping now and waving, his voice putting up a fight but with little chance against Robbie Williams. Jackie turned back to the bar, Brendan now standing behind him and mouthing to the music. No Daryl so far, the older brother noted, and although his smile at Maureen returned only a stare, he was relieved that she hadn't pointed to the door. From the other side the blonde barman appeared. He gave the arrivals a double-take but then swiped up a glass and left, and Jackie guessed that Wayne Boyd was looking after them, still worried they could spill his secret. After he was served, he turned to face Skin's now desperate screeches. They walked around.

'Come on!' Skin pulled two stools out from under his table, thrust them at Jackie and Brendan. He grabbed at their sleeves. 'Billy, sit down! You've...'

On hearing the name Brendan's legs seemed to give way, Jackie guided him onto a stool.

'Ye alright, son? Sergeant, is he alright?'

'He's fine,' Jackie said. 'Int ye, Billy? *Billy?*'

Brendan sat up, grabbed his drink. 'Aye.'

Skin slapped Jackie on the back. 'I knew youse would come. Just as well, that last roon.' He shook his head, gulped at his pint. 'Had me near chucking it.'

'Tough?' Jackie kicked Brendan under the table and nodded at the poster on the wall. *Pub Quiz.* A way to kill time, Jackie said with raised eyebrows. Brendan nodded back.

Skin nodded too. 'Wan right, I think. Pulled the phone oot for a couple, but that lot?' He shot the staff a glare. 'Eyes in the back of their heids.'

The first round's answers were read out, they told Jackie and Brendan how useless Skin was while everyone else clearly already knew. To howls and jeers, the pony-tailed quiz man revealed that Skin had thought the 'world's hottest temperature' had been in Spain, and 'the Zambesi' was a drink. Bristling at the catcalls, Skin fired back his own insults. 'Fuck them,' he muttered. 'I've got *wan*.' Then the guy revealed that the biscuit named after the Italian general wasn't the Jammy Dodger, and they all knew he had none.

With the roars and points and hoots, Jackie saw that laughing at Skin's ignorance was as much the entertainment as the quiz, and another glimpse at the poster told him why the barfly had bothered. The first prize was for match tickets, and it had probably been years since Skin had been to Ibrox. The captain pulled the brothers towards him, jabbed at the table like it was a treasure map. If there was a strategy however, Jackie didn't hear one, just *fuckings* and *points* and *hingmys*. He scanned for Wayne but failed to see him, he had to be up the back or in the office. He spied the Londoner again though, bored now and alone by his pillar. From somewhere a cry of

...*Fenians*...*!*, and it was followed by muffled shouts. Jackie and Brendan exchanged glances. Maybe being Skin's teammates wasn't the best idea.

But what was there to do but get the *heid doon and hingmy*. The Current Affairs round was next and Jackie knew his stuff, and Skin scribbled down the answers like some mad, frantic waiter. The Sport round was mostly football and it was Brendan who was on the money, then on TV even Skin's brain spluttered to life. Within the hour, Skin's chances of winning *Crawford's Friday Night Quiz* had gone from laughable to why not. But the climb hadn't gone unnoticed. In the absence of laughs the insults had resurfaced. Louder. More threatening. Catching his brother's eye, Jackie gestured *cut*.

Skin meanwhile banged at his head with the palm of his hand like an answer was cowering inside. He looked at his teammates. ...*Nothing?*... and the next question drew the same silence. Skin's head was in his hands now, and when a blank was drawn on another it was almost in his lap. 'We're almost done! Don't chuck it noo!'

In front of him, a young woman appeared.

'Would youse be needing some extra brain-power?' Britt asked.

'Aye...!' Skin was up and searching for a stool, grabbed one from another table. 'It's music, so it is! See...'

She sat down opposite the brothers. 'Are we in with a shout?'

Jackie mouthed a warning but Britt didn't catch it, Skin had grabbed her arm and was now pointing at the quiz man. 'Oh, I know this,' she said after he re-read the question, and gave her answer and spelled it out. She beamed back at the brothers, sipped from her glass of coke, then saw Brendan make the *cut* sign and shrugged back confused. A call of

'...*fucking getting it....!*' and she understood in seconds, shrunk back from the table and took in the rising tension. The only one with no idea was Skin. When Britt gave him a shrug rather than an answer to the next question, he stared at her speechless, then he asked if a drink would help her remember. Soon the veteran of a thousand failures was gazing at his teammates like an about-to-be-abandoned puppy. The chances of winning were gone, so Jackie threw the dog his final bone.

Third they came, and Jackie slapped the captain on the back. 'Well done. Enjoy your beers.'

Skin scowled, threw back his tiny shoulders. 'No done yet. We're going all the way.'

'It's no finished?'

'The final round! The solo!' Skin gestured to the space in front of the quiz man that two others were now approaching. 'Nae offence Sergeant...' He nodded at Brendan. 'This is a young man's game.'

Brendan shrunk back. 'What's he saying?'

'How many questions, Skin?' Jackie asked.

The barfly shook his head in admiration. 'Billy could win it in wan.'

Voices rose again. A chant was picked up around the room and being accompanied by slams and boots. Jackie looked around, two hundred stern eyes were on them. He leaned into his brother. 'Say anything and get back here.'

Louder got the singing.

Fiercer got the staring.

Jackie nudged his brother. Brendan finally got to his feet. 'Wha...what's the subject?'

'Nae bother for you, Billy-Boy,' Skin answered. 'The Gers.'

Too late to turn back and Brendan knew it. He walked to the floor, where the quiz man ushered him to a spot between a white-haired man and a young guy with a nervous smile. He stood there wide-eyed like the very last of the Celtic fans, hunted and captured to the point of extinction. Over calls then pleads the abuse continued, dying only after a roar from a hidden Boyd.

Brendan wouldn't stand a chance.

Neither would Jackie.

He lowered an arm and unzipped the rucksack.

Gripped a handle.

The quiz man stepped to the young guy, asked a question about Rangers in Europe, and the guy laughed at how hard it was and gave the wrong answer. Then the man turned to Brendan and asked about a Scottish Cup Final.

Brendan stared like he hadn't even heard, and Jackie wondered if he'd blacked out but somehow stayed upright.

He said, 'Duncanson.'

And the man said, 'Correct.'

The quiz guy turned to the third guy with a question, who gave a confident answer.

But it was wrong.

The quiz guy said, 'We have a winner.'

Skin jumped with a 'Yeeeesssss!' and crumpled to the floor, shook his fists at the ceiling and burst into tears. Dropping the hammer back into the rucksack, Jackie hugged Britt, and near bit his own tongue off when he almost shouted his brother's name.

The quiz man raised the winner's arm, and Brendan stood like a death row prisoner told to get a taxi up the road. From somewhere began a clap, then shouts of congratulations, and as Brendan reached his stool another song had begun. Again they were being watched, but all the aggression had gone.

Brendan flopped down on the stool. 'That's…It's…the…'

'What?' Jackie asked, both hands on his brother's shoulders.

'…First thing I've won in my life...'

Maureen placed down two pints and pointed across the bar. 'There'll be plenty more.'

Across the table, a wet-eyed Skin said he'd love to hug the hero but his heart might not recover. 'Eight years I've waited, Billy Boy,' he sniffed.

'Thanks.'

'Aye, man, ehm…Nae bother.'

Britt left to call Amy and Skin sobbed into his drink, and Jackie leaned towards his brother. 'So…?'

'What?

'*What*? Ye gonni fill us in?'

'I dunno, I just read about the Rangers round in a poster in the bogs. Had a terrible feeling man, was studying all day.'

Two shorts clinked onto the table. Above them stood Boyd. 'Luck of the Irish, eh?'

Jackie pulled over a glass. 'You've lost us. But cheers.'

Boyd held out a ticket.

'No. That's for Skin.'

'This isni the prize,' he said. 'It's for the morra.'

'The match?'

'Ye asked for a spare. Here ye go.'

'Right…' Jackie said. 'That's…'

'Course. If you're no quite as big a Bear as ye make oot…'

'I'll take it. Thanks.' He put it into his wallet. 'I'll square ye up the morra.'

'Meet us at half-eleven and we'll get tanked up. There's a team going.'

Boyd hobbled off, and Jackie hung his head back and sighed. 'Get back here, Shaun, wherever ye are.'

31

The drinks piling up on the table, Jackie and Brendan would smile a thanks to every donor, it'd be followed by a handshake, a backslap or even a photo. This was no problem to the brothers, the only hint of any trouble came from the drinkers who'd stick around for a chat. How long before a smartarse arrived to knock the new champion off his perch? Except no one was interested in talking about football, they only wanted to talk about Shaun. Hand on a brother's shoulder, some expressed sympathy for their sister, but in time she'd get over the ex-barman because the guy was a fucking dick. Others, through piercing an eardrum or spraying a face, would declare the Fenian to be dead the day he turned up again.

In other words, no-one knew a thing.

Soon the winners were forgotten, the only shouts now were at the singers on the Karaoke. Skin got into the freebies like they were the first course of an eight quid buffet, while the brothers started to worry if they could actually pull this off. Jackie was especially anxious. While his brother had stepped up when he'd been needed most, he had no clue how to keep themselves in the pub past closing. At least Britt he saw, was enjoying herself, had even had to apologise for singing too much. At half-past eleven she got up and headed to the tables by the windows, and at the second she beamed at the occupants and sat down. The two golfers glared back.

The brothers had noticed the men before but neither had thought it worth mentioning, not only had the pair been ignoring them, they were just no longer relevant. Brendan, chilled now after a few drinks, asked his brother what he thought Britt was up to. Jackie went to answer but he didn't get the chance, Brendan was up and shrieking, a hand over his face. Half-expecting an attack, Jackie jumped off his stool, but the assault when it came was both silent and invisible. It turned Jackie's insides and contorted his face, as a barmaid gagged and nearly dropped her tray. Among the cries of protest, Jackie noticed someone unfazed. In fact his face was locked in an ecstatic trance.

Brendan nodded at their team captain. 'What's he been eating?'

Jackie shrugged. 'Don't know. Get him a drink.'

'*Another*?'

He nodded. 'I've got a plan.'

Jackie headed for outside, and Brendan was almost after him until he noticed that his brother had left his jacket. He wondered if this was about the Londoner until he clocked him by the pillar, he seemed to be on the same pint as hours ago and was still messing with his phone. At last orders Brendan got Skin a whisky, then with the Karaoke finished Britt reappeared. She sat down, gave a subtle nod at where she'd come from. 'Are they still talking?'

Brendan glanced over at the muttering golfers. '…Aye…'

'Good. I'm recording them. I know I'm probably miles out but there's just something about those two. And tonight they're even more miserable than usual.'

Jackie re-entered with a parcel of food, took the stool next to Skin. 'Keep drinking, my man,' he said. 'Tonight will never be here again.' In front of the barfly stood an assortment of drinks, some near finished and others untouched. Jackie pushed forward the newest then sat back with a jolt, in Skin's orbit there remained the linger of his record-breaking reek. Skin himself sat slumped with eyes half-shut, and was mumbling, Jackie was sure, to his drinks. ...*thanks for the question*... Jackie thought he heard ....*But whisky, you were first*... He unfolded the parcel and placed on Skin's lap a smouldering kebab. 'Folk are getting jealous. Eat this before they nick it.'

Skin gave a secretive wink then apologised to his drinks, dug his hand in the parcel and ripped into the food. The saucy contents dripped as he devoured it in scoops, mumbling and burping and farting again. 'Don't forget the drinks,' Jackie said. 'Before it's too late.' Skin gulped at the whisky then threw down a vodka.

'Jackie, man...' Brendan said. 'I don't think...'

'Shut up.'

Maureen spied the kebab and Jackie apologised for their captain, the barmaid snapped they had five minutes and swiped up a couple of glasses. Skin got to his feet and Jackie made a scan of his arse, but he saw nothing doing so nudged him back onto the stool. At Jackie's request, Skin took yet another drink then shut his eyes. Only one opened again. 'I think I'm gonni...I'm *sure* I'm gonni...'

Jackie pulled Skin up and slowly, very slowly, led him by the arm, past the few remaining drinkers and into the toilet. One hand on his lips now and the other on his arse, Skin stumbled inside and lunged for the first cubicle. His body failed to move so he had another go, no clue that Jackie was holding him by the collar. His arse juddered and chugged, like a rocket trying to lift-off on a tank of milk. Then from his mouth shot a geyser, throwing both him and Jackie back.

Jackie's cry of disgust was heard in the bar. A moment later, splattered with sick and gasping for breath, he threw open the door. 'Bit of a situation.'

Boyd who'd been clearing up drinks, stopped and fumed. 'Has he fucking *puked*?'

'Among other things.'

Spitting and growling, Boyd hurried to the door, and catching a nod from his brother, Brendan stepped over too. Overwhelmed by the reek, Boyd stumbled back, he clattered into Brendan and his phone went flying. Brendan retreated to retrieve it, anything to escape the smell. He grabbed it and dropped it. Then, glancing at the screen, he grabbed it again.

'It's cool,' Jackie gasped. 'Me and my brother will get Skin's jeans off. But somebody will need to get him home.'

Jackie and Brendan stripped the semi-unconscious Skin of his shitty jeans and boxers. Or Jackie did, Brendan mostly stood whimpering like they were dismembering the guy's body. They then helped him outside to where his wife Margaret arrived with an overcoat, and fell against the wall and gulped liked fish at the night air. After that, they said their goodbyes but crept back inside and to the toilet, where no one now would be mad enough to go inside and check. In the less splattered but equally pungent second cubicle they waited, with not just their mouths mostly shut but eyes and noses as well. Jackie asked Brendan about Boyd's mobile that he'd grabbed. Did he read something? Something useful? That could hint that they were on the right track? Brendan said it was nothing, an incomplete text about football, and for ten more minutes they listened to voices, thuds and clinks. Then, finally there was silence. Brendan dived for the door like he was escaping a fire. 'Five minutes,' Jackie said, pulling him back. 'We've got *this* far.' They waited two more and stepped out.

Through the windows, lampposts and traffic threw dim and drifting lights. The brothers crossed the bar and headed through the strip-lit back, and at the steps to the cellars Jackie put a finger to his lips. The only sounds were of passing cars and the hum of electricity. He pulled out a torch and switched it on, and they started down.

Reaching the door of the old cellar, Brendan knocked.

Nothing.

No matter.

Jackie pulled out a screwdriver. 'Keep a look-out, I'll just-'

At the steps, a creak.

They jumped.

A beam into their eyes.

'Is there something I can help youse with?'

32

The office felt smaller to Jackie as he sat down on the two-seater couch. Maybe it was Brendan upright beside him, eyeing the man opposite and unsure whether to be scared or not. Or it could have been the man himself, back on his chair and hands behind his head with a grin near the length of the room. Since disturbing his intruders, Daryl hadn't spoken again, had just rolled his eyes and gestured that they follow him to the office. Now he sat there like he was expecting not just a confession, but a sorry and an arse-lick all rolled into one. He might have got the first if his smugness hadn't shut down Jackie's throat.

Having checked out the guy's purple fitted shirt and deciding he was more male-stripper than mad man, Brendan flicked over a nod. 'Long youse keeping us for, then?'

Daryl gave an aggrieved shrug. 'You want to go, I'm not stopping you. But it might be manners to explain first what you're doing on my premises after closing time. With a bag of fucking tools.'

Jackie glared. 'Obvious, I'm sure.'

'Trying to get in my cellar? I got that, thanks. I just happen to be wondering why.'

'Our brother, alright? We-'

'Brother? Not sister's girlfriend? That's fine, hey, at least we're getting somewhere. Although I was under the impression we'd reached an understanding about Shaun.'

'We did,' Jackie said. 'But it's your cousin.'

A faint smile grew on Daryl. 'My *cousin*? Well, someone's been doing their homework. So Wayne's the problem?' He sat forward. 'I'm biting. Reel me in.'

'Ye know what? Forget it.'

'Maybe I can help.'

'Kidnapping,' Brendan blurted.

Daryl's mouth dropped. 'Why do you…think…?'

'Gambling.'

He weighed this up with a nod. 'Serious, then. And what's brought you to this conclusion? Has your brother been in touch?'

'No,' Jackie snapped. 'We've come to this conclusion because…' He threw up his hands. 'Ach, ye know what? Either let us in or call the polis.'

'The *p*-…?' Daryl stared. 'You still don't get me, Jackie, do ye? If there's even the remotest possibility that a human being is locked up against their will in *my* pub, I want to know.' He got up, squeezed past them for the door. 'I want to know now.'

The brothers stood and followed Daryl into the corridor. He strode down the first set of steps then the other. At the door of the old cellar he stood back, arms folded.

'What?' Jackie asked. 'You've no got a key?'

He shrugged. 'I should think there's one somewhere, but to be honest at one o'clock on a Saturday morning I'm not gonni start looking. There are two of you, you'll get it off in no time.' He walked back to the steps then turned again. 'I won't be far away.'

After Daryl disappeared and they heard the office door close again, the brothers just stood, the rucksack unopened between them. While Brendan

224

waited for word, Jackie waited for a noise, the vaguest sign of life that could shake his growing doubts. If Boyd could be some pyscho abductor, why had his cousin just turned around? Because Daryl's concern was bullshit he knew, just indulging them until they left him in peace. For the first time, Jackie wondered if he and his family were as mad as some others clearly thought. With a sigh he pulled out two screwdrivers, passed one to his brother. 'Let's just do this and get home.'

Three twelve-inch-long rusted hinges, each containing four rusted screws. For twenty minutes the brothers worked away, prising, forcing and loosening, then two hinges clanged onto the floor and the last one quickly followed. They pulled at the door and it toppled, and as they carried it aside there was an escape of sour dampness. Stepping in, the beam of Jackie's torch swept round a lost, windowless dumping ground. In front of them lay a bashed filing cabinet, an electric fire and some dismantled tables, and scattered all around sat squashed or dented cardboard boxes. Brendan picked one up and its bottom collapsed, papers fell onto the floor and disturbed a layer of dust. As thousands of specks rose and danced in front of them, they stepped round the cabinet and walked further in. Then after several sweeping glances, they turned back round and left.

Daryl stood waiting at the top of the steps. He smiled. 'Hey.'

'What?'

'Don't forget my door.'

The brothers turned back again.

Ignoring the invitations of neds on the other side of the road, the brothers began their trudge in the direction of town. Brendan got out his phone, muttered he'd let Amy know, and as Jackie flagged a Hackney he hit *dial* on the phone.

'He wisni there,' he said, climbing into the taxi.

'Okay, youse did well. Just come back, Brendan.'

'Had a look, was all dust and shite.'

'I'll get the kettle on.' Her voice was sad but expectant.

'...Ye alright, Amy?'

'I'm fine. Britt's here.'

'Britt?'

'Yeah. Just get up as soon as youse can.'

33

'Means nothing.'

'Yeah, right.'

'They could be talking about a million things.'

'They could be talking about our brother.'

Sitting on the chair by the computer, Jackie made glances around the living room. He looked to Britt for a moment like he was planning an escape, but instead with a tired frown he turned back to his sister. 'I'm just not going to freak out about a few garbled words.'

'I'm not asking ye to freak out, I'm asking ye to consider the possibility that they were talking about Shaun.'

'Then we're just going round in circles, can ye not see? Wayne, Daryl, Wayne, Daryl. I'm saying we've run out of road. It's neither of them.'

'Ye don't know that.'

'We need to face it.'

Amy shut her eyes and took a calming breath. When she spoke again, her voice was quiet and strained. 'Ye think I wouldn't rather Shaun had been in that cellar? Alive? I'm facing it, Jackie, I need all of us to face it together.'

'A few words, that's all it is.'

'*And* their behaviour.'

'Ye weren't there.'

'No, but Brendan?' Beside Amy on the sofa the other brother sat slumped and twirling his cap with a finger. He gave Jackie a sheepish look then shrugged. 'I canni read minds man but they two were different fae the other night. Worried aboot something it looked like.'

'Their golfing. Their livers. Their fat arses.'

Amy took a tissue from her lap. 'Do what ye have to do, Jackie,' she sighed. 'Whatever that is. I'll just keep looking, and if I see the tiniest clue that might get me a step closer to Shaun, I'll take it, okay?' Her last words broke and she sobbed into the tissue. Brendan reached over, but almost immediately Amy sat up, and across the coffee table she smiled. 'Britt? Play it once more, please?'

Britt, she'd expected a bit of debate about the audio, it would have been crazy to think otherwise, but for goodness sake not while she was still in the flat. Jackie hadn't blamed her for this, not yet, but he would after she'd finally left. Maybe he'd be right to as well she thought, maybe those words did mean nothing, but although she felt embarrassed and even a bit guilty, she had no regrets about telling Amy. How could she? She owed this to her brother, James. She owed it to him to *act*, and the crucial thing now was that Amy acted too. God knows, if Britt had taken action a year ago after her calls had gone unanswered and her texts had gone ignored, James would still be alive. No, she'd never see her brother again. But help Amy find hers? It'd be *something*.

By the time Jackie and Brendan had got back, Britt had expected to have left, but the recording had upset Amy so much she really couldn't go. The brothers had listened once, then Amy had insisted they *keep* listening until they agreed the words were relevant, she also hoped that the surrounding muffle could somehow be decoded. It couldn't and only Brendan believed she might be right, and after that the discussion had got heated. Not that

Britt had made any effort to leave, for more than half an hour she'd just sat in near silence. The truth, she realised, was that she didn't mind hanging about. As reluctant as she was to admit it, she preferred to stay in the loop.

'The last time,' Jackie said. 'Britt, you don't need to be here. I mean, thanks...'

'Oh, I'm sorry,' Amy gasped. 'Did ye say you'd sent me the file...?'

'I'm fine. Honest.' With a gentle smile, Britt placed down her phone and touched *play*.

The recording's first seventeen minutes, a relentless, indecipherable blare of karaoke, had been endured by Britt on her own, and instead she'd presented what followed. Initially this was an equally incomprehensible cacophony of drunken shouts and laughs, then the sound of a nearby male drifted in and out. Unintelligible for nearly a minute, there followed a handful of audible words...*disgrace...fucking liberty...shame...*

Then, clear and unmistakable...

...it ever gets out? This pub won't survive...

There followed a response from another man, and again Amy and Brendan strained to hear. But they threw themselves back in frustration, Brendan punching into his cap. One line was all they'd have.

Britt got to her feet and put on her jacket, took back her mobile. 'I'm really sorry if this doesn't lead anywhere.'

Amy got up. 'God, no listen. Thanks so much.' She went to hug Britt, only to find herself embracing someone who was stiff and awkward. She smiled nervously and stepped back.

'How ye getting home?' Jackie asked.

'I'll flag a taxi,' said Britt, fixing her hair.

'I'll get ye down to the road. I fancy some chips.'

'And me,' Brendan said.

'Ye have money?' Amy asked.

Thrusting a hand into his jacket pocket, Jacki pulled out his wallet then a folded piece of paper. 'Back in ten.' Throwing on his jacket, he followed Britt out the living room, Amy and Brendan heard the opening of the front door.

They didn't hear it close.

A few seconds later Jackie reappeared, holding the sheet of now unfolded note-paper. 'What the hell's this?'

His sister moved towards him, took it from his hand.

She read.

Duncan Gardner and Keith Marshall know what happened to your brother

'Gardner and Marshall,' Jackie said with a shrug. 'The golfers.'

Amy nodded, open-mouthed.

He threw up his hands. 'I need to sit down.'

34

Jackie groaned, scratched at his head. 'I just don't know. The whole pub wanted to be our pal.'

'True, man.' Brendan threw the note onto the table. 'Never even seen half of them before.'

Still on her feet, Amy scanned her brothers for a clue. 'No one hung around longer than anyone else? Got that bit closer? Nothing weird happened under your noses?'

'Ye kidding, Amy?' Brendan threw back his head. 'I practically won Rangers fan of the year, and I'll be smelling of shite for a lot longer. Weird enough.'

Jackie sighed. 'Like I said, I was sitting on my jacket, would have been a piece of piss to just bend down and slip the note in.'

Amy sighed. 'Okay.'

'There's something else we should think about. Whoever this is might not be trying to help, might be throwing us off the track.'

'Like Wayne Boyd?' Amy asked with the hint of an apology.

'Maybe. Or his fat-necked pal.'

'Nah, he was nowhere near us,' Brendan said. 'Sure of it.'

'We should be careful.'

'So what about Skin?' Amy asked with hesitation. 'Could he have…?'

'*Skin*? He's practically the only one we can eliminate.'

'Then the barmaid? Maureen? She got us in touch with Margaret.'

'But she was upfront. This isni her style.'

'Somebody we don't know, man,' Brendan said. 'Got to be.'

Amy swiped up the note again, stepped across the room. 'Britt, do ye think this is a woman's writing?'

Still standing by the door, with a helpful smile Britt examined the handwriting. 'It's neat, so if I was to guess I'd say yes, but…'

'I know, I know…' Amy flopped back down on the couch.

'Britt,' Jackie asked, 'What made ye suspect Gardner and Marshall anyway?'

The woman smiled, gave an almost embarrassed shrug. 'I didn't want to make a big deal, Jackie, you had your reasons for suspecting the barman and I'd no intention of interfering. But those two, what can I say, they make a show of themselves in there, leers, catcalls, all that. But not tonight. Locked in a conversation, they were, worried seemed like, and when I last saw them on a quiz night, they didn't just do the quiz, they won it. I told you I'd try and record them so that's what I did.'

'Ye came from our table and sat at theirs. How did they react?'

'Uncomfortable, although to be honest I'm not even sure they *knew* I'd been with you two. It was maybe because I'd only ever rolled my eyes at them and there I was sitting down like an old mate. I asked them about tomorrow's football and that loosened them up, the smugness was still there but they seemed relieved to have something else to think about. I talked about James, they knew some of his story and let me go on for a few minutes. But it became obvious I was overstaying my welcome, so I hit record and hid my phone. A pity I only got one line. Just hope it's done some good.'

'Oh it has, Britt,' Amy said with a smile. 'The note on its own would have thrown us. But with the recording? It has to mean something.'

'Aye,' Jackie said. 'So we follow it up.'

Brendan pulled at a tuft of his hair. 'That place, man. *Again.*'

'What time's kick-off?' Amy asked. 'We can't wait until the afternoon.'

'Half-twelve,' said Jackie. 'We'll get there for it opening.'

'I doubt they'll be in Crawford's,' Britt said with a shake of the head.

'No? What did they say?'

'They'll be watching it in a golf club.'

'Don't suppose ye…?'

'No.'

'Shit.'

'No, hang on…' Britt took out her mobile, swiped a few times. 'See, I took their photo, I had to lay it on thick when I was trying to find *record*. I think…I'm not sure. Is that…?' She leaned forward, and the four crowded round a picture of the two seated men. Both middle-aged and bulky with thick but greying hair, one of the men was clean-shaven and the other had a moustache. Gardner and Marshall wore brightly coloured jumpers, one pink and the other yellow. On the yellow jumper there was, creased but visible, a crest. Britt enlarged the photo. They peered.

'Weathertown…?' Amy started. 'Windytown…?'

Brendan peeled back, got to work on his phone.

'Weathertop…?' Britt wondered.

Jackie shrugged. 'Willtown maybe.'

'Nah, it's…'

After a moment, Brendan snapped his fingers. 'Weatherhill. Weatherhill Golf Club.'

Amy stood back. 'Are ye sure?'

He showed her his search result. 'Nothing else with a name even close to it.'

'So where is it?' asked Jackie.

Brendan winked. 'South. No far fae that pub in fact. Few minutes drive.'

'Okay,' Amy said with a clap of her hands. 'We get there for eleven.'

Jackie shook his head. 'No. They'll be there to play golf before the match. Make it nine.'

35

Up on his back toes, the club swung past his shoulder, the man with the moustache stared at the ball soaring down the fairway then dropping yards from the green. His heart thumped as the ball bounced and trundled up the slope. But it slowed, stopped and fell back, then rolled with speed into a bunker.

'Fuck!' the man snapped.

'Yes!' his mate spat.

'Bastard!' Keith Marshall thrust the driver back into his bag. Then without a word to his mate, he began the journey on to his ball.

Duncan Gardner's sneer at the misfortune of his pal was nothing new, the two had been competitive since they'd met back at school. In their youth the game had been women, points would be won from snogging up to shagging, with bonuses for stunners and double-bonuses for *mingers*. After the two had settled down, cars became the competition, their sales jobs making one the flashier until he'd be inevitably eclipsed by the other. Then came golf. The Weatherhill Private Club was free of screaming weans not to mention unemployable Tims, and the sweetness of a Saturday victory would last the entire week. Then after two decades, the men again claimed sexual conquests, although now they were dubious snogs with gorgeous barmaids and not so dubious shags with troubled teenagers. By the time they'd reached their fifties however, their patter flopped with their bellies, golf was the men's sole competition.

But this morning Keith Marshall wasn't pissed-off because he was getting beat, his woefully crappy swinging was the least of his worries. What bothered him was the future, the future of the greatest pub in Scotland and the legends that sat inside. Because one thing was for sure, if this news broke then Crawford's would be finished, there was no way it could survive the fallout. But the question that had been doing his and Duncan's heads in for near a week was what they'd *do* about it, how they'd possibly manage to save everybody's arse. Then last night, at the end of a discussion that had got quite intense, they'd finally agreed. They do nothing at all. Since there was no way to avoid the impending disaster, they put their fingers in their ears and wait for the *boom*. Then, if the bomb somehow didn't go off? They'd keep their mouths shut until the day they died.

Ten steps down the fairway, Keith Marshall stopped and stood up his trolley. He stared ahead at the green, biting his lip, then nodded back to the clubhouse. 'Fuck this,' he muttered to his pal. 'Let's get the beers in early.'

At first, neither Amy nor her brothers had noticed that the men had abandoned their match after one hole. Once they'd entered through the gate and got suspicious looks in the clubhouse, they'd headed round the back and up a steep hill. The first tee lay at the top, and as Jackie and Amy set off in different directions Brendan waited for the men's possible approach. Although *being* on the course wasn't illegal, what Brendan did next was very much frowned upon. He couldn't help it, he'd no choice, the speedy drip of his kick-start coffees had him cross-legged in close to agony. Anyway there was barely a golfer around, what could possibly go wrong?

Whipping out his dick, he peed with a sigh onto the freshly cut fairway, then turned and gave a wide spray round the green. Crashing through the trees bordering the first and second holes, came the only people on the course to have seen him. 'You!' screamed one, face twisted and purple and with a club in the air. 'Fucking you!'

Brendan tucked himself back in and for some seconds stood gibbering, as the two men, middle-aged and brightly-dressed, huffed raging up the hill. He stepped back, these guys meant it, they looked like they've dreamt for years of finding somebody pissing on their course. He stepped back more. These guys really… Then he realised who they were and stumbled and fell. Marshall was upon him, drawing back his club, and Brendan could only plead and raise a hand in defence. 'Don't! Please…! I…!'

'Dirty tramp…'

'Hey!'

At the interruption of his swing, Keith Marshall peered above and past the pisser to the horizon of the next hill, to a man in a black t-shirt and black jeans hurtling towards them.

Duncan Gardner placed a hand on his pal's shoulder. 'We know them,' he muttered.

Slowly Marshall took in each of the invaders, as Brendan grabbed his displaced cap and scrambled further back. He nodded. 'You're right. The pub. Hey…it's that barman's fucking pals.' He rearranged his stance to allow a new swing for Jackie, flicked him a nod as he stopped in front of his brother. 'Ye want to be first?'

Jackie shrugged. 'No sure that's a good idea, there are probably some rules round here.'

'Rules, son? There are rules alright. What were ye up to on the fifteenth? Shiteing in the hole?'

'Was I...?' He shrugged, confused but close to laughing. '*What?*'

The other man now looked more concerned than angry, glanced between the calmness of the stranger and the rage of his mate. 'No bother, Keith,' Gardner muttered. 'We'll get the Fenians kicked out.'

'*Fenian?*' Having appeared unseen behind the men, Amy had slowed down from her jog, but on hearing that word she'd taken off again. 'I'll *Fenian*, ye!' Marshall spun round as she grabbed at the weapon, she wrestled it from his grasp and they tumbled onto the grass. The driver dropped beside her, she pinned him with both hands. 'Don't try it!' she screamed into his face. 'Enough of your lies!'

'*What?* Get aff me ya psycho...!' With a roar he threw her to the side, and as Amy landed with a thump he staggered to his feet. 'Getting you done, ya lunatic,' he spat, stepping back and brushing dirt from his pink and beige. 'Get youse all done. I *know* the polis,' he wheezed, stabbing at his chest. 'A visit to the station? One word from me and ye don't come fucking out.' He glared in disbelief at his mate who was staring in open-mouthed silence.

Taking a deep breath and a hold of Jackie's hand, Amy got up, rearranged her long skirt. 'We know youse know where my brother is,' she said, pulling grass from her hair. 'So youse better start talking.' She looked at her other brothers in expectation of support, but didn't get any. His hands balled into fists and eyes on the men, Brendan was still too wary to answer, while Jackie just couldn't back her up. The assault, he'd noticed, hadn't only stunned these guys but mystified them, they'd been shocked then outraged but not nervy or uncomfortable. Even now they stood glaring, not so much at Amy but *in* her, trying to make sense of the words that had left her mouth.

Finally with a look of both sympathy and disgust, Duncan Gardner sighed. 'If you say so, doll.' He took out his phone. 'Mon, Keith. Security will get this.'

Keith Marshall swiped up his club, and as Brendan and Jackie braced themselves Amy shrunk back a step. But the golfer paused, then threw back his head with a victorious laugh. 'Of course! The Taig's disappeared! And youse think it's to do with us!' He turned to his mate with a jubilant shrug. 'Ye getting this, Dunc? We're the prime suspects, big fella!'

Gardner cast a glance around the course and another back down at the clubhouse, two figures, a male and a female, were peering up. 'Aye, nutters,' he said with a scowl. 'Let's go.'

'But hey, I'm intrigued,' Marshall went on. 'Fair fucking flattered to be honest. What's your grounds for... Hang on, can I say what I *think* has happened? Somebody's tanned the wee bastard's jaw and he's bled to death up some pishy side-street. I'd like to think that was our lot, but sorry,' he chuckled. 'I'd just be speculating. 'It's the not knowing that kills ye, eh?'

Brendan stepped forward. 'I'll fucking kill *you*, ya bam.'

'An open invitation, come ahead!' he shouted, waving the club. 'Hey! Hold on. You won the quiz last night!' Again Marshall turned to his mate. 'What the hell is this world coming to?'

Gardner gestured at the man and woman now marching up the hill, purposefully enough to suggest to the family that they were staff. 'The police will be on their way,' he said, almost in pity. 'Best face the music.' Amy and her brothers looked down, but then back at the men.

Keith Marshall meanwhile neither listened nor looked. 'Felt good, didn't it?' He nodded at Brendan. 'Being one of us? Will never happen son. You're too ugly. Too Poor.'

'You bloody *know*!' Amy cried again, ready to fly once more.

He sized her up and down then rolled his eyes. 'Always the victims, you lot.' He nodded at his pal. 'Come on.'

'We have it recorded.'

He turned again. 'What?'

'What youse said last night,' Amy continued. 'It's all on a phone.'

At first there was a mystified but carefree shrug. Then the smile dropped from Marshall and the men exchanged worried glances. To the family, their minds seemed to start whirring back to the events of the previous night. Gardner shut his eyes and whispered, 'Shit…'

Marshall shrugged for an answer.

'That wee bird fae Belfast. Told ye she was up to something.'

A look of horror crossed Keith Marshall, then he appeared to try to keep a hold of himself. He smirked and he held it but his mind was elsewhere. 'So,' he eventually said. 'We were talking about the barman, aye?'

'Aye,' Amy answered.

Another pause. His eyes lit up. 'What did ye find out exactly?'

'We found out…'

Nothing, Jackie knew, which surely Amy now understood as well. 'About Sunday night,' he snapped before her.

'Sunday night?'

'CCTV's got ye following our brother as he leaves the pub.'

'Phones one second, CCTV the next,' Marshall sneered. 'Be drones in a minute, eh Dunc? Oh here,' he continued as the staff members arrived with nods. 'They think this a public toilet, Ralphy.'

'No even an apology,' Gardner said.

'We saw it!' Amy shouted, desperate now. 'In his office, we saw!'

The workers, the duty manager and an assistant, glared at the loiterers from a safe distance. Then with a lick at his lips, Marshall stepped to them again for one final shot. 'Your lies are a joke,' he sneered, face inches from Jackie's. 'Ye saw no pub CCTV.'

'The owner showed us.'

His mouth hanging open, for some seconds Keith Marshall only glared, weighing up whether to speak or not. Whatever his reason for keeping quiet, the temptation was just too much. 'I don't know what Daryl showed ye,' he whispered. 'But I can tell ye it wisni last Sunday night, not a chance in hell ye'd get a look at that. What I can say is you're having the piss ripped, and get used to it cos we'll be ripping it again on the park.' He stepped back with a grin, his morning round of golf not such a waste after all. Then he strolled past the managers to join his waiting mate, and went whistling down the hill.

36

Oblivious to the calm and confident threat of the duty manager, Amy, Jackie and Brendan just stared at one another. Then fists clenched, Amy ran. Jackie and Brendan followed her down towards the car park, and this time the oldest brother would know what to do. No trying to chill his sister out or make sense of this through logic, if that owner really had lied again then they ram his computer up his arse. Except who was he kidding, throwing punches and furniture would get them absolutely nowhere, it was answers they were after, nothing else would do. As they reached the car park, Amy pacing about with her phone at her ear, Jackie realised they had a weapon of their own that could force the owner to his knees. And it should have been pulled days ago.

The taxi finally reached them just before ten o'clock, after Amy had been pulled back several times from starting to walk the four miles. She'd only actually given up after Brendan had argued for arriving later anyway, if the owner turned up to see them hanging around, he might just get off his mark. Brendan had been feeling quite chilled since he'd heard Jackie's idea, one last visit might be enough and they could bolt before the place had opened. He had to right enough, ignore a few other thoughts fighting for control of his head, like where this idea might lead and if that golfer was just one more liar. Still as the taxi left the car park, the brothers and sister felt more or less the same, edgy but somehow sure that they were closer to finding Shaun. They got out near Crawford's and walked towards the door.

'Open up! Hey! Open up and talk!' Jackie and Amy were both quite taken aback at Brendan stepping it up, slamming his fist on the window of the door after he'd battered about with the handle. The place was locked but he was in there, the owner, a dim light shone from the bar and there were clunks and chinks of glasses. Brendan started booting the door then and Amy spun to face the road, with two hours until kick-off there were police vans crawling about. He finally turned round, back-heeled the door with a thud. 'Phone him, man,' he said to Amy. 'Gie him the ultimatum noo.'

Amy got out her mobile only for Jackie to nod past them both, at the man who'd chucked down his dishtowel and was now marching muttering for the door. He slammed back the bolt and pushed the door open. 'Half-eleven,' he snapped. 'That's unless…'

'Time to talk,' said Amy. 'Ye know what about.'

The owner blinked back in surprise at his visitors, and there followed the glimpse of an expression that the family now knew well. But while his top lip started to curl, that intrigued sneer didn't come, appeared to have been crushed by thoughts piling into his head. 'Youse are still barred,' he said, pulling closed the door.

'Up to you,' replied Jackie, blocking it with his foot. 'But ye might want to get your side of the story in first.'

'My *what*?'

'Our last throw of the dice,' Amy said. 'The police don't care and all you give us is bullshit, so we're going to the papers. Hey, it's hell for us but it'll be a jackpot for them. The big Rangers pub employing the Celtic fan?

The fan getting found out and going missing? The pub lying at every turn? I hope to God it'll help us find Shaun, but I know it'll ruin you.'

'Remind us,' Jackie asked, flicking him a nod. 'How many of your punters actually know Wayne deliberately hired a Celtic fan?'

Daryl shrugged. 'You want to ruin an innocent man? There's nothing I can do.'

'Oh spare us the clown act!' Amy shouted. 'We know ye lied about Sunday! We know ye doctored that CCTV!'

'I doctored the...*What?*'

She held up her phone. 'You've got five seconds.'

A Rangers chant went up on the other side of the road and Daryl gazed across. But he seemed oblivious to the appearance of the first supporters, appeared conscious only of the demand that had been made. When Jackie gave him a reminder, he still didn't give his response, just stood there silent and distant, gazing out ahead. Finally he nodded, and letting go of the handle, stepped back inside. 'You better come in,' he muttered.

Amy, Jackie and Brendan crowded into the office, as Daryl slumped onto his chair and switched on the computer. There were no jokes now, no offers of tea, the owner had eyes only on the screen, it flickered and sang into life. As Jackie and Brendan sat down, their sister stood in front of the desk, her gaze flitting between the screen and the owner, her nerves shooting all over. Daryl asked a question. It sounded like *Have you ever been in love?*, and no one answered.

He clicked the mouse a few times. 'Not even you, Jackie?'

'What?'

'Been in love?'

'Have I...?' Jackie scowled. 'Just show us the-'

'-Don't believe it, buddy. Not for a minute. Anyway, it shouldn't matter.' He turned around the screen, his finger hovering over the mouse. 'What we *do* share is a common humanity.' He held his gaze on the three, eyebrows raised.

'I don't know what ye want...' Amy began.

'I don't *want* anything, Amy. It's what I need.'

'Needing a skelp, mate,' said Brendan, almost off the couch.

'No, a promise,' Daryl said, with a calm nod at the younger brother. 'That what you see will go no further than this.'

'Let us bloody see it first,' snapped Amy. 'We'll be the judge.'

'Okay. But it's got nothing to do with your brother.'

'Then...?' She glared at him, then seemed to be looking for something to attack him with. Finally she shook her head. 'Fine.'

'Play it,' Jackie told him.

'Whatever, man,' said Brendan.

Daryl ran his hands through his hair, rested them on his head. Then he leaned forward and with a sigh, clicked the mouse. 'You're going to be disappointed.'

>*0648* The main entrance to Crawford's. A distant figure on the pavement, a smattering of traffic on the road.

'Your source was half-right,' Daryl continued, nodding at the screen. 'Yeah, I kept something back. But I didn't change the date. This is Monday morning. 0648.'

A bus trundles towards town, followed by a private taxi. The Crawford's door pushes open. At first it stays open, no one appears, then with a look one way then the other, a figure emerges. It's a woman, around her thirties or early forties, she's in an expensive, light-coloured dress and has a jacket over her shoulders. She rearranges the dress, scratches inside a strap of her high-heels, and draws a hand through her full, blonde hair. Then, unsteady for a second, she starts to walk.

After she continued out of sight, the family stared open-mouthed.
'That's…' Amy started.
'Mellissa West,' Jackie said.
'Yip. And this is me,' Daryl said, killing the screen and for the first time coming close to a smile. 'All out of secrets.'
'But…' said Amy.
He stood up. 'But …?'
'We…'
'What? Expected to see more than just my lover making a break before anyone saw her? No, I know it's nothing to you, why should it be? But it's enough to finish me a thousand times over. Hey, look at it this way, ye can finally score the bad guy off your list.'
He walked to the door but no one moved.
'Don't make this awkward, we're done now.'
Jackie shook his head back to reality. 'Aye…aye, we are.' He stood up.

'Biggest game of the season today,' Daryl said, winking and opening the door wider. 'Oh, who are we kidding,' he laughed. 'Beat your lot to win the league at home? One of the biggest in our history.'

One by one, the family left, Brendan even appearing to mutter a goodbye.

'Good luck, buddy,' smiled Daryl with a slap on his shoulder. 'Oh, actually, Jackie?'

The oldest brother turned round.

'I hear you struck it lucky with a ticket.'

'Aye.'

'My cousin.'

'That's right.'

'You're not going, obviously.'

'No...' Jackie shrugged. '...I'm not...'

Daryl nodded, drummed his fingers against the frame of the door. 'All the same, makes you wonder, doesn't it?'

'What's that?' Jackie asked.

'Those tickets, Jackie, they're like gold. In an hour's time they'll be killing each other down there for one.'

'And?'

'*And*? Wayne just offers one to *you*?'

*

Monday, 25th February (cont'd)

Listen, Wayne…

This thing you've found out, man. This temptation to make cash out of it, I get it, I do. But I get as well that it's tearing ye apart, and deep down ye know fine what the answer is.

I don't think telling ye this will help, I think the answer has got to come from you. But if ye fancy a longer chat, I'd like to sit down and listen.

We can go for a drink after this.

If you want to, I mean.

Nae bother.

It's cool, of course.

But I could help.

I'm here.

37

'I still think he's right,' Jackie said, swiping a few crumbs from the red-checked tablecloth onto the floor. 'It's mad. Trying to catch me out at the start of the week? Fair enough. But I don't think Boyd has *ever* believed we're Rangers fans. Giving me a ticket makes no sense.'

Taking her cup and swaying round the black tea, Amy gazed through the café window towards Crawford's. The pub had been opened a few minutes now, customers were trickling in, and traffic was building on the road and colour was filling the pavements. Amy's brothers waited for her to speak, to take a view and stick to it. But their sister was done guessing now and feeling devastated afterwards. Still staring outside, she shook her head at her own cluelessness.

'Look at it this way,' Jackie went on. 'He's either a vindictive bigot or he wants to keep an eye on me.'

Amy turned, shrugged at him to explain himself.

Jackie shrugged that he couldn't.

Emptying into his glass the last of his Irn Bru, Brendan eyed them both. 'There is something.'

'What?' Jackie asked.

'I don't know, man,' he started with a shrug. 'He's been in the clear, that prick, ever since that note turned up in your pocket. But that mate of his, I *know* I saw him in London. What? I'm just supposed to sit here and kid on that I didni?'

Amy pushed away her cup, slouched back on her seat. 'I don't know what we're supposed to believe.'

'But Jackie, you're right,' Brendan went on. 'Biggest game of the guy's life man and he wants a *Tim* sitting next to him? That's bonsai.' He emptied his glass and shrunk back, and with a self-conscious look at Jackie and Amy, pulled at his cap. 'The other thing...'

Amy's eyes widened. 'What?'

'Just covering aw angles, ye know?'

'Tell us.'

'Well....' He drew his hands down his face, took a breath. '...When Boyd ran in to the bogs last night, he dropped his phone, right? I picked it up, saw a text he'd been writing. I told ye, Jackie, mind?'

His brother nodded.

'*One match and it's all over*, it said, something like that. Obviously man I thought he was banging on about the day, how they get a result and that's it finished.'

'But it could mean something else?' Jackie's hands were on the table, like he was ready to jump if he had to.

Brendan shrugged like it was obvious, like he was pissed off to even have to explain. 'It's what we were getting convinced of man until that pish last night. *One match and it's all over.* The betting. The kidnapping. Us being on their tail. There's one game, could be *this* one. And when it's finished, they're done cos they'll be minted.'

There was a long silence as outside chants picked up, hands clapped and horns sounded.

Eventually Jackie nodded. 'Keeping an eye on me,' he said.

'It's what I'm thinking, man, so ye canni find Shaun until the game's done. It still leaves me and Amy,' he said. 'But maybe he thinks you're the man or something, I don't know…Amy?'

'Yeah,' she whispered. 'Why not.'

'So say this is all true,' Jackie wondered aloud. 'Right now where does it leave us?'

'It leaves us not screwing this up at the last minute,' Amy said, placing a hand on Jackie's shoulder. 'If Boyd wants to watch you, we let him.'

Jackie nodded, took a deep breath. 'Aye. And it means I better get a scarf.'

The Rangers Megastore, a silver-roofed building jutting out a corner of the red-bricked stadium, was easy enough to find, although getting inside was another story. With an hour and a half before kick-off, the growing support was milling round the grounds and the car park, until the clouds opened and they rushed in their hundreds for its doors. As the family squeezed through the entrance and among the sheltering supporters, Amy was the only one to march for the clothes. Jackie just wasn't sure about the idea, didn't see what was wrong with only a scarf, while Brendan had begun his protest the moment Amy had started to explain. It was for his protection, she'd insisted as she hurried past the first street vendor, nearly every fan was in a strip and Jackie couldn't afford to stand out.

Jackie knocked-back not only Amy's first choice of Rangers top but second one too, and for a moment she stood there glaring like she might just chuck them at him instead. He explained he wasn't being a pain but those were strips for the current season, a retro top on the other hand might seem like he'd owned it for a while. After Brendan moved towards them, dodging key rings and sweeties like he was in an aisle of infectious diseases, Amy took a red top and a scarf to the counter, as well as a Rangers pen and Rangers wine gums. Outside Jackie threw on the top, made a joke about When in Rome that seemed lost on his brother and sister, and Amy drew pen down the front and smeared wine gum around the back. Then, the denim jacket on again, the three passed back through the swelling crowds, heading once more to Crawford's.

The bar was the busiest and noisiest they'd seen it, both the blast of the beer and the roar of the drinkers threatened to flip Jackie's stomach as he entered. It propelled him into action as well, with a clap of his hands and a shake of his fist he shouted, 'Mon the Gers!' at the top of his voice. No one looked or even blinked, the punters either screaming along to a CD or shouting to be heard above it. His jacket half-off his shoulders to reveal the red of Rangers, Jackie gestured to his brother and sister that they should move further up the bar. He noticed then that in their neutral colours they seemed kind of vulnerable, and for a moment he even hung back half-expecting an attack.

Either impatient at his brother's uncertainty or disgusted at his needless shout, Brendan rolled his eyes and squeezed nearer to the bar. After they'd watched him move, impressed as well as surprised, Jackie and Amy gazed around some regulars. Propped up by an elbow Skin was gazing into his pint, while on a stool the ned chanted as he slapped a palm onto the bar. Maureen meanwhile shared a laugh with some pals, and the old man in glasses gave his usual nod. There was no sign of Boyd's big mate or for that matter Boyd, and Jackie supposed he'd be up the back, hidden by other drinkers. Within a few minutes Brendan reappeared, and they stepped further from the bar to the middle of the room. Then in front of them heads began to turn, peering straight past them towards the entrance. Amy turned as well, found her view blocked by a wall of supporters. A man and a woman emerged.

As Andy and Melissa West strode further inside, the customers in front of them parted. Some stepped on each other's feet and other's spilled neighbouring drinks, as the legend's name or ...*The Weapon*... gushed from supporters' lips. Leading his wife with a curled finger, bald and in a white muscle t-shirt, Andy West acknowledged some fans with nods while others got as much as a grunt. What no one received, Amy and now her brothers saw, was anything close to a smile. The ex-striker made for the bar like he was sniffing out a goal, his beady eyes narrowing, searching for space. Behind him meanwhile wrapped in royal blue and dripping in gold, Melissa West beamed at one woman and waved at another. She passed Amy and their eyes met, and as perfume reached Amy a hint of panic swept across Melissa. Amy's instinct was to give a reassuring smile but the woman had already turned away. She then stood near the bar holding her husband's hand.

'That's...' Brendan muttered.

Most customers might have been in awe of West, but they were also either quickly used to his presence or following pub protocol, after a minute just Brendan still had eyes on him. Jackie kicked at his brother's ankle. Then he felt a slap on the shoulder. He turned around.

'Ye made it,' Boyd grunted with an unimpressed nod.

Jackie laughed, shrugging back in protest. 'Told ye, Wayne, I wouldn't miss this for anything.' He dug into his pocket and passed a handful of notes. The barman gave him his ticket.

'Main Stand, we're in. Dead centre.'

'Right. Cool, that's…'

With a raise of the eyebrows, Boyd waited for more. But Jackie couldn't give more, didn't know one stand in Ibrox from another. Boyd nodded satisfied like his fun was just starting. 'A blinding seat,' he said with a wink. 'Plenty of Bears would kill for it, know what I mean?' Then he nodded under Jackie's denim jacket. 'Good memories fae that season, aye?'

Jackie looked down. '…Aye, it was…ehm…' Shite. Jackie had been so keen to look the part that he'd forgotten Boyd wouldn't be fooled.

'No!' Brendan blurted, glaring like Boyd was some part-time supporter. 'A nightmare of a couple of seasons. A cracking strip, that's aw it is.'

Lifting his pint, Boyd stared at Brendan.

Brendan held his own stare back.

'Aw part of the history.' Boyd then said, and took half a dozen gulps. When he came back up, he licked his lips. 'The pish with the magical.'

Amy forced a smile at her brothers. 'I forgot about Britt, by the way. She might want to watch the game here.' As she swiped her phone, Boyd eyed her up.

'That what youse are doing? Watching it here?'

She shrugged. 'Practically my pal's local. Why not?' But about to move for the door, Amy found herself rooted. This was hardly likely to be small-talk from Boyd. What did he care about where she and Brendan watched the game? Just like he needed Jackie where he could see him, he preferred *them* to be far from Crawford's. Amy now felt surer of this than ever, whatever her brothers saw in that cellar, she knew what *she* saw through the keyhole. 'Then again,' she went on with a casual nod to Brendan. 'We might move on after the first half.' She was only trying to conceal her nerves but it didn't matter, Boyd wasn't listening. He was gazing across the floor at Andy and Mellissa West. They were chatting to Daryl.

Amy couldn't help but gaze across with him. A hand lightly wrapped around the husband's forearm, Daryl was relaying a story that had the couple laughing aloud. His eyes were also mostly on the husband, yet Amy could see something between the owner and the wife. It was Mellissa, how her eyes soaked up Daryl's every word and move. If *she* could see it, Amy wondered, who else could? Boyd, it certainly seemed like by the solemnness of his gaze. As if hearing Amy's thoughts, Boyd then turned back round.

'Leaving in twenty, mucker,' he said to Jackie. 'Be ready.' He hobbled his way back to his mates.

Amy raised her mobile, 'Back in a minute,' she said. She headed for the door.

Brendan approached Jackie, leaned into his ear. 'Don't mean to freak ye oot, but...'

'What?'

'...The songs.'

'*Songs?*'

'The *Rangers* songs. The fucking....' He jabbed a finger up at a cacophony of whistles and drums, just as a fan screamed *Fuck the Pope!*

into his ear. He grimaced, shook the pain from his brain. '...I don't know,' he said, eventually. 'The Sash and aw that.'

'I've got my work cut out. I know. Thanks.'

'I don't just mean that...'

'*What?*'

He leaned in further, eyes flaring. 'What if the fucker tries to blow your cover? What if that's been he's plan aw along? Get ye in there and...'

Jackie shrugged. 'What can I do about it? At least I'll make the papers.'

Amy jostled her way back, explained that Britt should be arriving in time for kick-off. 'Listen, Jackie,' she continued, sipping at her glass of coke. Take my phone and text Brendan at half-time. When it's finished, get right back to mine.'

'I will,' he said.

'Then...' Her eyes dampened as she took a furtive glance around, then gave her older brother a hug. '...It might just be all over. We'll see Shaun walking through the door.'

'Let's go,' Boyd said, swiping at Jackie's leg with his stick.

He spun round. 'Now?'

'Change of plan,' Boyd grunted as some unsmiling mates appeared behind him. 'Getting there a bit early. Belt oot a few anthems.'

38

Eighty-seven minutes gone.

Eighty-eight.

....

Jackie again checked the scoreboard.

...

Eighty-nine.

He was nearly there, he'd get out in one piece. A minute plus whatever then he'd do one on the whistle. Taking deep and calming breaths, Jackie looked straight ahead and down, followed the ball as it passed between the players. The Bouncy, that had saved him really. The first song as he'd reached his seat, he'd just shouted *Bouncy!* and jumped about and it had actually helped him relax. Not that it had stayed that simple of course with the tunes he didn't know, forced to stand there and gulp at air like some stage-struck Loyalist goldfish. Then the other songs, for fuck's sake he knew *them* alright, his stomach had churned and his heart had sunk and his tongue had even gone on strike. An achievement getting this far, he knew, but one he wouldn't be looking back on. Every second of this afternoon would be wiped the moment it was finished.

Ninety minutes.

Now three minutes of injury time.

...

It was still a massive relief to be not sitting *next* to Boyd as he'd thought he would, but a full eight seats away, where even the surrounding Bears only noticed him in the sweeping insanity of a goal. So should he steal a final glance? To see what Boyd was up to? If he was watching his beloved team or sending messages on his phone? Because that was what he *had* been up to, Jackie had spied him a few times. Then he'd strode up the steps to clock his reaction once he'd noticed Jackie's seat was empty. And shite, was there a reaction. Jaw dropping. Eyes darting. Arse lifting. Then whole body sighing as Jackie reappeared. Not that this had given him any pleasure, it had only told him Amy was probably right. Until then, Jackie hadn't *truly* believed Shaun was being held by gangsters. He couldn't, it had been far too much to grasp. But with Boyd completely obsessed not with his team but surely, bets, there was just no other explanation.

...

Injury time.

Shit.

On his feet again.

The Bouncy.

No problem.

...

Down once more.

He was down, although not everybody was because the celebrations had started. Or they were continuing. Or they'd never actually stopped since Rangers' first goal in the fourth minute. The first of five. To Jackie, each of those goals had been like some psychotic sergeant major screaming in the face of an exhausted recruit. *Jump up! Roar! Hug!...Jump up! Roar! Hug!...* Don't like it? Too bad. Ye *don't* want to see the alternative.

The mad thing for Jackie about all of this…He shook his head, nearly smiled. *One* of the mad things… was that he'd never have dreamed he'd witness this again, never have dreamed he'd *want* to. Just last week he'd scoffed at Brendan when he was looking for a ticket, he told him that the game was full of nutters. On both sides. The bigotry. The chants. The obsession. They lived their lives to hate each other. So that made them the same.

But now?

Despite the obvious dangers…

Despite even losing *five-nil*…

This was beautiful.

He was watching his *team*.

Us against *them*.

He wondered how he'd lived without it.

He wondered…

The ball flew high..

Far...

Into the net.

'Ynhhyaassmnagh….!!!'

Jackie flew off his seat.

He grabbed it back, threw himself down.

He squirmed and slapped it like there was some faulty ejector.

Then he spluttered and gasped like Mickey Mouse with Tourette's.

A thousand eyes turned.

Somewhere a balloon burst.

He launched himself over three supporters, landed on the aisle.

He pulled himself up.

Raced down the steps.

Out of the stadium.

The final whistle sounded behind him.

39

With his cap on his chest and feet resting on the coffee-table, Brendan sighed as he gazed at the bookcase in front of him. Beside him his phone rang again, and by the window Amy spun round again. Feeling her glare starting to burn his cheek, he grabbed for it and checked. And just like he'd done with the three calls before, he hit *ignore* and tossed it away. Fair enough Brendan thought, Amy was cracking up, but they shouldn't be expecting a call from Shaun if he didn't have his phone. No, for the rest of the day and tomorrow as well, only Brendan's pals would be calling, the match finished half an hour ago but the humiliation was just beginning. However devastated they were though, however bewildered and raging, Brendan wouldn't be picking up. He wouldn't mention that match ever again or how he had to watch it.

Slapping his cap back on he sat up, even gave something close to a smile. It still made sense, the gambling stuff, with Jackie's news especially, this crap was finally coming to an end and life could start again. He stole a glance at his sister, a curtain wrapped tight around her hand, and when she turned away he sank into the couch once more. What was his problem? How could he no talk to her? Tell her it was still early and things would work out cool? Because of the result, that was why. That place and their celebrations. Aye, that or... Pulling down his cap like his sister might somehow see his thoughts, Brendan shut his eyes. He remembered he and Shaun as kids, how if anybody asked if they were telepathic they would either joke or groan. But now he felt like he was. He felt it clear. He felt like…He felt like Shaun was screwed.

Aye, but it was probably just the result.

As the rod began to creak above, Amy let go of the curtain and rested her head against the window. Condensation soon filled the glass until the roads and park were a blurry grey and green, and she wiped the window with a sleeve and stared out again. The view still a blur, this time she wiped her eyes, and clenched a hand and muttered that she *wouldn't* break down now. That creeping dread, Amy had felt it in Crawford's as well, where she'd glanced around, gone outside and even walked around for a couple of minutes. No one had followed her or even noticed her in the first place, every eye in that place was on only the match. And that had made no sense to Amy, if Jackie was a danger then surely they were too. She'd actually felt relieved once she'd read Jackie's texts. Yeah, Shaun was being held but at least he was alive.

In spite of what had been agreed earlier, Amy had decided against leaving at full-time, she'd wanted to stay until Boyd came back because then Shaun might reappear. Brendan hadn't even hung around long enough to be told, as soon as Crawford's had erupted he'd headed for the exit. Britt was the one who'd insisted Amy go home, *she'd* hang around and all night if she had to, and once Boyd turned up she'd watch him, let her know if he acted dodgy. Britt, Amy felt like she'd known the woman half her life, and not just because these days felt like years. She just had a way of helping when she was at her most hopeless, yet for all the love she gave she couldn't even accept a hug. She squeezed the curtain again. Who knows, she thought. When this was over they might even laugh.

Catching a glimpse of Jackie cross the road below, Amy headed into the hall. She waited then pressed the buzzer, held her finger until the main door opened. After she listened to Jackie bound up the steps, he appeared with a carefree smile. He looked to Amy like Shaun had returned months ago or hadn't even disappeared, but she knew this was just his way of hinting at her to be patient. Whatever, Amy thought, shutting the door behind him. She expected Shaun *now* and Jackie did as well.

In the living room Brendan jumped up open-mouthed and glared at his brother. Jackie just stared back, unsure if he was being checked for injuries or signs that he'd become one of *them*. He took off his jacket, threw it on the couch. Brendan shrunk back with a glower.

'Is there a problem, Brendan?'

Between a thumb and a finger, he held out part of his trackie-top.

Jackie looked down. 'Oh…' He threw off the Rangers shirt, tossed it in a corner. 'A decent shade of red, if I'm being honest.'

'So…?' Brendan started. '…What…?'

'How was my afternoon?'

'Aye...'

'No the best.'

'No?'

'Ice-creams a bit pricy.'

Amy returned, passed Jackie a t-shirt and retreated again to the window. 'It's been tough for all of us,' she muttered.

'Aye,' Brendan agreed, sitting again and swinging his legs back onto the table. 'Noo just a wee matter of waiting.'

Jackie made to move to his sister, but changed his mind and sat on the armchair. He swiped up the remotes. 'Let's find something decent to watch.'

An independent American movie started and then it finished, and in the time between none of the three had left their positions. Amy still stood by the window gazing down at the street and beyond, now clutching her phone in one hand and drumming on the windowsill with the other. When she'd heard the closing credits a weight had plunged inside, a whole film had come and gone and where the hell was he? Brendan was on the couch stabbing away at his phone, most other games were finishing and results were coming in. Maybe he shouldn't lose it yet because one of *these* could be Boyd's last match, no it didn't make total sense but it wasn't impossible either. Jackie was on the chair, arms folded and legs stretched out. He'd zoned out of that movie within seconds, its pictures and sounds just a blur and a drone. He zapped off the TV and jumped up. '…Takeaways?'

Eyes welling up, Amy nodded to the kitchen, where menus lay on the counter from a couple of days before. Shit, that wasn't what Jackie had meant. He wanted to get out again, get a chance to breathe. 'I'll call,' he said with a sigh. 'But here, Amy, listen. We just have to be patient. We-'

'-Don't…' she blurted without turning round, her body hunched and rigid like it could be broken by a touch. 'Don't.'

'Right,' he said. 'No bother.' He headed into the kitchen and returned with a menu. 'Thai?'

Each of them sat with their meal on their lap, gazing at the muted jokes of two creased-up entertainers. The brothers and sister spoke only to wonder how long the men had been around, and to agree that the food was good as they pushed it about their plates. From outside there was a euphoric scream and seconds after that a chant, celebrations were now spilling from the pubs into the air. Brendan swore under his breath at the partiers, and Amy swore under her breath at Brendan, then it was quiet but for traffic and forks scraping on plates. Jackie put down his dinner and bit at a nail. He looked at his sister, gazing swollen-eyed at her barely-touched red curry. He got to his feet. 'I'm going back.'

Without looking up, Amy nodded.

Brendan blinked back. 'Crawford's?'

'See Boyd, get some sense out of him.'

Amy gave a sad but grateful smile.

Jackie threw down a final forkful and grabbed his jacket from the back of the couch. Then he kissed his sister's cheek and slapped his shoulder's brother.

'Jackie,' Amy asked as he opened the door, her voice so low he could barely hear.

He turned around.

'Here.' She handed him a twenty.

'Right. Thanks.' Jackie put it in his pocket.

'And if ye don't mind…could ye, well…Could ye try and check that cellar?'

265

40

In search of a taxi, Jackie hit the pavement and jogged for the main road. The celebrations had now officially kicked-off, a Loyalist tune blasted out a window and a Rangers flag flew from a lamppost, and this was a quiet place Jackie knew, where everything was always dead nice. He neared a couple in Rangers strips singing and swinging a takeaway, then three young guys in baseball caps joined in from across the road. The couple barely noticed Jackie but the teenagers eyed him up, then crossed and bounced about the pavement waiting for his arrival. Jackie thought about flashing a grin or giving it ...*Some day, boys, eh?*... But he decided against it, shoved one in the chest and sped off down the avenue. For all their screams and threats, the neds were pretty wasted, and by nipping up and down a few streets Jackie lost them without much problem. He reached the main road, and right away flagged a Hackney.

The driver listened to the name of the destination then drove off without a word, Jackie was relieved he wasn't a Rangers fan, he'd get a break from playing games. As the cab trundled towards the river he banged at his mouth with his knuckles, what the hell could he say to Wayne that they hadn't tried before? That he'd expose him for hiring a Celtic fan now seemed pretty hopeless, this guy had to be in far too deep to worry about stuff like that. More to the point Wayne could expose *him* then get his mates to rip him to bits, taking a breath he reminded himself he might not come out in one piece. Then there was the cellar. Getting there just seemed out of the question, reaching the bar would be an achievement. But he'd need to give it a shot, Shaun *could* have been moved out then in again.

The taxi slowed, and digging into his pocket Jackie took in the surroundings. He'd been aware of singing for a minute or so but he hadn't expected this, Amy's place in comparison was like the end of some middle-England street party. On the debris-scattered pavements supporters staggered about, bellies exposed and arms aloft as they sang and stamped and clapped. Not everybody did. One guy was slumped by a shop in tears and another lay asleep on bin bags, while two men seemed to have crashed out standing up, leaning on each other's shoulders. On the road a woman with puke down her top was screaming at an empty bus stop, while two fans slammed their fists on a bonnet and another showed his arse to a bus. Still more were just zig-zagging about chucking kebabs at their chins, and others were pishing against doors a few steps away from toilets.

Jackie read the time on the metre. *6:48.*

He paid the driver and stepped out.

Opening the pub's main door, the twin wafts of beer and laughter slapped him and he shrunk back. He entered but stopped, blocked by a mass of bodies, and in every snatch of space between drinkers would be quickly swallowed up by another. The place wasn't just rammed but deafening, music vaguely pumped under his feet and he apologised and tapped on shoulders, but no one paid attention, no one cared or even knew. He began to shuffle forward, scanning around for Boyd, and at first he made no headway but then he used some force. With nobody seeming to mind being pushed he soon arrived around the centre of the floor, and eyeing the mural up the back he made his way towards it. Finally he reached a concentration of fans even thicker and louder than elsewhere. He tried to peer between some for a glimpse at the table behind. No joy so he shoved.

'The fuck ye daeing?' a fat, baldy guy shot back, thrusting out his pint out as beer dripped up his flabby arm.

'Sorry, I'm…'

'Dick.'

'Didni mean it, I'm trying to find Boyd.'

Eyes glazed under droopy lids, the guy sighed and slapped Jackie's shoulder, 'Aye, you're awright.'

'Ye seen him?'

He drained his pint and let out a championship-winning burp. 'No seen him aw day.'

Jackie made for the bar, a good bit closer but no easier to reach. Customers struggled around with drinks, and when he'd move aside for one he'd only drift further away. So he pushed himself forward, sidestepped and heaved, spilling drinks, knocking elbows and stepping onto feet. Then several nods, a couple of warnings and a feel of the arse later, he was almost touching the railing. He glanced about. There was no Boyd but there was Maureen, and freeing up an arm he got ready to wave. Except now of course he had his other task, to get back to the cellar, to boot that door and finally know if Shaun was being held or not. Arriving at the front of the queue, he casually moved a few glasses. Then, ignoring a familiar, friendly voice, he placed his hands on the counter.

He pulled himself up.

A hand slipped on a spillage. He swung a leg and it booted a pint. His other leg battered a chin and he scrambled over. To a shatter and a shriek he crashed onto the floor.

'What the…!' Maureen screamed, racing round and slapping him with a dishtowel. 'Ye think this is a free for all?'

Head throbbing, Jackie groaned and opened his eyes. '…Just trying to…find my…' His elbow ached. His thumb felt broken. Maureen was upside-down. She shouted again, but now her voice was drowned by the howls of several men.

Jackie raised himself, got close to sitting up.

He was seized by the legs.

Then the arms. 'Ye want to come wide wi *me*…?'

By the door of the twenty-four-hour newsagent's, Skin took a draw at his roll-up and shrugged. 'Who hisni done it, but? Jumped the bar to pour yirsel a fly pint? Hey, I stood on it wan time. The bar. Did a himgmy right across it, so I did. What was it called? Ye know what I mean, a fucking…'

By the roadside and grabbing hold of a bin, Jackie got to his feet. He took the damp dishtowel from his temple and examined the blood, then with a wince he placed it back. He moved his thumb. He straightened his elbow. He twisted at his earring.

'Wisni too chuffed aboot the boot to the chops, auld Den, was he?' Skin chuckled. 'Aye, but you're wan of us Sarge, end of story. Nae belting to be done by naebdy. Did ye no hear me shouting, by the way? Trying to get ye a pint? Ye widni have jumped if ye'd heard me…'

'Aye, well…' Jackie threw up a hand, stumbled towards the subway.

'Ye no going back in? Mon, my shout.'

Jackie turned round. 'Actually. Skin, have you…?

'Moonwalk!'

'What?'

The barfly shook a victorious fist. 'The fucking moonwalk! What I was daeing up and doon the bar! Gieing it…' He gave an impersonation of a clunking robot, and stopped and rubbed at his chin. 'Canni mind the reason, right enough. Must have been a good yin.'

'Listen, have ye seen Wayne? Since the match finished?'

Skin took another draw. 'Canni mind. How?'

'Ach, it's important.'

He skulked around the darkness of his head until he found a light. 'Saw him, aye.'

'You're sure?'

He nodded. 'Came in no long after full-time. A bit weird, by the way. Wayne's like you and me, Sarge. And Billy Boy.' He slammed the breast of his denim-jacket, nearly tripping over his feet. 'We've got it *here*,' he said, quickly recovering. 'Know what I mean?'

'So what was up? Wayne wasn't fussed?'

'It wisni that.' Skin strutted over to the bin, extinguished his roll-up and scowled at the painful memory. 'I think he's betting again. I mean the boy was totally raging.'

'I'm fine, honest, it's just a cut.' Jackie smiled at his sister standing over him in the kitchen, delicately padding his head gash with pieces of cotton wool. She stripped the plaster, pressed it over the wound, gazing at it silent and distanced. 'I'll get some paracetamol,' she whispered.

Throwing down the tablets, Jackie returned to the living room, chucked a remote to the side and sat down on the couch. From the chair opposite, Brendan shrugged what looked like an apology while Amy, hands in back pockets, stood gazing at them both. Brendan glanced back at his sister, huffed and looked away.

'Is there anything youse want to tell me?' Jackie asked with a scowl.

'Ehm...' Brendan scratched at his face. 'Just that text, man.'

'Text?'

'Boyd's. The wan I saw in the pub.'

'Aye.'

'We might have read it wrong,' Amy said, with a bit of defiance.

'Wrong?' Jackie sat up. 'How?'

'One match and it's all over.'

'One match and...' He shrugged. 'Sounds clear enough.'

'Yeah. But what if he didn't mean a *football* match? What if....?'

Jackie stared back. 'Are you...?'

'I'm saying a *match*, Jackie. To light a fire. One *match* and it's all over.'

'What...?' Jackie eyed them both up like he needed them to say he'd misheard. 'Are we really gonni go there? Is this all not torturous enough without just making stuff up?'

'I'm *trying* to get the truth,' Amy snapped.

'If this is what youse get up to whenever I go out the door...'

'I know how it sounds,' Brendan said. 'Mad.'

Jackie drew his hands down his face 'We just wait, alright? We wait.'

'The thing is,' Brendan went on. 'The guy would need petrol.'

'Petrol. Aye.' Jackie stood up. 'I'm gonni take a lie down.'

'And…'

'Back in half an hour.'

'…I found some.'

'What?'

'Roon the back of Crawford's,' Brendan said with a perplexed shrug. 'Yesterday, when I was trying to film the fire exit. I picked up this can, man. It said vegetable oil on it. But I smelled it. It was minging. Petrol.'

Jackie collapsed again on the couch. 'Let me get this right.' He looked at his brother then his sister. 'Wayne and they others are gonni burn down their pub with Shaun inside it.'

Amy started to tremble. Her face began to crease. But she stared at him, hard. 'It's possible.'

'To be honest, I'm struggling.'

'Really? You've been told Wayne was furious,' she said, glaring. 'Well, I've been listening to Rangers fans all day. Believe me, he's the only one.'

'You've got to admit,' Brendan muttered. 'It's no oot the question.'

'We know nothing about this man,' Amy continued. 'If his bets go wrong, do *you* know what he's capable of?'

Jackie got back to his feet. 'I just need to lie down.'

At first Jackie had wanted a rest, and then it had been an escape, but to his surprise he'd actually fallen asleep, woke again three hours later. Refreshed but no less anxious, he rose to get up for the living room, no choice now but to add his quiet to the already creaking silence. Amy couldn't have convinced herself yet that a fire was coming to Crawford's, maybe Brendan was holding her back but more likely it was time. And the more that passed Jackie figured, the surer that she'd be, until she'd freak completely and they'd all race back to Crawford's. And she'd be wrong, Jackie was now certain, she wasn't thinking straight, this Boyd might do a lot of things but surely *that* was beyond him. Savouring the solitude, he took a final, deep breath, then opened the door again to the living room. It was lit by a lamp now and a peaceful TV. He nodded at his brother and sister and they nodded back.

Within the hour Brendan had dozed off as well, and after a nudge and a whisper from Jackie he trudged to Amy's spare room. Jackie then suggested Amy take a rest, even just close her eyes on the couch, but she shook herself awake and flicked the TV channels instead. Amy refusing to sleep wasn't exactly a surprise, and it wasn't only because she knew she'd stay awake, Shaun's reappearance was supposed to be *today*, and nodding off would bring today to an end. An unwatched film finished and Jackie switched the TV off, searched the computer for music and pressed play. He sat next to his sister and as the album began he smiled, wondered if it would stir any memories. As kids, Amy would always borrow CDs from her big brother, but *he'd* borrow Dylan's *Blonde on Blonde* from her. She returned an exhausted but knowing smile and took and patted his hand. Then she dozed off on his lap.

Later, but for Amy's gentle snoring and the hum of electricity, silence fell again. Outside the occasional taxi arrived and the odd supporter sang or roared, but even for the biggest football fans the night was coming to an end. Jackie looked down at his sister. He didn't want her to wake. He wanted her to sleep for weeks. Or right until Shaun came back.

At 0318 a phone rang.

Amy's phone. On the coffee table.

She jumped up with a blurt, spun around looking.

Jackie pointed and she grabbed it.

She dropped it onto the floor and she grabbed it again.

Jackie read the name. *Daryl*. She hit *answer*. 'Hello??'

'Speakerphone!' Jackie shouted as Brendan bounded in. 'Hit speakerphone!'

'Is this Amy?' Daryl asked after a moment's silence.

'Yeah. It is. Do ye know something? About Shaun? Please, Daryl, you've got to tell me. I'm going out of my...'

'I know about my cousin, that's for sure.' Daryl's voice was slurred. He'd been drinking. But he hadn't been celebrating.

'We need to know. Please. Just tell me where he is.'

'I want to say I'm sorry, ye know? For not treating your...your concern as seriously as I should have...I...'

'I don't... What...? Where's...?'

'Wayne's, ehm...the thing about my cousin, when he's fighting his demons he *becomes* a demon. That's what ye need to understand. It's what we all need to under-'

'-What's happened to Shaun?'

'I'm sorry, I can't answer that.'

'But ye must!'

274

'I just know I lied. Didn't mean to fucking *lie*, just couldn't be bothered with your shit.'

'You lied about what?' Amy screamed.

'There was a key to the old cellar,' Daryl said with a sigh. 'Wayne took it a week ago.'

41

A phone was grabbed.

A set of keys.

Money.

The three raced out of the flat and down the stairway.

Into the darkness and onto the pavement.

They crossed the road for the avenue, Amy screaming something that her brothers couldn't make out.

But they understood.

Shaun might be trapped. They might be too late. He might not get out.

They hurtled down the avenue, almost ran into a slowing private hire dropping off passengers. A plea from Amy got a silent shake of the driver's head. A shout from Brendan got him hitting the accelerator.

On they ran, reaching the end of the avenue and hitting the pavement. Boxes crunched and cans clattered as they passed the neon of takeaway shops. They searched around for a Hackney, one way then the other.

The odd travelling hire. Distant home-goers.

But nothing.

'Rank? Is there a rank here?' Amy shouted at two young guys exiting a close. It was like she had no idea of the answer, like she hadn't lived there since before those boys were born.

Wide-eyed and laughing, the guys barged past.

Marching now, the three continued on, away from the lights and into nothing.

Then an orange glow.

A taxi.

They flagged it and jumped in.

42

Fifty seconds after it had entered the city's underwater crossing, the taxi emerged south of the river. Amy again sat forward. 'Could ye…Please, can ye…?'

The driver mumbled and put his foot down, and the taxi hurtled faster to its destination. But in seconds it levelled off again, the driver shrugging into the mirror. 'Got to stay in the limit. I'm sorry.'

Amy bit into her knuckles and took short, controlled breaths, Brendan bit at his lip, frantically snapping his fingers. Sitting back and staring ahead, Jackie noticed the driver steal glances at the three of them, maybe after something that could justify him risking his job. Jackie doubted that would happen after Amy's 999 call, when she'd shouted about a fire but hadn't known if it had started, and then asked for the police but couldn't explain why they were needed. She'd dropped the phone with a scream after that, unaware if they'd even come. No, the driver would be going no faster than this.

The roads were clear and the lights were green, and in five minutes they arrived on Paisley Road West. On the taxi sped, the roads and pavements busier, of cars and taxis and a bus and the occasional mangled supporter.

Crawford's was a minute's away. 'Sit down, hen,' the driver said. 'We're nearly there.'

At the first red light, the taxi stopped.

No smoke, thought Amy, craning her neck. No shouting.

Nothing.

But no.

An alarm.

Somewhere ahead.

Whooping and stabbing.

'Oh my God.'

'Hey, ye canni just…ye…Wait.' The driver pulled into the side of the road, let open the door.

Jackie chucked him a tenner and they hurried out.

43

With each step they made, the siren grew louder.

Amy prayed that it belonged elsewhere, her eyes searched building's fronts and roofs for billowing smoke.

Then in front of them, Crawford's.

The noise got louder still, piercing now and hooting.

Maybe it was from Crawford's. Maybe not.

Amy, Brendan and Jackie reached the pub and stopped.

They gazed at the thick blue, white and red horizontal stripes, stared at the flags on the poles. They scanned the windows, checked the entrances. The slogan, *THE WORLD'S NUMBER 1 RANGERS PUB*, stood above as proud as ever.

Then they realised.

The noise *was* from the pub.

But there hadn't been a fire.

'It's a burglar alarm,' Jackie said.

'Someone's broken in?' Amy wondered.

'That…Or…'

Brendan noticed first.

But he couldn't speak.

Near the top of the tenement-lined street, the one they'd just crossed, a figure.

A man.

In the distance, way beyond a line of lit parked cars then behind a van.

Visible again.

In a t-shirt.

Running.

Skinny.

Maybe young.

Probably bald.

Brendan pointed and stuttered.

Amy saw. 'Is…? Shau…Shaaaaauuuuun!!!'

The figure came to a stop, spun round and stared down.

Then, in the darkness and the blur of orange light, he was gone.

But it was enough.

That was their brother.

The three of them ran.

*

Monday 3rd June

Hi, everybody…

My name's Shaun and I'm…

I'm……

…I don't even know what I am.

I've thought about this for weeks, but I'm just not sure what my problem is.

But I know something.

I know that finally I need to get it out.

I need to tell youse…

So here goes.

44

They raced to the top of the street. Amy spun around the doors and the steps and the parked cars and vans. 'Where is he? Where did…?'

Jackie pointed to where he thought Shaun had run. Again they raced off.

'Shaun!'

On they continued up a wide, well-lit road, warehouses on one side and a line of trees on the other. They shouted and peered and searched through the darkness, into narrow lanes and wooden gates and iron fences. On they ran.

They came to a crossroads.

Stopped.

Straight ahead maybe or down to the main road, or else up towards a square patch of grass. Amy gasped for breath. 'Why is he…? It was him, wasn't it? I know it was…'

'Aye,' shouted Brendan, staring ahead, cap crunched in his hand. 'That's definitely Shaun.'

Jackie smiled, about to speak.

But he didn't.

To their left were hurried steps.

Then shouts. 'He's there! Get him!'

Emerging from trees in front of the square, two men raced their way.

They bolted past.

The brothers and sister could only stare.

They'd seen the men before.

They ran after them.

In time to see the collision.

In time to see Shaun bolting up the main road but then kicking into a binbag, sprawling onto the pavement and landing on his face. Blood spurted from his nose as he turned and lay flat out, as the smaller of the men reached him and got down on his knees. 'You're mine,' he hissed, pulling Shaun up again. 'You fucking arsehole.'

He launched a punch at Shaun's bloody, beaten face.

Then a second.

'Get off him, ya bastard!' Amy's scream caused the other guy to jump away in fright. As his friend spun round she kicked him in the leg. Then Jackie threw him against a wall.

'Shaun!' She fell to her knees, cradled his head in her hands.

Shaun's eyes were shut.

'Shaun!'

They flickered open.

'It's me. It's me, Shaun. Amy.'

He groaned, then he smiled.

'Oh, thank God.'

Amy leant down to kiss his forehead.

'You don't get to do that.' The first guy marched forward again and pushed her away. Shaun's head clunked onto the pavement. 'Not yet.'

Jackie made a lunge for the guy, but he'd already stepped back.

He kicked Shaun in the balls.

*

Monday 3rd June (cont'd)

I wanted to open up, open up right I mean, back in February. I did, it was honestly why I turned up here, I was dying to just…cleanse myself, get the past out my system. For a few months I wisni ready. But then finally I was.
Honest.
It's the truth.
At the start on that Monday night, sitting just over there, everything I told youse was true. My dad, my mum, my system, my escape, all of it happened man just like I said. But then, well…youse might even have guessed when my truth ended and my lies began. Me saying how worried I was about how ye'd react to my confession, then telling youse something that was probably quite easy to forgive. Don't get me wrong, ignoring a lassie's screams, no trivial, but it's something ye might expect from an addict, intit? Well, whether youse had your doubts or not, the truth is nobody killed that lassie. Nobody killed her and nobody ignored her. Nobody did anything cos she didni exist. The gangsters, they didni exist either.
Why did I make it up?
I just, I…
Oh I'll get there, but like I told youse I went to London for revenge. It's what I wanted most of all.
I hung about betting shops waiting to rip off gamblers, anybody at all more pathetic than me. How did I get on? No brilliant, couldni even get a potential victim to so much as notice me. Aye, I looked the part with the

moleskin book but really I was a joke, my system was a shitshow from start to finish. ...Actually I suppose it had its moments, and with self-control I could... see, there I go again, coming out with the crap I'd tell myself down there. Bet smaller! Bet less often! No, my system had major failings and it was in the wrong hands as well, the thirty-five grand from my ma was gone in a matter of months. What I want to say right is that losing didni teach me, it only got me angrier, more determined to see myself as nothing but a victim. Anyway I lost bad for a year or more, then one day I passed a sign for a meeting like this. Seeing it reminded me of what had happened that night I was here a couple of years ago.

Then I remembered something else about that meeting.

It's amazing, intit? The vibe there is? How nobody judges or disagrees with ye, nobody argues or accuses. Everybody just listens and supports, everybody's positive and warm. I felt it that night two years ago. Along with what Wayne was saying, it's what told me that I belonged. And it crossed my mind as well, I couldni help it, how easy it'd be to go and mouth off. About this yin stealing from his wean and that yin stealing from his work, this yin sleeping with her boss and that yin seeing a shrink. Trusting a room full of strangers with your darkest secrets man, it blew my mind. Then that night I forgot all about it.

And a year later it came back.

So, the truth?

My truth is this.

In London, I blackmailed people.

In London, I was a blackmailer.

See, a week after that meeting I'm sitting in another one. I'm quiet, just listening to people talking about their struggles and fears. Only but I've got my phone out and it's all on record, and sitting on my lap half-hidden under my jacket. Well, being a normal meeting I suppose it's just the normal stuff- debt, misery, guilt, all that. But there's gold to mine as well, I can hear it for myself, one or two folk confessing to nicking from their work. Blackmailing people in debt, eh, not the greatest money-spinner, but then it wisni about money with me and never had been. So the meeting ends and for all my plans I'm feeling queasy, my next step's making pals with a target and it just disni feel right. In fact before I change my mind I'm actually first out the door. But then somebody shouts me back, doing the decent thing.

He asks how I'm getting on, this guy, gives me words of encouragement, it's my first meeting and that, he says, don't judge too soon. But our talk's not about gambling for long, he soon moves on to football. He loves the game in Scotland, he says, blah, blah, blah blah blah... He's just .annoying me, the guy, far too pleased with himself, he's just admitted to stealing five hundred quid, now he's grinning like some mad bloody chicken. Aye. Greg, his name is. Poor boy as well, reaching out to somebody who disn4i deserve the steam from his shite. So he gives me his number, tells me to call whenever I want. Well, I call the next day. Ask if he fancies a pint.

Not exactly anonymous, our Greg, says he's a second-hand car salesman up the road, he gives it a bit of patter as well and even hands me his card. Well, after that I call again and give it to him straight, and maybe it's cos I'm on the phone but blackmailing's no that hard. At first he thinks I'm joking, actually starts to laugh, then realises the script and my ears are stinging with his verbal. I tell him I want a grand, a hundred every week or the recording will get sent to his work, so what can he do but agree. So over the next two Fridays man I meet him in a park. I'm on my bike and I spy him and I grab his envelope and I'm off. He knows not to be clever, knows it willni be worth it, knows the recording's on a laptop and when he pays up I'll delete it.

So, there youse go.

No, actually. Maybe not.

A second victim.

The meeting's in Camden this time, a different night but the same story. And as much as I hate to say it, the second time's no as tough, once you've downed that poison, it just sort of goes, the fear. So he's another one who's stolen from his work, this guy, another one with a lot to lose, difference is his job's in banking and it's twelve thousand quid. I justify this by telling myself he can afford it and I'll actually be doing him a favour, maybe with nutters like me around he'll even sort himself out. Disni look like a banker this guy, if anything he's more like a hooligan, big and fat with Union Jack tattoos, a guy ye might even avoid. He's got this sneer as well, Will his name is, but it's really just a nervous thing, he canni smile, that's his problem, got nothing to smile about. I get his info and pull the stunt and he disni even seem surprised. He just whimpers man like his time is up and I'm the bloody good guy. Same script, hundred quid a week. Different park.

Then, well...

There's a third.

Or supposed to be.

From a meeting in Forest Hill.

Jimmy, he's called. Jimmy is, well… look, by this point I've met Greg twice and Will once, and I'm starting to have my doubts, suppose I'm feeling some humanity, or more accurate, like shit. I'm no really sure why I'm at the meeting, why I've bothered my arse, it must just be my bitterness, still there, still simmering. Anyway I hear nothing useful, only marriage problems and debts, and there's Jimmy who's just worried that his family will find out about his gambling. I like Jimmy, I mean he's got Monty Python on his phone, loves his Indie music, in another time I think me and him could be mates. But he tells me about his family, how he canni be seen as a failure, and I'm trying not to feel sorry for him cos I'll soon be looking for his sister on Facebook.

Aye.

I threaten to tell her if he disni come up with the goods.

Then when I hear those words coming out my mouth, I put down the phone and go to pieces. This is what I've become, what it's taken to make my life worth living, except I'm a million miles away, in fact further away than ever. So I don't meet this guy, or Greg or Will again, I don't go to any other meetings, I just try and turn things around. I go to my work and I put in a shift, and it feels kind of rewarding, Then for the first time in months I talk to my flatmates, we go out to a couple of pubs. I'm back in touch with a lassie as well, one from a year before, and I think I might even like her and feel lucky to get another chance. Okay, I'm still gambling but I don't feel myself obsessing, and that system's feeling more trouble than it's worth. It feels like, no that I'm expecting it to be easy but…like I'm entering a new world.

Then two weeks into this new world, Brendan visits. He's been sent down by my sister cos she's still dead worried, for all this new me I've no got round to telling her. He's no in great form himself, Brendan, starts asking about my system, and since it's one of my more difficult days I've no got a lot of patience. So we argue a lot and I kick him out, then I go for a drink with my flatmates. Then we're back and see the flat's being broken into and the place has been turned upside down. Except no, only my room's been trashed and just a laptop and books have gone, and the door's no been tanned either, somebody strolled in. I canni work this out, no completely anyway, just know Greg or Will had found me and waited for their moment.

They'd no idea that I'd left the blackmailing behind.
Why would they, I didni think to tell them.
So there I was, crapping it in case the police came next.
I got the first train home.
Thought finally my life would change.
Didni for a minute think I'd see them again.
Had no idea how it'd be even possible.
Greg and Will.

45

'Get away from him, ya prick!' Brendan lunged forward, kicked the man in the ribs. With a cry and a thump, Greg hit the pavement, his head landing by a squashed box of discarded chips.

Expecting the other one to make his move, Jackie stood in his way. But Will made no attempt to approach, stood rooted and silent by the road.

In front of Shaun, fists clenched, Amy thrust a hand into her pocket. 'I'll get the police…I'll…' She grabbed out her phone, swiped it to life.

'Yeah, great idea,' Greg snapped, wincing as he tried to get up. 'The police at last. You *dirty*…' he hissed at Shaun. '…scum.'

'What…? Just…!' Amy bent down again, an arm around her brother. She touched the swell above his eye, took him by the hand. '…You're okay now.'

'No,' Will now stepped towards them, eyes wide and trembling.

Jackie shrugged back. 'What do ye mean, *no*?'

'Not everyone's here for starters,' Greg butted in with a sneer. 'Spent the last week searching for this shit, you think we're just gonna let him walk?' Eyes narrowing, he rose to his knees. Then Brendan marched his way and raised his fists. Greg sighed, shrunk down again.

'I want to go home,' Shaun muttered, his hand over a swollen cheek.

'No,' Will snapped again. 'An apology.'

'An apology…?' said Jackie. 'What ye talking about?'

'For blackmailing us,' Greg hissed. 'Your brother. The scum of the earth.'

'No, it's….you've…' Amy tried to pull Shaun by the arm. 'Come on. Let's get you home.'

Shaun didn't move. Instead, to the first Englishman then the next, he nodded. 'You're right…'

'What?'

'It's true.' He turned back to Amy. 'What he said.'

Greg nodded, angry but satisfied.

Will was groaning, he took rapid, calming breaths.

'What do ye mean, Shaun?' Jackie asked.

'If he doesn't fill you in, don't worry,' said Greg. 'Wayne will be around in a minute.'

'Wayne…?' said Amy. *'Boyd?'*

Shaun nodded. 'Aye.'

Amy shrugged. 'We don't…'

'Wayne must somehow have told them,' he whispered. 'It's the only explanation. I'm sorry,' he said to Greg and Will again. 'What I did. I'm just sorry.'

Ignoring him, Greg grinned. 'Here he is. Right on time.'

They peered along the main road to the block of tenements before Crawford's. To the figure of Wayne Boyd limping towards them.

Boyd paused for a moment, took in the sight.

He continued on.

*

Monday 3rd June (cont'd)

So aye, I'm back living at Amy's and I'm keeping my past to myself. I know that as far as the burglary's concerned, my brother Brendan's the key. But whatever...I'm putting it all behind me, just trying to settle down again, and work-wise it isni easy but there's only one person to blame for that. One positive but is that I don't have an appetite for gambling, I'm focused on getting a flat and I'm looking at restarting uni. By January I've found a job in a supermarket so things are looking up, but the trouble with looking up is, well, I feel the urge coming back to bet. So what I do is I take off to a meeting, my first up here in two years.

I've made my mind up now to spill the truth, relieve myself of the burden, it's something I canni even tell Amy but I'm prepared to reveal here. So that night, a Monday, I look about for Wayne, he's no around and it's a pity cos I really liked the guy. Then the Thursday he's here and I'm like-magic, we'll have a chat, I'll even run my confession by him before I tell the others. But before I get to speak, he starts talking to the group, and I canni believe what I hear, he says he's considering blackmailing somebody then bolting with the cash. The whole thing just sounds terrible, so...I don't know, extreme. So I give Wayne my support, it'll pass blah blah blah... But I feel myself changing my mind, how can I admit I actually followed through on blackmail? No, I decide to keep my mouth shut, nobody will ever know. Problem with that but is I've given a drum roll already, canni just drop my confession. So at the next meeting, what can I say. I make up a lot of shite.

That's that, far as I'm concerned, nobody bats an eyelid. Me and Wayne, we go out for a drink and pretty much hit it off. I mention I'm skint and he's got an idea, some shifts in the pub that he runs. He's kidding, man, youse know the deal, right? The very idea is just mad. But we keep blabbing and end up serious. Wayne wants to help and we're both up for a challenge, might even be a laugh. So we shake on it man, our mental wee secret. But well, it isni a laugh, working in that pub isni funny in the slightest. No offence, Wayne, ye'd be the same yourself, the two of us should just have known better. Still but, one Sunday I'm through another shift and the money is stacking up nice, there'll be one weekend to go then I'll have some stories to tell my brother. But that disni happen cos I'm dumped on my arse, accused of nicking some charity tin. Total lot of shite and I wisni paid for the shift either, so I'm really pissed off. Like we'd arranged, I head up to Wayne's.

We're soon firing down drinks, spirits I've never heard of, and I know it's no Wayne's fault but I'm no very happy. Before long Wayne starts on about his cousin, Daryl, his name is, he's the owner of the pub. He's bitter, Wayne, about Daryl I mean, said when he was drowning in debt Daryl stuck the boot in. I've guessed by now that Daryl's the potential blackmail victim he talked about but I think the temptation's passed, Wayne's been on better form these days and there's no mention of blackmail. But...I don't know, I'm wasted and that so I ask about the secret, I ask what he's holding then say fuck it let's screw him over. Wayne mumbles he's no interested and at this point I should drop it. But I don't man, I push it, and

I push it too far. Blackmail's not as bad as ye think, I tell him, I know because I've done it. Puts his glass down, Wayne. He stares. I try to backtrack man but the damage is done.

He starts shouting and balling, telling me to get out, and I'm screaming as well, losing the plot. Next thing he's throwing punches man so I tear it down his stairs, drop my phone halfway down and run back up for it. Except he's there first and boots it, then he's jumping and smashing it up, so I'm out of there, no phone or cash and my face totally throbbing. Wayne man, probably battling that demon every day. Then the demon's mate just turns up and says hello.

Well, I pass Crawford's again, launch some missiles and shout abuse, then I'm banging at the door cos I know I left my jacket. I don't really expect him, I don't really expect anybody.

But Daryl appears.

I say- I know about you.

46

Ignoring the staring sister and brothers, Wayne stepped towards Shaun in silence. Drawing his eyes down him, huddled ashamed on the bin bags, he gave a slow nod. 'Well done,' he said.

Greg grinned. 'Thanks for the call, Wayne.'

The barman winked back. 'Team effort.'

Amy jumped up and faced him. '*You?* What are...? Will somebody tell me what's going on?'

He prodded Shaun with a foot. 'Maybe this yin can. What do ye say, Shaun? Up for it?'

Under the words and the glare, Shaun shrunk further. 'What I did to Greg and Will, I'm just sorry.' He turned to them again. '...I took advantage. I'd no right and I've got no excuse.'

Eyes reddening and trembling still, Will took a step forward. 'That's what I came here for. For you to look at me in the eye and say those words.'

Shaun took a breath. He paused. 'I'm sorry, Will.'

'And I came to kick you in the nuts,' Greg declared with a sneer. 'One for the road I think...' He stepped forward again and swung back.

Jackie rushed in front of him. 'You had your shot.'

'I'm getting my money back an all.'

'Aye. I'll make sure of it.'

'So that's it?' Amy asked. 'Do you have what we want, more or less? Because I've still got no idea what this is about but I do know my brother's been missing a whole week. And I *really* need to take him home.'

Boyd chewed the idea around in his mouth, had a pick at his stubble. 'No.'

'*No?*'

He shrugged. 'No everybody's here.' He prodded Shaun with his stick. 'Hey. Somebody *really* wants to meet you.'

Monday 3rd June (cont'd)

I don't know jack shit about him of course, just fancy my chances, like I say I'm in a hell of a nick. Old Daryl disni take this well, in fact he stands there speechless, but then he realises I'm at it and he lets out a laugh. Well, I go for him man and he skelps me, so time to move on I think, I stumble off again towards town. But a few minutes later a car drives up, it's Daryl and he's got a proposition, no a trick or anything he says, just wants me to hear him out. I suppose Daryl had guessed I was a Celtic fan, thought I might be off my nut…Anyway, he wanted to find out.

Wayne boxed my ears so I think I'm hearing things.

But no, my hearing's fine.

Daryl wants me to set fire to his pub.

Aye. One night through the week, he's asked me to douse the place in petrol and set it alight. He needs the cash he says cos he's starting a new life in the sunshine, and putting it up for sale's a no-no cos he canni afford to to raise eyebrows. I've got no idea what this is about and I'm sure he's no gonni tell me, although the way he's a bit smug and that I'm guessing that a woman's involved. I realise that's probably the secret, actually, the thing Wayne could have blackmailed him about. Anyway, he's got it worked out, he says, a plan that canni fail, and if I agree to help him then he'll hand me twenty grand. I'm just trying to make sense of this when he claps his hands man and whoops. Says worst case scenario the polis will look at ex-employees, and since I was never even on the books I'll be gone man, a ghost.

I don't know. Obviously the answer's no cos you're talking ten years for arson, plus what sort of nutter goes round setting fire to pubs. But then again I'm thinking, twenty thousand quid, the thought of what I could do with it sends me all dizzy. I can only really gibber and Daryl says take my time, even drives me back to Crawford's where I crash out and sober up. I get more details then. It's got to look sectarian, he says, after like, genuine threats he's received. So we'd do it on the Thursday after a Celtic game on telly, and rather than smash windows we'd burn it from the inside. And that, he says, is where we'd be off to a flyer. Since I've already come in through the back, Daryl explains, I've avoided the CCTV. So if I decide I'm in, the job's already half-done.

I take this all in man, look for holes, but everything Daryl says seems on the money. A sectarian attack will have the polis checking back only on the night before, for a customer entering the pub then no leaving again. Plus, in the event I do become a suspect, even Wayne knows no more than my first name, so no matter how I look at it this really canni fail. Only thing but is Daryl wants me to spend three days in an old cellar and I'm no really up for that, but he'll look after me, he says, feed me and that, it'll be a doddle, part of the job. What do I do, man, I fight off my instincts, I shrug and tell him aye. Then I go to my phone to spin a tale to my sister, how I'll be gone a few days. But of course there isni a phone, I last saw Wayne destroying it, so I want to bolt for a bit and tell Amy face-to-face. Daryl says no chance, too risky, just chill, it'll all be done in just a few days.

Looking back, Daryl was worried that I'd blab. But whatever, I tell him I'm in.

So time pure kills in that cellar and I feel guilty as well, I get by through dreaming of what I'll do with that cash when I've got it. Daryl gets pretty jumpy, he needs this job done quick, and the way he's so careful when he asks about Amy I get the feeling she's been in. Then Thursday comes and he postpones it. Man, I hit the roof. But he's right, the Rangers Celtic match is just two days away and the violence after it will be a gift. But just as I can see the end, sitting playing a game on my burner, I hear Amy on the other side of the door. I'm dying to scream that I'm here, dying to tell her I'm fine, it takes all my resolve and greed to just and listen to her sobs. My family come back later as well, take off the cellar door. I've been moved so I don't know this but widni care either, I just want this done.

So man as agreed, at three-fifteen on the Sunday morning I get the buzz. Daryl's unlocked the cellar and placed the petrol in a cupboard, I'm to begin pouring it round the front door and go on until I reach the kitchen. Then I'm to light it. So I make a start, go round the front, looking out the windows all nervous and that. That's when I know. See, hung by a window there's a framed top of a Rangers player, a Danish guy, he was brilliant, disni matter what team ye support, he just was. I scan round the programmes as well, and all the scarves and pendants and that. And I think, no. I canni dae this. It's history, intit? No my history, to me it's a load of pish, but for some it's a museum and I canni just destroy it. So I decide Daryl's on his own.

Next thing I'm booting in the fire escape and running into the streets. I want to go home. I want to see Amy. I want to start again, again, again.

Soon I slow down and I clock a wee guy in front of me. It canni be, I think, my eyes are screwed fae that cellar, plus it's dark as well so he really could be anybody. But he recognises me, Greg, his eyes all flare up. Then he shouts 'Will!' and I know the two of them have found me.

I run but Greg's fast, I canni shake him off.

I fall on my face.

I don't get how they've teamed up or how they've managed to find me.

I don't get either why Wayne arrives on the scene.

Then they say somebody else is coming.

I think, who?

Jimmy?

Jimmy??

What does Jimmy want?

I didni even go through with his blackmail.

47

The barman took the phone from his ear, nodded up the main road. 'Coming now.'

A taxi approached.

It slowed down.

With a creak the door swung open and a passenger stepped out.

Amy rocked on her heels, her mouth opened but at first she couldn't speak.

'*Britt?*'

Britt stepped slowly towards them, appearing to stare through every one. Then she stopped over Shaun, her face trembling and reddening. 'You bastard,' she hissed.

Shaun gazed back, broken but blank. Then he shrugged and stared down at the pavement.

'How…do you know my brother?' Amy asked.

'I don't,' Britt said, still glaring. 'I wish James hadn't either.'

Turning again, Shaun's question was barely a whisper. 'James?…'

'Jimmy.'

'I…'

'He trusted you. He let you into his life.'

'But…'

'You blackmailed him.'

'No…' Shaun's eyes pleaded, first with Britt then with Amy. Then Boyd and even Greg. 'I didn't…I… Where…Where *is* Jimmy?'

Eyes flaring, Britt took a deep, juddering breath.

Then with a scream, she threw herself on top of the blackmailer.

Monday 3rd June (cont'd)

The threat of Jimmy's parents finding out about his gambling was enough to tip him over. Hung himself, Jimmy did, left a note explaining why, or a note explaining that he was being blackmailed anyway. His sister, Britt, she did some digging, found out about his problems.

James, she called her brother.

She decided to hunt me down.

First she sent emails to groups around London looking for other victims, and Greg and Will read them and they all got together. When they saw I'd done one they knew I might have come back to Glasgow, they fired up warnings about the potential blackmailer. For weeks man it hung on the noticeboard, neither me or Wayne even saw it. Then the night after our fight, Wayne strolled in and...

He called Britt right away.

The blackmailer was here.

Greg and Will shot up from London and Britt flew over from Dublin, and she'd end up saying she was from Belfast to sound believable. I'm sure Wayne thought finding me would be easy, especially when he managed to get my phone working again, but by that time I'd vanished and he was lost as my family. Of course, he could have given them the script but I'm sure that seemed too risky. Instead they, or I should say Britt, tried to stick to them like glue. Aye, Wayne and that assumed Amy and my brothers would find me in the end, just had to make sure they kept them on track. I think but after nearly a week they were getting pretty desperate. That's why when they raced out the flat, Britt was standing outside. She alerted Wayne to where they might be heading. Wayne told Greg and Will.

So, that's me.

Guilty.

Soon, anyway.

Greg, he got his kick at my face.

Will, he got his apology.

But Britt wants more than that.

I've been charged, I've given my statement.

My lawyer says...well, it's complicated.

I don't want to go to jail.

But I think I will.

I know I should.

Aye.

That's it.

My name's Shaun and I'm a fucking idiot.

48

'Brendan? How's it going?'

'Jackie! Hey…' Swinging his legs off the sofa, Brendan jumped up. '…Not bad. Just watching some fitba. How are you?'

Two floors below, the horn of a parked car stabbed the peace of the afternoon. Jackie stepped away from the balcony. 'Good. Done for the day. A bit of reading in the sun.'

'The sun, aye. Sounds nice.'

'So what's new?'

'No a lot, that's the problem, Jackie. The season's started and there's no new signings.'

'I know, I've been following.'

'Really?'

'Course. No need to panic yet, they've got their problems as well. How's our sis?'

Brendan stepped across his room to the window. He took in the bulging sky and the water streaming down the glass. 'Better. She was out on Saturday night.'

'Really? That's great to hear.'

'With her workmates. I didni have to ask either, Jackie, I got the full rundown yesterday. She had a right laugh. And ye know what's mad and what I didn't know? She'd never been out with them before. I mean *ever*.'

'Moving on, Brendan. She's moving on from a lot of things.'

'Aye. And we're all made up you're coming back, we thought it widni be for another year.'

'I had to make the effort, and Reem's got to meet everyone.'

'Will be magic to meet her.'

'It will, aye. So what about Shaun?' Jackie asked. 'Still no date?'

'A matter of waiting. Had his first session with the counsellor, right enough. Paid for it himself. Do ye think the court will look upon that, sort of…favourably?'

'…I'd say that's a stretch.'

'Ach, was just wondering.'

'Won't do any harm, put it that way.'

'Here,' Brendan said. 'My heart was in my mouth there, I thought you were that mad wino again.'

'What mad wino?'

'That Skin character. Six times he called over the weekend. *Oh Billy Boy*… he was giving it. …*What's happened to ye? We need to hingmy*… No chance, man. No. Chance.'

'Ha Ha! How did he get your number?'

'Nae idea. It's about those tickets we won. Inter Milan it's against. Like I'm gonni do what you did. Like I'm gonni go there as a *hobby*.'

'Inter Milan? Ye knocked it back?'

'Don't start. Just the thought of reliving those days gives me a panic attack. What date are ye back anyway?'

'August the eighth.'

'There ye go, game's on the twelfth. It's yours.'

'…I, well…'

'Ha ha, fucking…'

'I'll maybe just call Skin, say hello.'

'Glad you've settled back in anyway. Still loving it over there?'

The horn below now stopped, Jackie stepped back onto his balcony and into the sunshine. The gentle chatter and smell of shisha rose from the coffee house below, as a cyclist carrying a tray of bread trundled past a woman selling herbs. 'Aye, Brendan. I couldni live anywhere else.'

Brendan squinted up at the sky, wondered if this rain would ever stop. 'Me neither, Jackie man. Couldni imagine it for a minute.'

Really hope you enjoyed the book.

Would appreciate a review on Kindle!

Cheers.